BELLA BATHURST

SPECIAL

A MARINER ORIGINAL

HOUGHTON MIFFLIN COMPANY

BOSTON • NEW YORK

First published in 2002 by Picador, an imprint
of Pan Macmillan Ltd.

For information about permission to reproduce selections from
this book, write to Permissions, Houghton Mifflin Company,
215 Park Avenue South, New York, New York 10003.

Visit our Web site: www.houghtonmifflinbooks.com.

Library of Congress Cataloging-in-Publication Data
Bathurst, Bella.
Special / Bella Bathurst.
p. cm.
"A Mariner original."
ISBN 0-618-26327-6
1. Teenage girls—Fiction. 2. Female friendship—Fiction.
3. Dean, Forest of (England)—Fiction. 4. Teacher-student
relationships—Fiction. I. Title.
PR6102.A785S6 2003
823'.92—dc21 2002191263

Printed in the United States of America

QUM 10 9 8 7 6 5 4 3 2 1

ACCLAIM FOR **SPECIAL**

"*Special* is unlike anything I have read about the contemporary plight of being an adolescent girl. More than any recent sociological tracts, it gives us an inside look at the cruel stratagems, fierce sexual pressures, and budding romantic longings that mark this group. By turns wise, funny, and horrifying, it describes their tribal customs with casual but deadly accuracy. Part *Lord of the Flies*, part *The Prime of Miss Jean Brodie*, this inexorably unfolding drama will haunt you long after you put the book down."
— **Daphne Merkin, author of** *Enchantment* **and** *Dreaming of Hitler*

"A work of brilliance and insight . . . Bathurst has pulled off the often difficult transition from nonfiction to fiction with panache . . . sharpened by acute observation and artful characterization." —*Telegraph*

"This troubling, fascinating, and intense novel is like *Lord of the Flies* meets *Picnic at Hanging Rock,* with hints of Ian McEwan's *Enduring Love* . . . Strikingly accurate." —*Times*

"A striking debut . . . a fully adult read . . . Bathurst's series of vignettes and scenes ring achingly true . . . She has conveyed the world about which she writes with excruciating faithfulness."
—*Independent Magazine*

"Exhilarating to read . . . vigorously entertaining . . . contemporary and fresh. It explores, with great sensitivity, the discovery of personal identity, and marks a fine beginning as a novelist for Bella Bathurst." —*Spectator*

"This authentic, stingingly accurate novel . . . has captured something important; shocking, yet familiar and real."
—*Scotland on Sunday*

"It is often said that teenage girls are crueler than teenage boys, but never have I read a novel that explores this idea more convincingly and chillingly." —*Independent on Sunday*

"A thoroughly absorbing read . . . Will no doubt earn comparisons with Golding's *Lord of the Flies*. Like that tale, *Special* focuses on group dynamics as adolescents struggle for power, with their own sexuality, and, finally, for their own survival . . . The Spice Girls this ain't."
—*Scotsman*

For Lordy, with love

One day when we [Johnny Rotten and Bob Geldof] were both in Cork, he on holiday visiting his relatives and me picking up an Irish pop music award, we met in a pub. A man came over and put his hand on Johnny's arm and began asking him a question. Johnny interrupted him half-way, turning around with those laser eyes and said, 'Don't touch me. I'm special.'

BOB GELDOF, *Is That It?*

MONDAY

It was quite late when they saw the accident. They'd been driving for almost three hours, ambling down the M4 at a humiliating 55 mph. The minibus – a rented Ford with a broken wing mirror – had been making shrieking noises for a while now. When Jaws changed gears or accelerated the shriek crept upwards, close to hysteria, choking Hen's thoughts. On the level, moving along the slow lane as they were now, the noise subsided a little but the sudden switches of volume had prevented any of them from dozing off.

The minibus was arranged like a coach with seats running parallel down its length and an aisle in the middle, but this was not like any coach Hen had seen before. Normal coaches were designed with some token understanding of the human body. They had seats covered in carpet and armrests one could lever up in order to sleep. This thing had seats covered in gaffer-taped plastic, a floor speckled with old chewing-gum spots and a smell of sweat and fried rubber.

Jules leaned over the gap between the front seats and glared at the speedometer. 'Doesn't it go any faster?'

'Play something,' said Miss Naylor. 'I spy with my little eye.'

Jules mouthed 'Wanker' at the back of Miss Naylor's head and turned to see if anyone had been watching her. She caught Hen's eye, grinned, and began picking at her cuticles.

The heat and the finicky driving were beginning to make all of them restless. It was one of those tight flat summer days without sun, and the heat rising up from the road seemed to get thicker with every mile they moved. It was making Miss Naylor's foundation leak. Hen watched a trickle of sweat creep down the side of her cheek and disappear into her shirt. Miss Naylor had a broad, bland face, small eyes which bulged a little when she was angry and dyed ginger hair. She usually wore yellowy make-up slapped on thick as fish batter. The make-up clashed with the ginger and the result was so compellingly unattractive that Hen often had to suppress the urge to ask Miss Naylor if she'd ever considered surgery.

There were ten of them crammed into the minibus, eight girls in the back and two teachers up at the front. Things had started well enough. They had stood by the school gates waiting for the other two groups of girls to leave. Mel and Mina had been arguing, but as the last van turned the corner, they stopped and gazed after it. In the silence, Hen had glanced upwards and noticed that someone had left the porch light on even though it was now bright day. The light shone without anything to shine for, and there was something about its wasted usefulness which made her feel sorry for it. She felt empty for a second, a feeling almost like homesickness.

She wondered if she ought to feel jealous of the others. One lot was supposed to be going to Warwickshire and the other to Norfolk. She had no idea what either of these places was like, except that they involved countryside and undignified exercises, but it was possible that the countryside and the undignified exercises would be more interesting in Warwick-shire and Norfolk than they would be in Gloucestershire.

Two minutes later, Jaws came round the side of the science block in the minibus. She was smiling. The smile dwindled as she drove closer.

Jules jeered. 'We can't go in *that*.'

'Why not?'

'Because,' – poking an accusatory finger at the tyres, – 'it's embarrassing.'

'So how else are we going to get there?'

'Maybe we . . .'

'It's either this or walking.'

'. . . could just stay . . .'

'No. Definitely not.'

Caz picked up her bags. 'Come on. It's bad, but it's not as bad as here.'

And so far, she seemed to be right. Just to turn out of the school drive and onto the main road had given them all a flip of exhilaration. The minibus might be old, but it worked and the day was warm and every inch they drove was an inch further away from school. Izzy had brought along several tapes and taken control of the stereo, overriding Miss Naylor's desultory protests. Hen had leaned back against the open window and felt the beat going right down deep into the back of her skull.

They'd chattered for the first hour or so, and then, as the temperature rose, had slowly fallen silent. Just after they passed the Swindon junction, the traffic slowed and then stopped.

Hen leaned back in her seat, shifting from thigh to thigh to stop her bones from aching. As they crawled round a curve in the road, she could see blue lights and the stripes of police vehicles ahead. An accident. The minibus screamed as Jaws tried to put it back into gear. The traffic was squeezing into the slow lane; once in a while a sunburned arm poked out of a car window, waving at Jaws to make space. Hen saw a carful of small children making faces out of the window. One of them stuck his tongue out and rolled his eyes at her. Next to him, a little girl in pigtails raised a single obscene finger and giggled, her mouth shaping insults silently through the glass.

For the next half a mile, they stopped and stalled and started and then stalled again every few yards. A van which had been blocking their view moved over and Hen felt the blue light slam against the back of her eyes. The scene assembled itself into a recognizable disorder – three cars, one upside down with its back axle resting against the twisted central barrier, and another two crumpled beyond sense. Fragments of windscreen glass spangled prettily from the fast lane, and a fireman sprayed the bonnet of each car in a shining grey-green arc. Someone had scattered sawdust over something on the tarmac. There were two fire engines parked by the verge, an ambulance with its back doors swinging open, and three police Range Rovers. One of the policemen was standing near the flow of the traffic trying to direct the cars past the scene. Most drivers seemed too diverted by the possibility of gore to pay him any attention.

Hen was not sure where the figure came from. She only knew that she turned and saw someone running from the hard shoulder towards her. The person ran without purpose or direction, with no regard for where it was going or how it got there. It blundered into a shrub on the verge, pulled free and then ran on, almost as if it couldn't see the line of cars, the motorway, the ambulance doors swinging open. There seemed no sense or reason in the figure's trajectory, only this mad stumbling rush straight into the path of the traffic.

At the last minute, just before the figure whacked head-long into the side of the minibus, it stopped. Perhaps it had finally seen the white metal looming up in front of it; perhaps it had simply exhausted itself. It stood with its shoulder to the window, crowding up against Hen's vision. In the stillness the figure reassembled itself. It was a woman, dressed smartly, as if for a wedding. She was wearing a tight, livid pink suit with a miniskirt that barely covered the tops of her thighs and a pair of vicious-looking black stilettos. Underneath the skirt, she had on a pair of scarlet tights which had ripped as she'd run. Her legs seemed absurdly thin and stringy, as if they shouldn't have been able to support the person on top. The woman's face was obscured by a huge cartwheel hat on which she'd fixed what looked like Valentine's Day decorations – huge papier mâché hearts, a plastic red rose.

Hen could hear the woman singing, repeating something over and over. And then she turned and the huge hat knocked against the window of the bus. It spun off, tripping over the road onto the verge. Hen saw, all at once, the woman's face. The face was hideous: a huge sick purple moon, a chunk of rotting meat painted to look like a woman. On her cheeks there were pits and lines like the marks on something diseased. Her lips were slashed with scarlet lipstick and her gaze was high and hectic, as if nothing of the scene in front of her had registered at all. All the colours were wrong – the pink jacket, the scarlet lipstick, the face dark and raw as butcher's liver. On top of the face, false and garish, was what looked like a black wig. Strands of dark hair hung down over the huge decaying nose, groping around her neck. The woman looked straight at Hen, and straight through her.

One of the policemen had seen the woman and was weaving through the ticking vans and people carriers towards her. As he got to the side of the van, he extended a hand. 'Come on,' he was saying. 'Come on. We've been looking for you. Over here, love.'

The woman turned towards him. Hen saw the policeman stop. She saw the look on his face shift from hurried concern to incomprehension to a kind of blank-eyed terror. She saw his hand hesitate and his body go still. Then he gathered himself and touched the woman's arm. 'Over here,' he said unhappily. 'Come on.'

The woman stopped singing and looked down at his hand on the sleeve of her pink jacket. The silence stretched out. All the noises from the other cars seemed to have stopped; all the sirens and the racket of the crash dwindled away. There was just this policeman, and Hen, and the woman, standing there, watching the policeman's hand.

Then the woman giggled coquettishly and began to walk away from the minibus, allowing herself to be led over to the police cars. As she moved, Hen looked down at her legs. And saw that her ripped scarlet tights were not tights at all. The woman's legs were slathered in blood.

At the same moment, the minibus lurched forward. The policeman who had been directing the traffic appeared at the opposite window and then vanished behind them. Hen heard the crunching of the gears and the sound of the engine accelerating. She looked out of the window at the verge and saw the woman's pink hat with its hearts and roses lifting and falling in the breeze. The motion of the hat made it look as if it was breathing, as if it too was alive, and just waiting there. She watched the hat until they were past, past the ambulances and the crash and the policemen and the hurting blue lights. She felt the wind against her face as the landscape changed and the green verge began to flick past as it had before. She shifted in her seat and found that she was shaking uncontrollably.

The rest of the bus seemed unconcerned. Jules had begun to say something and Miss Naylor was trying to reassemble the broken mirror so Jaws could see out of it. Ali, who was in the seat two spaces in front of her, sat up. She had been resting her head on the window and gone into a trance, staring fixedly at a spot somewhere up in the clouds. She didn't seem to have noticed the window rattling against her head.

'Hen.'

No reply.

'*Hen*.'

Hen looked up. Jules was leaning over her, prodding her arm. The breeze from the windows had ruffled her hair out of its clip and it swung loose over her face. As she bent over Hen her eyes seemed larger than normal.

'Space chicken.'

'What?'

'Hel-lo. Hel-*looo*. Earth to Planet Hen. Hel-*lo*.'

Hen looked down at Jules's finger. 'What?'

'Fit policeman.'

'What?'

'Fit police. Didn't you see?'

'Where?'

'The *policeman*. The policeman directing the traffic.'

'What policeman?'

'Back there. With the accident. Oh, never mind.' Jules

7

sighed and sat down in the seat next to Hen. 'You look weird. You OK?'

'The woman. The woman with the blood.'

'Woman? Woman with blood?'

'On the road. Out there. The woman with the hat.'

Jules bent down and peered past Hen out of the window. 'Where? Can't see.'

'She was there. Right there, by the window. She had on this hat . . .' She swivelled round to look out of the rear window, knowing that the woman was far behind them now but wondering if she might not appear again, smiling crazily through the glass.

'Amazing crash,' said Jules cheerfully. 'Really heavy.'

Hen realized that she had probably been the only one to see the woman properly. All of the rest of them had been looking out of the opposite windows at the crash. Perhaps she'd imagined it. Had she seen the woman? And if she hadn't, if she'd just daydreamed her, boiled her up from old sick bits of imagination, then how had it seemed so real? She turned away and stared out at the verge again. She was still shaking; she couldn't stop.

Jules touched her arm again. 'You OK?'

Hen yanked her sleeve away. 'Yes. Fine.'

And then, a couple of minutes later, pawing at her stomach, 'No. Going to be sick.'

+

By the time they'd stopped the bus, watched Hen as she vomited weakly into a hank of shrub, clucked around for a bit, asked Hen fourteen times how she was, got back in the bus, stalled, driven a few more miles, stopped for petrol, let Hen off the bus to clean herself up, let Jules go with her because she insisted, waited, torn Jules away from one of the arcade machines, stalled again, and pulled back to the road at a scorching 45 mph, they were late. By now, it felt to everyone as if they'd been on this stinking bus for most of their lives. Up ahead, Hen watched the immense H-shaped struts of the old Severn Bridge creep closer. The red lights on the top shone placidly at her. She felt woozy and light-headed, although the shaking had stopped about an hour ago.

'Very dangerous, the Severn.' Miss Naylor didn't seem to be talking to anyone in particular. 'Quicksand. They say you can walk across the whole river in some places at low tide, if you know where the sand is. In most places, it's very shallow. The channel where the water really moves is quite small, considering.'

'Weird.' Jules swivelled round in her seat and looked down. Hen saw a silvery glimmer of water and a toy-sized tug boat far away in the estuary. The water moved in thick slow circles, over and under itself. Only the width of the estuary told Hen in which direction it flowed. Out in the mouth of the river the currents crept round each other, meeting and parting without rhythm or direction. Something about the water seemed misleading to Hen. Over there in the distance the river looked harmless. Only when she looked down through the railings of the bridge could she see how fast it was going. You'd never know until you were dead that it might kill you, she thought.

'Doesn't look like it's dangerous. Just looks like a river.'

'I wouldn't expect you to think anything different.'

Jules glowered at her. 'Cow.'

Hen kept on watching the road ticking past. A flicker of

scarlet caught her eye; just a shop sign. When she closed her eyes the woman came back. When she opened them again the woman stayed there, just at the corner of her vision. She wouldn't go away.

. . . MONDAY

Ali could see everything from her place in the tree. If she stood with her back against the trunk and turned a little to the right, the struts of the Severn Bridge beamed back at her through the heavy afternoon light. When she turned on the branch, feeling the bark catch against her fingers, there was the river. Most of it was obscured by industrial clutter: warehouses, sheds, the detritus of old cars and farms, the kind of stuff that silted up over the years without anyone really noticing. Maybe it had once been possible to see an unbroken stretch of water from here, but now the only sign that it existed at all was in the gaps between the buildings. Somewhere over on the opposite bank a cooling tower exhaled clouds.

She had been sitting here with one leg dangling languidly over the side of the branch for about half an hour now. The discovery of the tree had been an accident. She had been following one of the paths behind the Manor and come across a branch sagging over the shrubs. At first it hadn't seemed connected to a tree at all; the branch was so long and swung so low that she assumed it had fallen and been left uncleared. The tree itself was a London plane hunched with age. Half its branches had already died and the rest had swivelled

11

themselves into impossible knots and twists. The bark was covered in small ochre scabs falling away like sunburned skin. Ali found the sight of the peeling tree with its strange snakey limbs both comforting and a little bit sinister. In climbing terms it did not seem much of a challenge, but she found something about its age and its indifference to standard tree decorum interesting.

She turned back to face the Manor. Directly in front of the house was a slab of buckled tarmac and then a rectangle of lawn bordered with tubs of geraniums. Below the lawn the ground sloped downwards into what must once have been an elegant landscaped vista leading halfway to the river, but which had gradually run wild and was now a tangle of self-seeded birches and weeds. A high rusting chain-link fence marked the boundary of the grounds. Ali could just trace out the shape of the gardens as they must once have been. In places there were still gaps in the trees and someone had been fighting to keep some of the pathways open. Perhaps the people here had once felt secure in the division between the town and the country; perhaps when it had first been built the Manor had stood splendidly alone. But during the last hundred years the world had sidled closer and it wouldn't be long before this place became part of the suburbs of Stokeley. Time and neglect had collapsed the divisions between the natural landscape and the artificial one, and Ali had the impression that it would only be a matter of a year or so before the lawn itself slipped back into the wild.

When the minibus had finally shuddered up the hill and into the drive, Ali felt a brief flicker of anticipation, and then – having taken in the thin curtains waving at them from an upstairs window and a glimpse of a beaten Parker Knoll armchair – subsided back into indifference. The house itself was horrible. It was a large asymmetrical building, constructed from the type of Victorian red brick that made Ali think of rain and cold Sundays. It had evidently been built as an institution and had remained one, unloved and unlovely. There were Gothic arches above the windows and dark stains down the front of the building where the gutters had leaked. Four or five trees overhung the roof, blocking out most of the natural light, and two tubs of dead conifers leaked earth on either side of the front entrance. The whole place had a scrappy, passing-through feeling to it. It looked like what it was, thought Ali: a school away from school.

According to Jaws, who had found the place for them, Dean Manor had been built in the 1880s as a private asylum for the insane. A Glasgow speculator with a rich, despairing client list and a faith in fresh air had bought up much of the surrounding land and equipped it with landscaped grounds and its own arboretum. His enthusiasm for the area had survived for as long as it took him to build the asylum, admit the first generation of patients, watch the local landlords hack down much of the nearby forest for timber, and slide abruptly into bankruptcy. Much of the land was sold off, until all that remained were the landscaped lawns with their distant view of the river and a small patch of struggling pine plantation. Since then the building had gone through various incarnations, each a little more dishevelled than the last: a medical supply depot during the First World War, a training centre for missionary priests, a school for evacuees during the Second World War. For a while the local council had considered turning it into a hostel, but most backpackers and tourists found the choice between a hand-crafted castle and a leaking

Victorian ex-lunatic asylum remarkably easy to make. The rooms weren't large or modern enough to attract the local conference trade, so Dean Manor and its part-time staff of three disaffected local women got by on the proceeds of school groups and trade associations in need of somewhere cheap, quiet and uncomfortable from which to conduct meetings. Two or three evangelical Christian groups used it regularly for prayer and counselling retreats, and a small ecological organisation took it for three weeks in late summer. And so the Manor had remained largely as it was – part hostel, part barracks, part derelict.

Ali, who had initially been interested by the frisson of insanity, sat back and absorbed only as much of the history as was necessary to figure out two things: where to find solitude, and how to escape.

'Upstairs,' said Miss Naylor, hauling open the doors of the bus. 'Supper's at six. We'll do the timetable then.'

Hen sat where she was, staring sightlessly out of the windows.

'Lola. *Lola.* Out.'

Jules nudged her. 'You all right?'

Hen nodded.

'Beds,' said Jules offhandedly, picking up her case. 'Get you one.'

When Ali walked into the hall, she found it dark as winter. Long ago, when the building was still an asylum, it must have been decorated to give the impression of authority and competence. It had been built rich and ugly, and was now poor and even uglier. Sometime in the last twenty years, the walls had been painted a gynaecological pink. Three dusty rectangles indicated where paintings must once have hung, and one of the rectangles was partially covered by a cork noticeboard. There was a table to the right with copies of rules and instructions, and a payphone jammed into a corner. The doors leading off the hall had been replaced at some point with plywood substitutes and above her two striplights gave off a liverish glow. From down below Ali heard the tickle of a radio. Otherwise there was silence.

At the other end of the hall, a door opened. The man who entered had on a pair of grey lace-up shoes and a black T-shirt with a drawing of a large mechanical insect on the front. He seemed preoccupied, and as he came in he kept adjusting his glasses. Ali put down her bag and extended her hand. The man walked to the other end of the room, opened another door and stepped into the passageway beyond. Ali stood for a moment where she was, gazing at the door, her hand still outstretched. She was not surprised at being ignored, but somehow it did not encourage her to go and explore the rest of the building. She left her bag where it was and walked out into the sunlight.

+

Hen found their bedroom by listening for Jules's voice. Jules was always louder than everyone else, particularly when she had a grievance.

'You're there.' She pointed to one of the middle beds.

Hen jumped experimentally on the mattress to test its bounciness. Her knee hit what felt like solid rock, a bed as austere as the building itself. 'Fuck! God. That's supposed to be a *bed*?'

'Vile, aren't they?' Jules flung out a foot. 'That's mine.'

Hen was aware that she ought to say something in order to cover for the stuff in the minibus. She wanted to sound bright and careless, but she seemed to have lost the knack. She couldn't think of anything to say, so she opened her case and began unpacking. There wasn't much, just the usual photographs, her alarm clock and a book with a gun on the front which she didn't intend to read.

'You OK?'

'Fine.'

'The road—'

'*Fine. Really.* What's it like?'

'OK smoking, OK drugs, need to sort men and drink.'

'Town, isn't there? Stokeley?'

'Yeah. Check that out.'

'Where's Jaws and Naylor?'

'First floor. Main block. Nowhere near us.'

Neither of them noticed Izzy standing in the doorway until she put her bag down. Hen looked up, considering her for the first time in a while. It wasn't really that she was fat, it was just that she seemed that way. Big square bones and defeated shoulders, a long face, small slapped patches of eczema at the elbows. Puberty had not been kind to Izzy. Instead of giving her a waist and breasts, it had given her the beginnings of a moustache and a set of weird growths stretching from neck to hip. Izzy lacked definition, somehow; she looked as though she'd been assembled out of spare parts of someone else. She was tall, but height had only spread out the lumps and growths over a larger area. When her mother looks at Izzy, wondered Hen, does she think she's ugly, too?

'Iz,—' said Jules, 'there's three rooms. We could space out.'

Izzy sniffed. 'Means you don't want me.'

'There's masses of space.'

'You don't, though.'

'It's . . . easier if we all space out. Less cramped.'

Izzy sniffed again, picked up her bag and walked out of the room.

'Pfffffff. That was close.'

Hen bent her head.

'Just want to get some decent sleep. The scratching . . .'

'Mmmm.'

'She goes on and on. I didn't sleep at all last night.'

No question, Izzy was a pain; she scratched, she snored, she extruded. Somehow all Izzy's bodily functions seemed more complicated than anyone else's. Blowing her nose took application and thought, eating had to be approached with stealth, sleep was a nightly wrestle against intransigent skin and disobedient breathing. She had asthma, she had eczema, she had syndromes and malfunctions which flourished like bacilli. Every term, she brought back some new triumphant disorder. The others would arrive with their trophies – a jacket, a different haircut, an upgraded grope in the shrubbery of some anonymous garden – and as they chattered and compared, Izzy would coyly unfurl her latest complaint. Psoriasis perhaps, or an outburst of suspected dyslexia. An allergy to the outdoors one year, an intolerance to dairy products the next. Trouble with household pets or a suspected case of Attention Deficit Disorder. Sometimes they changed – the dyslexia had faded as suddenly as it had appeared, and the allergy to dairy products had lasted just long enough to refuse three packets of chocolate and a slice of someone's birthday cake – but sometimes they remained the same. The scratching, the snoring and the sniffing were old and faithful associates now; Izzy without her sniff – particularly in times of crisis – was as unthinkable as Jules without her temper.

But Hen still did not want to be drawn. Some cloudy understanding told her that Izzy was necessary. Izzy performed a valuable function and should be acknowledged for it. Izzy was the scapegoat and the punchbag, Izzy was the scratching post against which they all relieved their itches. Izzy was necessary, because it was always necessary to have someone to hate. If it wasn't Izzy, then it might have been someone else. And, as Hen was aware, that someone might just have been Hen.

Izzy appeared in the doorway again. 'I've got to sleep in here. Jaws said there's only two rooms we can use.'

Jules shrugged. 'Whatever. Caz's in that bed.'

'S'pose you want me to go miles away?'

'*Whatever.* It doesn't *matter,* for fuck's sake.'

Izzy went over to the bed furthest away from Jules's corner and placed her case gently on the mattress. Then she turned away.

+

'That cow,' said Jules loudly. 'That cow always has it in for me. Always.'

'Not you specifically,' Caz turned a page of the magazine.

'The way she looks at me. Can just tell she's so completely longing for me to fuck up, do something so she can kick me out.'

'Not just you.'

'Is. Naylor loves you. She wants your babies.'

Caz looked up.

'No question, she fancies you. Her eyes go all like sheepy when she sees you. You and her and some hot lezzie action.'

'*Jules.*'

'You can just see her thinking about it. You and her and a

candlelit dinner, all the lights down low, squeaky violin music . . . Creamy.' Jules smirked.

'*Please.*'

'You've just got to accept it. Naylor loves you. She hates me.'

'You'd rather she fancied you instead?'

Jules looked momentarily appalled. 'No.'

'Well, then.'

Jules was wearing a sleeveless black T-shirt she'd borrowed earlier in the day, which had been fine when they'd been stuck in the fug of the minibus but wasn't enough for a breezy evening on an exposed roof. Caz could see her arms beginning to mottle with cold. Not that she'd ever admit it; pride, vanity and the pleasure in temporarily possessing the T-shirt would prevent her from complaining until she was blue to the bone.

Jules was pretty in an unremarkable way. Blue eyes, good skin, average height, a temperamental mouth. She'd been dyeing her hair blonde for several years now, and her darker roots were beginning to show. They made her hair seem greasy even when it wasn't.

The usualness of her looks made them less noticeable. Only the thin crescent-shaped scar scything from the bridge of her nose to the tip of her left eyebrow marked her out. She'd got the scar, she said, when she'd been having a row with her youngest sister. She'd thumped Anna, so Anna had flung a video box across the room at her and been gated for a week. The video was of her cousin's wedding, and every time weddings were mentioned Jules told the story of her scar.

They were out on the roof after supper, considering their instructions. Miss Naylor's account of the next two weeks did not sound encouraging. Walking for the next four days, swimming on Saturday and Monday, cycling for the rest, other forms of exercise as and when Miss Naylor saw fit. Up by 7 a.m., church at 9.30 on Sunday, no going anywhere alone, no impromptu visits to Stokeley, one half-day on Wednesday, kindly remember that they were ambassadors for the school and that their behaviour etc. etc. etc. The only remotely encouraging thing about the lecture was that Jaws looked just as miserable about it as they did.

As they smoked, the shadows began to blur over the Manor. Down below they could hear the sound of a car and an occasional crack of gunshot. Jules leaned back on the tiles, letting the warmth of the day seep through to her skin.

She had found the roof when she was checking out potential smoking places around the grounds. Out at the back, there were several well-hidden patches of shrubbery and a couple of rhododendrons so dark and overgrown that the branches vaulted high above her when she crept inside. With the light creeping through the leaves and the decaying flowers soft under her feet, the bushes made her feel safe but a little daunted. Once within them, she couldn't be seen from outside, but approaching them meant a straight walk across the lawns in full view of anyone looking out of the building.

When she re-emerged she looked up at the Manor. From the back it was shaped like an upside-down J, with the kitchen block as the bar at the top and their bedroom at the end of the curve. Directly opposite the main building was a smaller parallel wing joined by a flat roof. When she got back upstairs, she discovered that one window opened directly onto the roof through a small cleaning cupboard thick with the reek of disinfectants. Outside Jules could see rooftops, slates and a chimney crazed with splits through the mortaring. It seemed perfect; they could see without being seen, and as long as they kept quiet there was no reason at all why anyone should find them. At the edge of the flat roof was a low wall, more ornamental than practical, which protected them from the sight of anyone in the main building. Time and ice had broken down a few of the stones in the wall and the gap fell in a straight drop three floors to the drive. Someone had tried to patch the gap with wire and a few unmatched bricks but, since no one except workmen were expected to be up here, the wire had rusted and the bricks begun to fur with moss. Over the river, Jules could see an office building far away catch the sunlight and signal it back over the river. There was something about the light – reverent, with a hint of dodgy pink – which reminded her of album covers or boring paintings.

Caz perched upright on the tiles and began flicking through the magazine again. It grinned brightly back at them: fat men and their desperate wives, women in heels and diamante dead-heading flowers.

'Bike. Bike. Bike. *Utter* bike. *God* look at that.' She picked up the magazine and turned it round. 'Hideous.' The picture was of an empty-looking woman in a wedding dress.

Jules couldn't see anything wrong with it. The woman was a bit tanned for her liking, but the dress seemed fine. 'Gross,' she said obediently.

'She looks like chicken in tinfoil. God. And her, look.' A woman at a party in a low-cut dress. 'You could tie knots in those.'

'Sad.'

'Falsies. They're so obvious'

'Wonder if it'd be worth it?' Jules pulled out the neck of her T-shirt and stared downwards. 'Could do with help.'

'No. Yours are fine.'

'They're not. Not even poached eggs. They're like two little pins on a wall.'

'You're *fine*. Shut up.'

Both of them inhaled deeply and stared upwards.

'What's up with Hen?'

Jules shrugged. 'She was talking about some woman with a hat and blood.'

'Blood?'

'Mmmm. Something to do with that crash we passed. Some woman.'

'Are you sure?'

'Mmmm. Was why she was so weird. That was what she said.'

'Think she's all right?'

Now that Jules thought about it, she wasn't sure. Hen had been odd recently, her presence somehow more insubstantial than normal. Jules kept getting the sense that she had interrupted something, as if Hen had been having an invisible conversation with someone just out of sight.

'I don't know,' she said slowly. 'She's been strange lately.'

'She's always strange.'

'Yeah, but. This is different strange. This is *strange* strange.'

'You don't think she's becoming . . . ?'

'No she's not. She's fine.'

'She is,' Caz said carefully. 'You know she is.'

'She's not. She's the same as usual.'

'No. Just watch.' Caz did not elaborate, just picked up the magazine and melted back through the window.

Jules remained on the roof, smoking a cigarette she didn't

want and gazing up at an unpleasant sunset. If Caz said to watch, then she would watch. She just wasn't sure that she wanted to see.

+

Hen was awake. The beds were so thin and stiff that she couldn't get comfortable. If she lay on her side then her shoulder hurt, if she lay on her back then the mattress jabbed at her pelvis, and if she lay on her front she ended up worrying about smothering herself with her own pillow. She'd been twisting in circles for what seemed like hours now. Outside, the sky had turned brown from the lights of some distant city. The lights seemed wistful, a suggestion of something possibly exotic.

Two beds down, Izzy made a faint whistling noise through her nose and began to scratch. Hen turned again and stared back into the bedroom, picking out the shapes of bodies and the silhouette of their dressing gowns on the back of the door. Six beds, three down one side of the room and three down the other, with a chest of drawers next to each. Bare walls, squared heaps of blankets, a fire regulation notice by the door.

The bedroom was the last of three on the top floor. It was halfway along a a passageway with a small bathroom opposite and a toilet at the end. She had noticed that the plywood door of the toilet had been kicked several times at the base, and that the tiling round the bath was rimed with mould. The bedrooms themselves were identical – large, with low ceilings, bars on the windows and walls painted the same hungover green as a hospital ward. There was a cloud-shaped patch of damp on the wall underneath the window where the paint had blistered and the plaster underneath bulged with decay. At the end of the corridor was a noticeboard giving details of prayer meetings, mealtimes and safety drills, and pinned at the top was an orange handwritten banner instructing the reader to 'Let Go And Let God'. Let God what? Let him hang out here and see how he liked it?

She could hear the building muttering to itself. There was a steady ticking sound from the roof, and the scud of water down a drainpipe somewhere. Lights came on and went off. Someone on some recent cost-cutting drive had filled the building with economy lightbulbs and fizzing striplamps. They gave the rooms an eery tinge. When Jules had turned towards her earlier, two dark shadows had formed under her eyes.

Hen was not sure what she thought of this place. She did not like the way the women in the canteen had stared at her or the religious notices on the walls offering salvation or the joys of Wales. She got the feeling as she walked through the blank corridors that people with more turbulent histories had been here before. Buildings had atmospheres, and this one made her feel restless. Were there ghosts? Sinister things still locked in cupboards? Had its previous occupants been happy here, or had they been kept against their will? Were the bars on the windows left from the time when this had been an asylum?

The trouble was, if she started thinking about asylums, the painted woman came to mind. Every time she closed her eyes, there she was, crowded up so close to Hen that she could almost feel her breath clouding and unclouding on the window. Somehow the way she'd looked straight through Hen made it worse. She saw the face again, saw it rot before her eyes, saw the hair around her neck begin to writhe. She saw the expression on the face of the policeman as he'd leaned over to take her arm. That raw fear, the sense of everything real fading away, the blood slipping down her legs onto the road . . .

She sat up abruptly. This was ridiculous. She couldn't lie there all night giving herself nightmares. She couldn't even be sure she'd seen the woman – no one else seemed to have done. Maybe she was no more than imagination. Maybe Hen had just dozed off for a second, and the woman had loomed out of the shadows of some sad dream. Was she really going to spend the next two weeks worrying about some illusory old bat she might or might not have seen on the motorway?

Hen was breathing fast. She pulled up her legs and began to rub the feeling back into her knees. Sleeping seemed to be getting more difficult recently, whatever the bed was like. Sometimes she'd find herself wide awake in the middle of the night with two aching red welts on the side of her knees from where they'd been pressed together. She could feel the bones now, the way they grated together under the skin. She went on rubbing them for a while, not looking down. As she lay there, trying to warm up her legs, she realized what seemed so disturbing. Hen was intermittently superstitious – she'd walk under ladders but step over cracks in the pavement – and there was something about the woman, unseen by everyone else, appearing out of nowhere, monstrous and already half mythical, that seemed like a message. Like a single magpie or a broken mirror, the woman on the road was bad luck.

TUESDAY

'Wakey wakey, rise and shine.' Miss Naylor pushed her face up close to Jules. 'Tchk. Late night, was it?'

Through the thick light of the canteen, Jules could trace the line where Miss Naylor's foundation ended and her throat began. Why did she bother with that hideous make-up? She'd always look like roadkill, anyway.

'Never very bright in the mornings, are we?'

'No.'

'Nothing like a good hike to wake us up then, is there?' Pause. '*Is* there?'

'No.'

Through the corner of her eye, Jules could see the men at the other end of the dining room. They had their backs turned and were bent over a large archaeological site map. The men seemed oblivious to the girls in the corner. When she had met one of them upstairs in the passageway, his eyes had flicked once to the right and then he'd scurried downstairs. None of them was remotely fit, and all of them were well over forty, but there was something odd about the way these men didn't acknowledge them at all.

Miss Naylor turned back to the table and began handing

out a pile of papers to the group. 'Maps. Forest of Dean, Tintern, Stroud, Chepstow. If you're thinking of losing them, don't. There are no replacements. Are we all suitably equipped? Trainers, anorak, decent socks, rucksack, penknife?' The group nodded. 'Good. Today,' – she smiled – 'we will be walking ten miles. Tomorrow maybe more.'

Jules whimpered.

'We have a problem with that?'

A small black beetle was trying to clamber out of one of the carved grooves in the table. Just when it was nearly out of the groove, it kept catching itself and falling back.

'So *far*.'

'By which I take it we are too idle to manage much more than to shuffle from one smokers' corner to another?'

Silence.

'You're not here on holiday. Any other complaints?'

'Where's lunch?' said Izzy sadly.

'Packed. We'll stop on the way.'

'Is there any free time?'

'No. Not until tomorrow. Anything else?'

All ten of them sat with their heads down, glaring at each other's trainers. Jules picked up a fork and crushed the beetle. It left a wet brown stain on the table.

'Right. Onwards. Onwards and upwards.'

+

Ali couldn't admit it, but she was enjoying this. She liked the sunlight and the whispering trees, this intriguing new landscape all rucked up into folds and tucks. The forest was weird. She'd never come across a place like it before. There were so many miniature valleys and summits, and so many intriguing shadows. It looked as if the whole place had been squeezed into a space too small for its size, and the only way to fit it all in was to pleat the ground up tight like corrugated iron. There was something furtive about it, something concealed within its lush respectability that she found fascinating. The darkened gaps where the ground fell away, the blue-green ivy creeping up towards the sun, the soft leaf-covered dips. All the colours in this patch of the forest seemed a little more vivid than they did elsewhere, the light more shiny, the darkness more complete.

She hadn't expected this. She hadn't expected anything. The trip was only ever supposed to be a way of using up the time between exams and the end of term, a cut-price kind of parole. But now they were here, she was pleased. There was no use explaining to anyone else that she liked the place, no point in confessing a fondness for fields or valleys or places that didn't have men or alcohol as their ultimate ends. But there were places to explore and things to find out, and that made the next two weeks a much more bearable proposition.

She tucked her legs underneath her and inspected her packed lunch. They were sitting in a clearing on a pile of logs, gazing round at the sky and the sunlit foxgloves. Someone had been felling trees and there was a good-sized patch where the sun had warmed the wood.

Mina had sat next to Vicky on one of the logs until she saw a spider. '*Euwww!*' She leapt up.

Jaws watched her. 'What do you think it's going to do? Poison you?'

'It's *hairy.*'

'Since when are there poisonous hairy man-eating spiders in England?'

'There are snakes. Whole place could be full of poisonous stuff. Could be mutant.'

'Right.' Jaws took a cigarette out of her top pocket and tapped it on the packet. 'Sure. In the meantime, how about eating your lunch?'

'There aren't man-eating spiders in England,' said Izzy. 'There just aren't. Everyone knows.'

Mina curled her lip. 'Yeah, right. "Everyone knows." '

'Leave it,' said Jaws, closing her eyes. 'Eat your lunch.'

A short, fraught silence.

'I'm just saying,' murmured Izzy, 'just because it's hairy doesn't mean it thinks you're breakfast.'

Jaws opened one eye. 'Izzy . . .'

'You didn't see how huge it was, anyway.'

'So? It's not the big ones which are scary. It's the little boring ones.'

'Oh yeah? God, you really fucking know it all, don't you? You really—'

'Mina! Eat your lunch!'

A longer silence, broiling with possible retorts. Ali stared upwards. Most times it was like this. Most times she treated it as a form of aural wallpaper, something so familiar it was simply part of the background. It was the same way people described living next to airports or motorways; sooner or later what had been unbearable became tolerable and then merely ordinary. She didn't like the endless arguments, the slow corrosive pickpickstabstab of claim and counter-claim, but she had, she supposed, got used to it.

As long as it didn't involve her it was fine. And most things didn't. Sometimes Ali felt like wallpaper herself; something unfashionable which only got noticed when someone remembered to look. She was present, but somehow she was also perpetually absent. The best that could be said of her was that she didn't irritate people the way Izzy did. She didn't scrape at their frustrations or say the wrong thing at the wrong moment or have that dogged eagerness to be part of things. And the worst? The worst was probably that people ignored her because she wasn't worth speaking to.

Ali wondered if Jaws felt the same way. When Jaws had arrived two years ago, no one had been quite sure what to make of her. She had a wry, rather sarcastic way of saying things which made people suspect that she was laughing at them and a habit of making jokes that skimmed straight over the heads of most people (including, Ali suspected, many of the other staff). She tended to stay a little aloof and to prefer her own company or that of the sixth-formers. In part, her separateness must have been connected to her age. Jaws was twenty-eight; the majority of the other teachers were into their late forties or fifties. She did not look or act like the others and it still surprised Ali that she should have chosen to come to the school.

Perhaps it was something to do with the way she looked. Her dark hair had been cropped back in a practical cut and lightened with a few desultory blonde streaks. But her hair would never be the part of her people noticed. Some genetic misfortune had given her a chin which was always shunted too far out. When she smiled or shouted, it was her lower teeth that appeared, maggotty-white and shining. Ali had never quite forgotten the sight of her at the annual Christmas party all done up in lipstick and sparkly earrings. She had looked, thought Ali, just like a transvestite. No wonder it had taken all of two days before Miss Collins, history teacher, MA (Cantab.), DipEd (London) had become simply Jaws.

She stood up. 'Come on. We'd better get going.'

Mina got reluctantly to her feet. 'How far?'

'Distance is a relative concept. If you think it's going to be far, it will be far. If you think it's just round the corner, it will be round the corner.'

'*What?*'

Jaws smiled. 'Never mind. It's just a possible way of thinking about things. If you programme yourself to find something easy, in all likelihood you will find it easy.'

'Like exams,' Izzy butted in. 'Like if you say Eng. lang. is easy, you'll probably pass.'

'Yeah, *right*. Like you would. Like you're so smug that always happens.'

'I'm not. I'm just saying, if you think—'

'So you go into something completely stupid like maths or physics and think, I'm going to pass this one, so you do. That's so completely typical.'

'I wasn't—'

'Just leave it,' said Jaws, heaving her rucksack onto one shoulder. 'My God, you two could argue for Britain. Let's just get on.'

They set off down the path, Jaws up ahead, Mina and Izzy kicking and scraping behind. Ali heard Mina fall into line with Vicky, and the discordant rise and fall of her complaint. Izzy, looking around for someone willing to listen, caught Ali's glance for a second. No, thought Ali, dipping her eyes. Not me. Not now. I don't want to be recruited. She felt the first drops of rain sting her scalp.

+

'Gym? As well? Why?'

'Because,' said Caz, 'because it's possible.'

'So there's the walking, and the biking, and the swimming, and now there's gym as well? What does she think we are?'

'Under-occupied. Or dangerous. Or both.'

Jules lay face down on her bed, arms out to the side, mock-crucified. 'And you're just going to go? You're not going to say something?'

'No use. I tried.'

'She just wants to get you in a short skirt. Told you. She's just after your body.'

Caz smiled, lifting her clothes up and letting them fall.

Hen, sitting cross-legged on the opposite bed, stirred. 'Isn't a gym here. There's just a big empty room with a load of crap in it. I looked.'

'That's it. Next to the kitchens.'

'Don't believe . . .' Jules tailed off. 'Can't we just say we don't have any kit? They didn't say we had to, so we didn't bring it.'

'You think that would make a difference? She'd get us doing handstands in nothing but knickers if she had a chance.'

'She can't!' Jules's voice rose. 'It's wrong! It's against our rights.'

'Um . . .' said Hen, 'which rights?'

'Our rights as people. Our rights as normal exhausted human beings who've just been on some stupid cross-country forced march. Just rights, for fuck's sake . . .'

Fifteen minutes later Jules's voice, rising like the scream of a kettle, followed them downstairs, through the darkened passageways and into the rec room. As a protest, she had changed into the most impractical clothes she could find: a pair of trousers so tight they left red seams down her skin when she took them off and a T-shirt with 'SAVAGE' written across it in glitter.

The rec room was an immense rectangular space with french windows stretching from ceiling to floor down one end and an odd, half-vaulted ceiling painted white and brown. Perhaps all the arches and crenellations were supposed to give a sense of the divine. As it was, the room felt like a chapel without a cause, an ugly space which had long outlived its gods. Bare bulbs hung along the length of the ceiling, and two ropes dangled from hooks near the windows. Along one side there was a set of wooden wall bars so shiny with age they must have been put up during the war for the evacuees. Someone had dug out what looked like a set of thin foam mattresses of the kind used for sofa beds.

Somebody had brought in a portable stereo, and Jules could hear the hiss of the home-made tape. Miss Naylor turned the volume down. 'Dressed for action, are we? Right. Izzy and Vicky, put the mats out; Ali, see if you can open one of those windows. Go on then. Chop-chop. Julia, get back upstairs and put some proper kit on.'

'Haven't got any.'

'Find something.'

Jules glanced once, bitterly, at Hen. Then she turned and vanished back upstairs. In the bedroom, she sat for a moment staring at her drawers. She didn't want to do gym. It wasn't the same as walking. Walking didn't risk anything somehow. Gym did. She pulled open the drawer and changed into a horrible pair of old jogging pants she'd only brought by mistake. When she returned downstairs, the others were doing warm-up exercises: stretching and twisting, swaying and bending.

Jules took her place on the empty mat. She was still wearing the T-shirt and she could feel its neckline pulling irritably at her throat. Hen, deep in the safety of a vast tracksuit, looked over at Jules and smiled. Izzy was out of time with everyone else, and Mel and Mina had placed their mats so close together that when Mina flung one arm out to the side, she whacked Mel's wrist. Jules picked up the rhythm and began to move. She was still furious. Her arms went up and down jerkily, pulling at the unaccustomed muscles. Hen, lost in the slow rhythm of each separate limb, did not look round.

As her arms began to move, Jules remembered everything she hated about gym. In the effort of a trampoline or a wall bar people exposed something of themselves, showed something other than their usual indifference. Gym forced them to want and to find that they would never be satisfied. All the time and effort that went into looking as if nothing ever took time or effort, all the exhausting hope. All the glimpses of other girls' bodies and all the knowledge of the glances they were sneaking at her. Jules had got used to being watched; was, in fact, so conditioned to it that when she lay down to sleep at night she curled herself into the sort of position that she thought other people would like to see. But at times like these she remembered how unbearable it was to have someone's eyes on you all the time. And there was something sad about the knowledge that if she tried, she might just be good at it.

She stopped watching Hen and looked over towards Caz, who was standing on the mat in front, semaphoring her arms slowly up and down. Not for the first time Jules found herself checking for errors that didn't exist. Caz's shoulders were perfect, square enough to suggest strength, but still feminine. The flesh at the top of her arms swelled and then dipped inwards as if she'd been working out every day for months. In the cavity of her collarbones, it would have been possible to drop two little pools of water and watch her carry them forever undisturbed. From her shoulders, difficult strappy dresses clung like a second skin. Jules had never understood why clothes, like everything else, seemed to love Caz so much. Caz could put on anything – an impossible skirt, a bikini, cut-throat shoes – and it would seem instantly richer. She would always have expensive hair and a hollow stomach. Her breasts had never been through an awkward phase, her eyebrows somehow plucked themselves and her legs stretched from here to December. Where Jules felt puffy and unkempt, Caz looked perfect. Caz always looked perfect. There was a delightful uniformity in her appearance, as if looking this good was the only possible honesty. Near the end of term most things became stale: sharp hair would have blunted, fine threads would have worn, clear skin would have silted. But Caz just went on gleaming, day after day.

Caz, conscious that she was being watched, turned and smiled. Jules stared straight ahead.

Miss Naylor was watching them both. 'Arms up,' she said, gripping one of Jules's wrists and sweeping it above her head. 'Right up to twelve o'clock. Put some effort into it.'

Jules tried to wring her arm out of Miss Naylor's grasp. *Fucking lesbian,* she thought. *Fucking lame old dyke.*

'Right.' She let go. 'Thirty star-jumps, all of you.'

Jules stood up. As she did so, she saw a shadow slither over the window frame. A man. One of the beardy people who had been staring at maps in the canteen that morning. He was standing by the window, looking in, half turned towards the lawns. She could see the curl of his collar round his poky neck.

What a creep. What was he doing, standing there, staring at them?

Izzy giggled. 'Eurrgh. Look. Perv alert.'

Miss Naylor walked over to the window and flapped a hand at the shadow. The bulging figure vanished. 'Right. Thirty star-jumps, starting now.'

Jules felt the floor shudder beneath her feet as the others began to move. In front of her, Caz's arms flew up and down. Jules knew she shouldn't really be watching her but she couldn't help it. There was something compelling about Caz, something that drew people to her. And she wanted what Caz had, no question. She wanted a wrist like that, skin like that, assumptions like that. She wanted her hair to swing out like that when she bent down, she wanted those breasts that seemed always neither too big nor too small. When she laughed, she wanted to laugh like Caz did, knowing she was lovely, instead of fearing that she was wrong or inappropriate or too loud or too childish or that her teeth were bad and her lips were not the right shape and . . . She wanted not to spend so much time being afraid. She wanted to feel the warmth of other people's glances. She wanted to have it all and take it for granted just like Caz did. She wanted to make everyone jealous of her. She wanted to take Caz apart, examine the machinery that made her tick, see why she ticked so much better than everybody else. She wanted to know how they could both have the same number of fingers and toes and eyes and legs and dreams, but still Caz was first class and she was only economy. For a second Jules felt desire so strong that she could scarcely breathe. But though she looked at Caz with passion, it was not love that Jules felt. It wasn't even close.

Caz looked round again. This time, she did not smile, just

kept on looking for a couple of seconds longer than necessary. There was understanding in her gaze, and something else as well. Not unkind. Something almost equal. Almost like a challenge. Not the way she usually looked at Jules at all, no distance, no benign superiority. Her gaze was hard and bright, like an invitation. Jules, disconcerted, swung her arms round a little harder. She wasn't sure what she'd been caught doing, but she knew obscurely that it was something wrong.

When she looked round again, Miss Naylor was watching her. Jules understood the message there, no problem. Pure straightforward dislike. That, thought Jules, is pure sad lesbian for you; she's just pissed off because Caz was looking at me and not at her. Something uneasy swam through the corners of her mind and then vanished.

Miss Naylor crossed the room. 'Have you always been malcoordinated, or are you doing it deliberately?'

'No.'

'It is deliberate?'

'No.'

'So you're just naturally stupid, then?'

Jules felt the shiver of loathing as something physical.

'Do you think you could try to keep time? Or is that too complicated?'

Outside, rain was pouring from a hole in the guttering and a puddle had formed on the right-hand side of the lawn. A figure was standing close to the side of the Manor, holding an empty Tesco bag above his head. The bag was doing nothing to prevent the rain from soaking him, but he did not seem to feel it. He was watching the figures in the gym. Further round this time, near the back of the building where they couldn't see. The man stood close to the windows, guarding his own silhouette, being careful not to let it fall where it shouldn't be. And as he watched, the rain slipped down the back of his shirt.

+

'Do you think,' said Mel through the darkness, 'that Jaws ever has sex?'

Izzy giggled.

'She must, though.'

'Who with?'

'Dunno. Someone.' Mel paused. 'She doesn't . . . She's not frustrated like Naylor is.'

'How do you know?'

'Because frustration makes people vile and paranoid. She's not as vile as Naylor is.'

'The Pope's not vile and paranoid, and he's not getting it much.'

'That's different.'

'Why?'

'Because he's married to Jesus or something.'

Izzy sat up, guffawing. 'What, like a gay wedding?'

'No. Doesn't matter. Point is, is Jaws getting it?'

'Never seen her with anyone.'

'She was with one of those beardy men earlier.'

'Yeurgh. Why?'

'She was talking to him.'

'Was asking him about the best walks,' said Hen, half muffled by a layer of bedclothes. 'Hardly counts as full-on cunnilingus in the canteen.'

'How do you know?'

'Because I heard.'

'No one snogs men with beards,' said Izzy. 'They can't. They've got food in them.'

'Somebody does. Even beardy guys must reproduce.'

'No! Be like snogging someone's lunch.'

Hen propped herself on one elbow. 'She's probably got a thing with beards because of the history. Everyone had beards in history. And she's obsessed with dead people.' Her mind spun off. She pictured Jaws alone in a wood-panelled room, bending over the corpse of a man in a periwig, lifting a glass of something to his lips. For some reason, the image didn't seem freakish. It seemed – well, tender, almost. Oh God, thought Hen, maybe I'm into dead people, too.

'Like who?'

'Like everyone. Henry VIII, Shakespeare, Disraeli.'

'And no toothpaste. Vile. God.'

'James I!' said Izzy suddenly. 'He had psoriasis! And bad breath!'

'He was—' Hen stopped. She had been about to say he was Scottish, but decided against it. 'He was gay, so he'd only have been snogging other men.'

'He had children, though.'

'So? Maybe he used a turkey baster.'

'They didn't have turkey basters in history.'

'How do you know?'

'Perhaps,' said Mel, feeling that they were losing the point somewhere, 'she's having a thing with Miss Naylor.'

Hen ignored her. 'Ye Godly Miss Collins,' she said, in an urgent voice, 'I find myself most pursuivantly persuaded with your excellent chin, I find myself coming over all dribbly at the thought of your dulcimer voice, it reminds me of my one-time lover Mr James the First of England who wore tight breeches in bed . . .'

'No. Or,' said Izzy, 'she got really overexcited about Charles the Second. The way he had meetings while he was shagging his mistress.'

Hen dangled a shirt which had been lying on the back of her chair. 'Madame Jaws, I'm so desiring of spending moments in your company. I have incredibly stupid hair and I look like some kind of dog, but if you slip into my flouncy starchamber, my foreign policy is really interesting.'

She was talking quite loudly, hoping that the conversation would rouse Jules from under the duvet. It was uncharacteristic for Jules to be silent, particularly during any discussion of sex and sexual matters. But she didn't stir. She hadn't said anything all night; she'd been offish at supper and odd upstairs. Even Caz hadn't been able to provoke much response. She'd suggested going for a fag up on the roof, and Jules had looked at her as if she'd been offering a spot of recreational crochet. Hen wondered what she had done. Was there some reason why Jules was pissed off with her?

'That's it!' said Izzy. 'Cromwell. Cromwell and his warts. She had a thing about that too. She's a necrophiliac.'

Silence. Finally Mel said reluctantly, 'The fuck is that?'

'Someone who sleeps with dead people.'

'No *way*. No one sleeps with dead people.'

'Some people do.'

'How do you know?'

'They just do. I read about it.'

'Jaws sleeps with dead people? No *way*.'

'She might. Doesn't sleep with anyone alive. So maybe she has a thing about dead people.'

'God's *sake*.' Hen was impatient. 'Get real. She doesn't. She had one conversation with a man with a beard, and you're saying she hangs around graveyards at night and bags off with the undead?'

'The dead.'

'That's what I mean.'

Izzy, taking offence at Hen's tone, got high-pitched. 'You said . . . all that history . . .'

'Shut up, Izzy. Get some sleep.'

Izzy looked for support from Mel, found none, and sank abruptly under the bedclothes. Hen turned on her side, wrapped herself over the hostile mattress and said no more. Whatever was wrong with Jules would have to be sorted in the morning.

Sooner or later, all of them slept.

WEDNESDAY

They had been walking for about two hours, Ali at the front, Jules and Hen murmuring along together and Izzy at the back. The track led through a large plantation of conifers, and through the gaps in the trees Ali could see stripes of sunlight. The trees had all been planted a set distance one from the other, and she was enjoying the way the trunks kept arranging themselves into straight lines and diagonals as she walked. The branches twitched with hidden life and she could hear the birds making the kind of summery racket she hadn't heard in months. Once in a while a plane drew lines across a sky of absolute blue.

Behind her, Ali could hear the rise and fall of Jules's daily complaint. Sometimes – as now – her words carried the distance, but Hen's voice was lower and less easy to make out.

'. . . will *not* die because my liver fails. You have to drink like a whole bath's worth of drink every day. Then your liver fails. Not now.'

Hen mumbled something.

'There was a man once. We used to live next to him. He got liver failure. He used to drink a whole bottle of Peugeot every day. It was really funny; he used—'

'. . .'

'OK, fucking *Pernod* then. Whatever. Used to come out every night into his garden and start smashing up the plants. Yell at them. Every night. He'd just lay into these things like they were alive or something. All these flowers and bushes and stuff. I saw him once in the winter and he was just standing there bashing the snow with a stick. Yelling at this stupid rose bush. My dad said it was really sad. He said he'd been like that since his wife left him. She'd made the garden and that was why he was angry. He died eventually.'

A pause. Then Hen's voice shouted, 'Ali! Iz! We're having a break!'

Ali turned. Jules and Hen had sat down and were feeling around in their backpacks.

'How much further is it?'

'Two, three miles. Probably. Don't know.'

Jules groaned and lay back on the grass. 'Three miles? *Three fucking miles*? Got your compass, Hen?'

Hen passed over a small plastic object on a bit of string. Jules stood in the middle of the track and turned a full circle first to the left and then to the right. She frowned at the compass and then sat down again. 'Doesn't work. Batteries must have gone.'

Hen looked at her for a while. 'I did learn,' she said eventually. 'My brother taught me.'

'Who's got food?'

Hen and Izzy rummaged. 'Coke,' said Izzy eagerly, 'Red Bull, prawn sandwich, cheese from yesterday . . .'

'Shouldn't eat anything.' Jules patted a virtuous thigh. 'So fat at the moment. Give us the Red Bull, will you?'

She passed the can over to Hen, who drank. 'Ta,' she said, handing it back.

Izzy turned it upside down, and a few drops pattered onto the track. 'You drank it all,' she said sadly. 'That was mine.'

'You offered.' Jules leaned back and untucked her shirt. 'Need my vitamin C. So pale I'm practically invisible.'

'It isn't,' said Izzy.

'It isn't what?'

'It isn't vitamin C you get from sunlight. It's vitamin D.'

'So?'

'So,' – patiently – 'you got it wrong. It's vitamin D you get from a tan.'

Jules sat up again. 'I think,' she said, 'that you are mistaking me for someone who *gives* a fuck. You sound like fucking Naylor sometimes.'

Izzy sat down a few yards away, turned her back on Jules and Hen and set about gaining the maximum possible tan with the minimum possible exposure. She lifted off her shirt and clamped it over her chest, rolled her trouser legs up to the knee, shuffled off her trainers, scratched, and lay back.

Time passed. Ali watched a dribble of sweat run down Izzy's forehead. She had begun a kind of rhythm – she would sniff hard and then scratch. Sniff. Scratch. Even at this distance Ali could hear the hollow rasp of her nails on her skin.

'Izzy,' said Jules, 'can't you shut up for a second?'

Izzy heaved herself upright. 'It's eczema.'

'Yeah, well. Can't you fuck off and sunbathe further away?'

Sweat had pasted Izzy's hair down flat on her forehead. She shoved one foot back into her trainer, tried to put her shirt back on without anyone seeing her breasts and walked off down the track.

'Thank fuck for that. Was really beginning to piss me off.'

'Mmmm.'

Ali watched Izzy go. She should follow her. Izzy had no compass and, for all she knew, no map either. And, given her complete inability to get from one place to the next without making an idiot of herself, no sense of direction. On the other hand, what was the point? She would either come back or she would get lost. And, since it was Jules who'd upset her, Jules could fetch her if she did disappear. She lay dozing for a few minutes.

Finally Jules got up. 'Fucking flies. Come on, I want a drink.'

They set off again towards the swish of distant traffic. The track kept on straight for a while and then curved to the left through a clearing already strident with fireweed. A few yards further on, Izzy sat hunched by a tree stump, pawing at her face with a shirtsleeve. Ali saw her darkened hair, the rumpled shirt, the red mark on her ankle where the trainers had rubbed at her skin. She crouched down beside her.

'You OK?' Perhaps she should put a comforting hand on Izzy's shoulder. Perhaps she was supposed to give her a hug. But she didn't want to touch Izzy. There was something about her that felt as if it might be contagious.

Izzy smeared at her face. 'Hayfever.'

'What's wrong?'

'Nothing.' Pause. 'Jules. What is it with her?'

'Dunno. Just born that way, probably.'

Izzy twisted her hair around one finger until it was tight and ugly over her face. 'Don't mind usually, but when it's not my fault she gets to me. Not my fault about the eczema.'

'Can go home soon.'

Ali turned as Jules walked up. 'All right?' Her face was bland.

Izzy kept her head bowed.

'There's a road near here and the road goes into the village. Hen's got a map.'

First we've heard of it, thought Ali.

'We're going. Jaws'll be somewhere down there. Maybe see you later.'

Izzy did not look up again until they were almost out of sight.

+

'Stop looking at yourself in the mirror.'

'I'm not.'

'Are. You're always looking at yourself in the mirror.'

'I'm *not*.' Hen yanked her chair around until she was facing in the opposite direction. 'You're sitting in front of it. Can't help looking in it.'

'Crap. You were looking in it because you wanted to see yourself. I saw you. You were checking your hair.'

'I was *not* checking my hair. My hair's shit anyway. Stopped looking at it years ago.'

'No, you haven't. All the time you stare at yourself in things.'

'I *don't*. I don't look at myself. Don't *like* looking at myself.'

They were sitting in a cafe up one of the side streets of Stokeley. It was one of many in the town and there was a good chance that no one would find them here.

When they had reached the end of the track, they'd found Jaws waiting for them. She'd looked hot, bedazzled by the sunlight and the resinous scents of the wood. They'd told her where Izzy and Ali were and waited while she deliberated.

'Right,' she said eventually. 'You can go. Back by five. And there'll be one of us around, so don't try anything too depraved.'

Jules had turned and began walking backwards towards Stokeley. She pulled off her jersey and waved it above her head like a football strip. 'We'll be good, I promise. Promiiissss.'

'Think I'm vain?' said Hen now.

Jules considered. 'Yes. Sometimes.'

'I'm *not.*' Hen yanked her chair further to the left. 'The opposite of being vain. It's *worry.*'

Jules smirked.

'It's true! If I don't look in the mirror, how can I tell if I'm covered in spots or hair or whatever? That's not vain. Anyway. You're just as bad as me.'

'I'm not. I couldn't give a shit about the way I look. I'm so fat and slobby and horrible at the moment there's no point in worrying.'

'You're not fat. Not half as fat as me.'

'I am. Look.' Jules plucked at her thigh. 'Bleeurgh. Look. It's disgusting. It's all slobby and white and pale and it bulges all over the place.' She lifted her leg slightly so it looked thinner.

'That's not fat. That's normal. That's muscle or something. Look at mine – that's fat.' Hen pinched the skin on her hip.

Jules could see the pale crescent nails biting into her skin. 'You're way too thin. You're disgustingly thin. Look. That bit. That is no way fat. Just skin you're pinching.'

'Not.'

'No, really. You're dead skinny. Not normal skinny, weird skinny.'

Hen kept her face impassive. 'I am not.'

'You are. You know you are. You're getting anorexic or something.'

'I *am not* fucking anorexic. There is no fucking way I am anorexic. God, I wish I was.'

'Well, you look weird,' said Jules, offhand. 'You don't look normal any more.'

'I do. I look completely normal. I look as completely shite as usual.'

'You don't eat.'

'Course I don't eat. Not that shite they give us. So gross nobody could eat that stuff.'

'No.' Jules looked suddenly unsure of herself. 'Right.'

'Order?' said the waitress, coming over to them. She was a girl not much older than them, wearing too much make-up. They ordered coffee and, as Hen looked up at her, Jules considered Hen's face. Her hair had been pulled out of its clip, making her widow's peak more pronounced than usual. Something about the shape of her face made Hen seem more virtuous than she actually was. People – parents, anyway – spoke to her tentatively, as if she might look through them and see their sins. Jules felt it too. Sometimes she'd turn round halfway through a conversation and see a stranger looking back, a girl with a face like a church. And then Hen would say something in that odd cross-bred accent of hers and the sensation would go.

'Jules?'

'Mmmm.'

'You know yesterday?'

'Mmmm.'

'What was wrong?'

Jules narrowed her eyes. 'D'you mean?'

'In gym.'

'Nothing.'

'But you . . . last night . . . were you all right?'

'Yes.' Abruptly. 'Fine.'

The connection was gone. Hen, not knowing how to continue, hunched deeper in the chair. 'Something to do with Naylor?'

'Doesn't matter.'

'Was it Caz?'

'Doesn't *matter*.' Frowning. 'No.'

'You would . . . you can say stuff. To me, I mean. You trust me, right?'

Jules pushed her chair back. 'Where's our fucking coffee?' Hen bent her head slightly, paying penance for an unidentified crime. They sat in silence as the waitress watched them.

+

Fuck, thought Ali. Now I'm stuck with her.

'Ought to go.' Izzy clambered upright, picked up her stick and stood facing in the wrong direction. 'How far is it?' There was a childish note in her voice like a toddler stuck for too long in a car.

'Dunno. Don't know till we get there.'

They walked on. The track bent and twisted, widening in places where the tractors must have been and then receding back into grass again. The sound of cars came whispering through the wood, sometimes almost silent, sometimes so loud Ali wondered if they were only a few yards from the road. She felt the trees creaking above them, saw the refractions of the sunlight and thought that actually she didn't much mind how long it took to walk. She was warm, the wood intrigued her and this felt like a kind of freedom. Even with Izzy. Who had started scratching her elbows after a few paces and was now trying to negotiate rearranging her backpack, keeping hold of the stick and scratching all at the same time.

'There was a story once.' Ali's voice sounded small in all this space. 'In a book I read. A book when I was younger. There was this boy called Edmund, and the other three were always getting pissed off with him. Edmund went off one day and got stuck in a dragon's lair. The dragon had died but there were all these bits of jewellery, diamonds and pearls and stuff, lying around in his den. And Edmund thought this stuff was amazing, so he stuck one of the bracelets onto his arm. And then he went to sleep. And when he woke up the bracelet was biting into his arm and he realized that while he'd been asleep he'd become a dragon.'

She stopped. Why was she saying this? Izzy didn't read. Not properly. Izzy's idea of reading didn't stretch much further than sleeve notes. When she read, her lips moved. 'And he cried and he wailed and he banged his tail up and down and eventually he just gave up and waited. And eventually someone came along in a dream and told him if he wanted to go back to being a boy, he'd have to take his skin off. Like a snake. Shed it. So Edmund the dragon scrapes off one of his skins and he's still like a dragon. And then he scrapes another one off and he's still a dragon. And he keeps on scraping and scraping away at his skin and he still goes on being this dragon thing. And finally he gets so pissed off he takes a really big bite into his skin, right down deep, and peels this huge lump of stuff off of himself. And it really hurts – it's like peeling himself from the outside in – but when it comes off, he's a boy again.'

'So?'

'So,' said Ali lamely, 'it's like you.'

'Me?'

'Listening to you at night. Scratching and scratching. You sound like Edmund. You sound like you're trying to take off your own skin.'

Izzy stopped. 'I can't *help* it. One of the *symptoms* of eczema is scratching. It's medical. It all comes up like blisters and then you scratch it and then it goes away. Sometimes.'

'Didn't mean that. I know it's medical.'

'It's not my *fault*.'

'I didn't say—'

'It's got nothing to do with books.'

Ali just stood there, waiting. She'd known it was pointless telling Izzy that story. She knew it as soon as she'd started talking. But she kept on, hoping – really, stupidly hoping – that someone one day would understand what she meant. That one day she'd have a proper conversation with someone instead of just a series of audible misconnections.

Izzy whacked the stick against the ground. They walked on again. This time the silence between them seemed less easy to shift. Ali felt the flicker of the breeze up her sleeves and studied the sharp colours of the leaves, the way they could turn six different shades of green just by rotating slightly in the wind. But it didn't work any more; it couldn't work with Izzy plodding resentfully along beside her. The best thing was not to say anything, just walk along pretending it was an easy companionable sort of silence. Izzy started whacking the ground again. Step, whack, step, whack, step, whack.

Ali could feel Izzy's scowl without even looking. She turned. 'What is it?'

'Jules and Hen hate me.'

'They hate most people. They hate most people who aren't blokes or Caz or them. Does it matter?'

'If I knew why, it might be different.'

'It wouldn't be different. It would be the same. They don't hate you for anything you do, they hate you – us – because they've got to hate someone. It's just the way it works.'

'Why?'

'Don't know. There's a theory in some book . . .' She reversed. 'There's a theory that people need scapegoats. You have a group of people and there's a leader and there's a good person and there's the sort of person who everyone ignores and there's someone who they all . . .' She had been about to say 'hate' again, but decided that Izzy might regard theory and reality as one and the same. '. . . someone they all make into a scapegoat. Always like that. Been like that since we started.'

'But *why?*' It came out as a wail, high and unanswerable.

'I don't know. It just is.'

'I would like . . . I would really love, one day, to be someone in a group.'

'Why?'

'Don't you want to be in one, just once?'

The question irritated Ali. She wasn't sure why. Partly because it was its own confirmation. It sounded so childish, so Izzy-ishly needy, that Ali wanted to shout, There! See! That's why people get so annoyed with you, because you ask questions like that! And partly, when she thought a bit further, because she wasn't in anyone's group or gang and she never had been. She was out on her own. But there seemed some enormous significant difference between knowing it and saying it. 'No,' she said shortly. 'No point.'

'It's different for you. People know you're not a groupy person. People think you're a weirdo. They leave you alone. People are scared of you.'

'I'm not weird.'

'All that going off on your own. Climbing trees and stuff. People think it's weird.'

Ali found herself becoming angry. 'It's not weird. It's just what I like to do. They're the weird ones.'

'They're not. They're normal. It's us who's weird.'

'Well, if that's normal, then . . .' Ali was having difficulty with Izzy's use of the word 'us'. She started walking faster.

'But you must.' Izzy stumbled to catch up. 'Must want to belong somewhere. Just once.'

'I don't.'

'Well, I do. I want to belong somewhere.'

'Yeah? Who are you going to get to join, then?' Ali was almost running now.

Izzy subsided, panting. 'Don't you want it? Just to see what it's like?'

'Doesn't *happen* like that. None of it happens like that. I'm fine.' Her words trailed out behind her. '*Fine*, OK?'

'Wait,' said Izzy. 'Please. Wait.'

But Ali fled on alone.

+

'Look!' Jules jabbed at Hen's arm. 'Look! Over there. Men! Live, free-range men!'

Hen turned round in her seat and followed Jules's finger. Walking past the cafe down the lane she saw a red-haired woman tugging at a scratchy toddler and a man with a spaniel on a lead. 'What?'

'*Duh.*' Jules poked her tongue into her cheek. '*Challenged.* Over there, retard.'

Hen looked again. Opposite the cafe was a record shop. Its facade was painted black, but some of the gloss had chipped off with time and the pale undercoat now leaked through. There was a large spinning disc in its window and the word 'DiVinyl' in Gothic lettering above the door. Inside she could see figures moving about and a man by the front window flicking through a crate of old LPs. When the coffee machine in the cafe stopped grinding, Hen could hear the thud of a deep bass beat. As she watched, two more figures appeared in the doorway and began to walk off down the lane. One of them had a plastic bag in his hand and was peering into it. The other was talking animatedly.

Jules grinned. 'Nice one. Let's go.' She took a gulp of her coffee, whacked a couple of coins onto the table and got up. 'C'mon.'

'Now?'

'Yes. Now. Come on.'

Hen put her hand up to her hair, put it down, squinted into the mirror and got up. Then she sat down again. 'But I'm all hot and red and crap.'

'Come *on.*' Jules began to giggle. 'Stop fucking fussing.'

'Haven't paid.'

'Doesn't *matter.* Stop staring at yourself.'

'Coming. Just wait.'

'God's sake.' Jules raised her voice slightly, so the rest of the cafe could hear. 'If you weren't so bloody vain . . .'

'Not vain.' Hen hurled the rest of her stuff back into the

rucksack and swung it over the chair, rattling the coffee cup in its saucer. She snatched at Jules's rucksack. '*Not fucking vain,* right?'

'Right,' said Jules, giggling frantically now. 'Only a little bit vain then.'

'Not vain! Take it back or I won't come with you.'

'So? How vain is that?' Through the corner of her eye, Hen could see the waitress looking up from her magazine.

Jules yanked herself away and pulled the door open. They bundled out onto the pavement, tugging at each other and laughing. It felt to Hen like the squelched sort of laughter she sometimes got in parents' meetings.

'How could you *do* that? In the cafe. Saying I was vain.'

'You are.' Jules assumed a caring expression. 'Just need to get in touch with your vain side.'

Hen made to kick her on the shin but she dodged. 'I'm not the one with twenty-seven lipglosses, am I? And the make-up bag so huge it takes a fork-lift truck to pick it up, and the sneaky mirror in your pencil case . . .' She ran across the road, giggling. They barged through the door of DiVinyl, shrieking, intoxicated.

From the moment they walked into the shop both of them were struck dumb. The shop was smaller than Hen had thought it would be, just one room divided at the back by a counter and painted black. Coming from a street full of light and movement, it seemed to Hen as if they had stumbled into polar winter. Each aisle was lit only with a couple of spotlights and the posters on the walls made the place seem dingy. Most were cheap photocopied fliers advertising spare guitar parts, band placements, sorry-sounding gigs. Hen stared at one of the sheets on the door. *Succubus plus Special Guests*

Sold Out, it said, over a picture of a man and a woman wearing chains and looking away from each other. Some weird music came banging through the walls. It sounded like a Japanese man talking very fast over the sound of trains departing.

This, thought Hen, was a man's place: run by men, frequented by men, meant for men. Girls didn't come here. Girls weren't meant to come here. She nudged Jules in the back. 'Perhaps we . . .'

Jules ignored her and walked over to the corner furthest from the door. Soul, R&B, Dance Compilations A–G, said a sign on the wall. She put down her bag and began going through the stacks, feigning interest.

Hen stood paralysed by the doorway. If she moved, she'd have to push past one of the boys. He was fat, or if not fat then he gave the impression of bulkiness. He had dark hair and a T-shirt with 'HARDCORE' written across it. From where Hen was standing, she could see the little black bristles on the rolls of flesh at the back of his head. But if she went the other way, down the Pop/Rock N thru' Z aisle, she'd have to pass the other boy. All she could see of this one was the back of his shirt and a bit of indeterminate blondish hair. There was something unfriendly in the set of his shoulders and the way he slouched so assuredly among the covers.

Hen felt the blood pulsing in her ears. She wondered for a second if she was going to faint. She wasn't ready for this. She hadn't had time to think about it. If Jules hadn't skittered off down to the other end of the shop, she would have left immediately. She walked down the Pop/Rock aisle until she was standing a couple of paces away from the blond boy. Put down her backpack and stared at the little signs above the

CDs. OASIS, OFFSPRING, OMD, ORBISON, ORB, ORBIT, ORBITAL, ORTON, OXALIS, PAGE, PARLIAMENT, PAVEMENT, PEARL JAM, PIXIES, PRETENDERS, PRIMAL SCREAM, PRINCE, PROCLAIMERS, PROCUL HARUM, PROJECT 2, PROPELLERHEADS, PUBLIC ENEMY, PULP. Oh God. She'd only heard of two of them. Perhaps those two were useless. Perhaps the blond boy would see her and know she knew nothing about this stuff. If she started looking through the Oasis section he might look over and think, what a loser. She picked Procul Harum, the one with the most obscure name, and began flicking through it, hoping it looked as if she knew what she was doing. It seemed to be a standard rule of musical appreciation that the weirder the band's name, the better they were considered to be. Was she looking dismissive enough? Did it look as though she knew anything about music? She rarely bothered buying stuff. She either taped other people's CDs, if she liked them, or she was forced to listen to the obscure shite that her brother bought: bands with names better than their songs, like Slipknot and Penetration. Maybe they'd get thrown out if they didn't buy anything. Maybe the shop owner would get so irritated with them just standing around that he'd tell them to go. That would be the final humiliation – kicked out of a record shop for not knowing anything. It'd be like walking around with a sign on your back: *Hen is Thick. Hen is Thick as Mince. Hen Couldn't Tell a Guitar from a Root Vegetable.* She imagined herself on Princes Street on a busy Saturday, doomed to bang up and down forever wearing nothing but a sandwich board. She'd be like the sad men advertising golf sales, or the Hare Krishnas in their pink nighties. She put down the Procul Harum and yanked out one of the Oxalis CDs. It had a swirly graphic on the front like the rat's innards in biology textbooks. Out of the corner of her eye, she could see Jules saying something to the fat bloke.

Hen turned slightly and saw the third boy, the one she'd seen from the cafe going through the box of LPs. All she could see of him from this angle was a pair of elaborate black and orange trainers and a few wisps of pale hair on his right arm. The trainers made him look as if he was wearing hamburgers on his feet.

The arm reached over and took the CD out of her hand.

'Like them?' He was skinny with a pale, girlish complexion and scary white-blue eyes. He had the fairest hair Hen had ever seen, as fair as her sister's white rabbit. She wondered if he might be some kind of mutant albino freak. 'Yes. Cool.'

'They're crap.' He dropped the CD back into its place. 'No originality, crap sampling, lousy tunes. Can't even dance to them. Just sit there and listen to them tossing off for twenty minutes.'

Hen burned.

'Just rip off other people's ideas. Totally derivative.' He had a little white spot just under his chin. It was almost ready for squeezing.

'*That*,' the boy said, picking out a disc and waving it at her, '*that* is serious music. Get that.'

Hen took the CD. It was evidently so hip it didn't bother with titles or track listings. I don't want it, she thought miserably. I can't even play it. 'Um,' she said. 'Can't take it. No point. Friend's already got it.'

'Cool, isn't it?'

Hen nodded, speechless.

'You got their other stuff?'

He took her gulp for a nod. 'Which ones?'

'God, can't remember. Got so many. Really difficult to keep track of them all'

'Yeah, right. I know.'

Hen watched his spot go up and down. *Pop it*, she thought. *Go on.*

'How many you got?'

'Hundreds.' Hen ran one hand casually over her hair. 'Been collecting since I was about eight or something.'

'Hey,' said the bloke. He looked almost impressed. 'Love to see them. Got thousands myself.'

'Yeah, well,' said Hen modestly.

He didn't say anything more, just turned back and began his interminable flicking again. Did she do something wrong? Did she say something that pissed him off? She could see the man at the counter watching them, bored but appraising. She didn't want to be here. She wanted to be somewhere quiet where there wasn't this noise, and this bloke standing in front of her wanting answers to things she didn't know about, and Jules's expectations. She tugged at the Celtic cross around her neck, swinging it tight.

'You live round here?'

'Sort of. We're staying. Couple of miles out of town.'

'What's your name?'

'Hen.' She giggled; no reason, but somehow the saying of her name sounded ridiculous.

He extended a hand, mock-formal. 'Adrian. Adey.'

'Where do you live?'

'Not near here. Only here for a field trip.'

He could be quite nice. If she'd been into crazed mutant albino freaks. 'We've finished exams,' she said. 'They don't know what to do with us. Sent us to this dump to do some shitey activity thing. Came down here to hang out.'

He nodded. 'Same here. Half-day. Come down here on Wednesdays during the afternoon. This place is OK. Rest of the dump's a dump.'

Hen felt something tugging at her arm and turned. Jules. She gave Adey a bright impertinent smile, whispered, 'Fat one's boring. Let's go,' and dragged at Hen's sleeve.

Hen frowned. 'Hang *on*.'

Adey watched her. He looked annoyed. She must have done something to upset him. Jules pulled her towards the door. Hen looked once more at Adey and then let herself be bundled outside. The sunlight was so bright it made every-thing – the street, the pavement, the people walking past – vanish into whiteness for a second.

'Don't fucking *do* that.' She wrenched her arm out of Jules's grip. 'So fucking *annoying*.'

'OooOOOooh. You fancy him?'

'*No.*' Hen was still rearranging her skin the way she wanted it. 'No. Not *that*.'

'He ask you out?'

'No.'

'The fuck were you banging on about then?'

'Doesn't *matter*.'

'You fancied him.'

'I was just *talking* to him.'

'You were standing really close to him.'

'No!' Things didn't seem to be ordering themselves the way Hen needed them to. 'No. *Hang on!*'

'Didn't look that tasty to me.'

'Just *shut up!*' Hen walked off down the street.

Jules caught up and started tugging at her backpack again.

Hen whirled round. 'Look, just *stop touching me! Leave me alone!*'

For a second, Jules looked bruised. Then her face went hard. 'All *right*. Stupid cow.'

Hen swung the backpack round, settled it onto her shoulders and walked off so fast that Jules would have had to run to catch her. When she reached the corner of the street, Hen let her hair swing over her face. She tried to push the tears back down her throat, but they wouldn't go. She had to keep holding her breath and then letting it out in a rush. She felt beset by the jangle of the traffic, the scream of rusty brakes, the man at his stand rasping out the late final of the local paper. The sunlight blattered down on her head. It made her skull hurt.

As she reached the next corner, she looked back. Jules had disappeared. She must have gone into one of the shops. Hen turned and kept walking. She'd have to take some kind of back route. She couldn't risk being seen by Jaws or Miss Naylor and she didn't want to bother dreaming up lies and excuses for where Jules was.

When she got to the traffic lights at the edge of the town, Hen turned right and began to walk down one of the lanes. It was quieter here, less oppressive. The shadows from the houses on either side made the sunlight seem less cruel. The sound of birds began to replace the crashings of the traffic. Fucking birds, thought Hen, just fucking piss off. She kept on going, not looking back any more, feeling lonely and daft and obtrusive, rushing down a lane on a sunny day in a place she'd never been before.

She passed a church with a noticeboard pointing out

towards the lane. It had a poster printed to look like the front page of a newspaper. *Come and Hear the Good News*, it said. It made Hen think of another poster she'd seen outside a kirk when they'd gone to visit her uncle near Aberdeen. *The Church is Full of Hypocrites*, it had said. *Come and Join Us.*

Hen began to cry. The tears wouldn't let her stop them any longer. She crushed her wrist against her face, pushing them away. But they kept coming, kept burning down her face. The worst thing was, she didn't even know why.

. . . WEDNESDAY

From where Ali was sitting, she could hear someone pacing back and forth, calling occasionally. She couldn't hear the words, only the tone. The voice sounded unsure of itself.

Ali stared at the wall. It was dark down here, but once her eyes had adjusted she could see enough to pick out the shapes of the stone. It wasn't the sort of place that Izzy would look. She would be too frightened by the darkness to come crawling down here. Ali could see two or three little ferns growing out of the walls, and the remnants of what looked like a rusty iron ladder.

When she had walked away from Izzy, she hadn't known where she was going. She had turned and seen Izzy looking back the way they had come and then plunged off the track into the wood. She thought of Izzy spinning in the white glare of the sun, alone. Then she moved on, deeper into the trees.

The landscape was odd around here. There wasn't much undergrowth except for a few brambles which clawed at her trainers, snagging her into reverse. The ground was covered in pine needles, and it was so dark in places that she could no longer sense the sunlight behind her. Once in a while the ground would dip down into a cavity surrounded by tree roots and ivy. Some of the cavities were large enough to have created gaps in the canopy of pines and birches where the sunlight slipped through. The shapes of the trees, the mutable light and these hidden caves all made Ali think of the useless story she'd been telling Izzy. Maybe down where the stones became shadows there were things living.

When she got to the third or fourth cavity, she paused. This one seemed bigger than the others, a deep hollowed-out space in the wood softened by fallen beech leaves. From where she was standing the ground dropped abruptly fifteen or twenty feet. At the bottom of the cavity there were two large boulders and a crumple of plants. Somewhere beneath, there was probably a decent-sized cave. She walked round to where the ground dipped more gently and slithered downwards, first on her feet and then on her haunches. At the bottom of the dip, all she could hear were the sound of wind in the leaves and her own crunching steps. When she looked up – right up, to the sky – the clouds toppled over her. At the back of the cavity there was an open space in the rock. Something about the way the light filtered across it made it seem more opaque than it should have been. Ali examined it, intrigued. She walked towards the space and felt her feet slide away beneath her.

When she put her hand down to stop herself, her fingers gripped nothing but air. Her hip cracked against something under the leaves and she flailed outwards with one foot, unable to stop herself. The light became darkness. Her foot jolted against solid rock and she stopped. She'd slithered down no more than about four or five feet, but it felt like miles. She wasn't in the outside world any more; she was in the cave.

When she levered herself upright, inching each foot along unseen footholds, she felt her limbs shiver. Lifting her hand up towards the light, she could see it shaking like the hand of a drunkard. When her eyes had adjusted, she found she was standing on a hollowed-out shelf of rock. Behind her, it dropped away into blackness, but she seemed safe enough where she was. She sat down tentatively and stared up the way she had fallen. Here, suddenly, it was silent: no birds, no planes, no traffic, no Izzy, no evidence of an outside life at all. The only sound came from the back of the cave: the sound of something softly dripping. In this place no one could find her unless she chose to be found. Which, just for the moment, she didn't.

She sat back, feeling the letter in her pocket crumple against her side. It had arrived in that morning's post, and she had read it, despite knowing exactly what it would contain. It was always the same. And, as the letters remained the same, so too did Ali's reaction to them. This one contained the customary domestic progress review with her mother's long-hand views on the areas in which she felt there could be improvement: numeracy, scientific ability, organizational and IT skills, appearance, social graces, catering, tidying up. The words themselves were friendly enough, but there was a thin undertow of dissatisfaction which had more to do with her mother's state of mind than it did with any genuine failing on Ali's part. Ali had, apparently, sat for too long in her room, had failed to appreciate the seriousness of her mother's endeavours, had not offered enough domestic or secretarial assistance . . . She supposed it was Ruth's way of letting off steam, and it wasn't as if Ruth never wrote anything nice to her, but still.

Ali was an only child, the unintended product of a wasted marriage. When her father left home for America, Ali remained at home with her mother. Perhaps if there had been another child, Ali's mother (Ruth. Always Ruth. Never Mother, or Mum, or Mummy, never anything small or cute or personal. As her father put it, that was Ruth as in Ruthless.) might have conceded more. As it was, she behaved as if Ali's childhood was an awkward phase to be tolerated but not encouraged, and her only concession was to speak in slightly shorter sentences. Ali didn't particularly mind, but she had occasionally found it difficult. It *was* difficult, aged seven or eight, to give a considered and informed response when Ruth asked her what she thought of the position of women at the English bar or how best to handle the financial aspects of divorce. Ali got used to listening, and to interpreting the lurches and slumps of her mother's temper. At junior school Ali had been taken aback by the softness of other children, the way their childishness was preserved and revered. It made her feel grown-up, knowledgeable, wise beyond her years. It also made her very bad at getting on with her peers. Now, of course, it was fine; Ali had long ago grown tall enough to meet her mother's gaze and didn't need explanations any more. Or didn't seek them, anyway.

When her father had finally left, driven from the house by one slammed phone too many, Ali's mother had floundered for a while. If Ali remembered that time at all, she remembered it for the smell of her mother's car, a temperamental Fiat hatchback that Ruth used to ferry both of them to meetings with lawyers and bank managers. In the end, all that time with the car and the lawyers had been put to good use. Her mother had found the legal process so tedious, so hostile to women and so unnecessarily disputatious that she had taken a degree in law and then set herself up as an advocate of women's legal rights. What had begun as a series of letters typed on a wheezing

Amstrad in the kitchen had become a major business with a publishing imprint and a well-regarded Web site. Now when Ali went home, she no longer found Ruth slamming courgettes against the side of the pan and fuming over conveyancing disputes, she found a place humming with technology. They had moved twice in the last five years, first to a larger flat in Stoke Newington and then to a house in Camden. The ground and first floors were entirely given over to her mother's offices, breezy white rooms full of purpose.

Perhaps it would have been different if her parents hadn't divorced. Had they once loved each other? She used to try to imagine the pair of them in a quiet restaurant, her father's face warm with hope, her mother stroking the side of her wine glass with the tip of one anticipatory finger. She wondered what they would talk about – books, work, food – but the images didn't come. It was beyond imagination now. She couldn't visualize her mother having any other form of discourse with her father than the one she had always seen: stony, disillusioned. If there had been love, then it must have been of the most fragile kind.

Ali did not think her mother would marry again. She gave the impression that the marriage to her father had been a youthful lapse of sanity and anyway, Ali couldn't see what possible role any man could fulfil in Ruth's life. Men, in her mother's view, were difficult and expensive to maintain. When Ruth talked about men, she always sounded as if she was considering some antique historical curiosity, like pirates or the Black Death. As far as her mother was concerned, her father no longer really existed, not even as an insult. He had been reduced to souvenirs and fripperies, to the occasional excitable present and to the promise, often given but rarely fulfilled, of visits to America. Ali thought about writing to him now. But even if he did send a ticket and even if she was allowed to go, her father would spend his days in the office and Ali would be condemned to the company of Mary-Anne, her father's new wife. Mary-Anne was younger than her mother, and blonde. She plainly found Ali as incomprehensible as Ali found her. 'How's school?' Mary-Anne would ask when she came to the phone. 'How's the weather in England?' Ali would tell her that school was school, and that the weather was still the weather, and that would be it. 'You must come over sometime,' Mary-Anne would say, sounding unconvinced. 'Come shopping.' Ali could never think of anything polite to say in response, so she would say nothing at all. Through the silence she would hear the plasticky click of Mary-Anne's rings on the receiver as she passed it back to her father.

She touched the letter in her pocket again, rubbing the corner of it under her nail. Last time she'd had a letter like this, it had felt just the same. She had read all the ways that her mother would like her to be different and felt so stifled that the only response had been to find air from another source. So she'd gone upstairs, packed a couple of things into her money belt, taken her jacket from behind the door and left. It was no more planned than that; she had needed to go, so she had gone. It was mid-April, and most people were outside on the lawns playing football or reading magazines by the copse.

Nobody saw her go; no one was looking. It had taken two and a half hours for anyone to notice she was missing. Even then, her habit of getting deliberately lost stood her in good stead. They had wasted a further hour searching under beds, up trees, in cupboards, even – for God's sake – peering hopefully into the waters of the pond. And then, when it was almost dark, a couple of teachers had got into their cars and gone looking for her. One turned right, and the other turned left.

Perhaps she had reason to be grateful that it was Jaws who had found her walking along by the side of the road with her jacket tied round her waist. She had heard the sound of a car slowing, and felt with a slide of inevitability that this was it, that there was no going forward, there was only going back. The car stopped. Ali stood by the side of the road with the other cars rushing past and the rhythmic click of Jaws's hazard lights flicking on and off.

Jaws watched her through the glass of the passenger window. 'Get in.'

Ali did as she was told.

'You walk fast. Could run marathons, the speed you were going.'

No reply.

'Took them a while to notice you were missing. Do you want to tell me about it?'

'No.'

'Something from home?'

'No.'

'Something bothering you? Work OK?'

Silence.

Jaws sighed. 'If you want to talk to me about it, you know you can. Any time. It doesn't matter. I have to mark papers in the evenings, so I'm usually in my study.'

Ali watched the headlights of the cars coming towards them. There was something irresistible about their brightness, the blinding white dazzle just on the edge of pain, the way they swallowed up all the oxygen in her mind. Every time she watched those inexorable lights they made her want to lean over, grab the steering wheel and drive straight into the middle of that whiteness. She wanted to do that now. She wanted to turn round, take the car away from Jaws and just drive in one smooth fatal movement right into the path of the oncoming car.

After a while she said, 'You didn't tell my mother, did you?'

Jaws shook her head. 'No. We would have done if we'd had to look much longer. But no, we haven't.'

She dropped Ali by the back door, telling her to see the head teacher. As she stared out of the window at Ali, she raised the palm of her hand towards her. That raised hand looked almost forgiving, like an acknowledgement or a blessing. Ali turned away, towards the steps. As she walked up the stairs towards the head teacher's office, past the girls who turned to stare, she thought about Jaws. Something in that upturned palm made Ali wonder if Jaws wouldn't have liked to run away as well. If she'd had anywhere to run to.

+

The passing cars glittered in the late afternoon light. People returning from shopping or school runs, a couple of caravans swinging seasick from side to side. It was turning into a perfect July evening, one of those days that turned everything to gold. The leaves had become temporarily translucent, and the flowers along the verge seemed bright enough to hurt the eye. From somewhere nearby came the faint scents of hay and cattle dung, and in the coppice on the hill the insects crackled with life. It was full summer. In a couple of weeks all of this would be dusty and overblown, but for the moment it looked like a perfect English postcard.

Jules was not conscious of any of it. She didn't like countryside, anyway. Or rather, she couldn't see the point of it. She found the notion of people voluntarily electing to stay here bizarre. Country people spoke funny, looked funny, dressed funny, and there was always something beaten about their expressions, as if they'd evolved to exist without visual stimu-lation. They had wind-proof figures and they walked at a slant as if pushing into a soundless gale. They only ever wore clothes in different shades of mud and they didn't seem to care about extraneous facial hair or furry teeth. Worst of all, they sounded like a soap opera. The first time she went to Yorkshire, Jules had been convinced people were taking the piss. No one could speak in an accent like that – not seriously, not for real.

Instead, she was practising speeches. Long, beautiful speeches all designed to devastate. Perfect speeches, full of truth and brilliance and not one single mistake. Perhaps this time she would get it right. Perhaps this time she might actu-ally be able to say what she meant instead of spitting out nothing but heat and a few acrid tears of frustration. It always happened. Every time she was angry, all her words ganged up against her, clotting in her mouth like a faceful of stones, coming out in the wrong order, too fast, too slow, gobbled up, munched to bits, ludicrous, incoherent. More than anything, Jules prayed for the gift of articulate rage; to be able to lose her temper beautifully, to slash and burn with the power of speech. Just once, it would be so wonderful to open her mouth and say the perfect sentences printed on her mind.

But for now, it all sounded just right. Hen would be shocked at what she had to say. Jules pictured her rooted to the spot, ripped into silence by all the things Jules had to tell her. Like how fucking *stupid* she was, and how Jules had *no fucking idea* why she bothered being her friend, and incidentally didn't she know she looked rough as hell and no one wanted to hang out with her any more. Like how fucking *dare* she leave Jules and run off like that. Like she could just fuck off back to Edinburgh and never come back, for all Jules cared. Like Jules only ever talked to her because Hen smoked. Like she should realize a whole lot of things about herself, stuff that it was about time she knew. Like her clothes were shit, her hair was an embarrassment and there were moments – lots of them, actually – when Jules only bothered because she felt *sorry* for her. Like she'd been such a fucking wimp in the music shop with the men, like she was always a fucking wimp when it came down to it, when it really mattered.

And then, when she'd said all of that, when she'd pulled Hen into very small pieces and put her back together in a different, better order, she'd present the fait accompli, the final devastating evidence that she, Jules, was a whole lot fucking smarter than Hen would ever be. She'd just say it quietly, like a throwaway line. She'd just say something like, oh, by the way, I went back to the shop. And we're meeting the boys on Friday. Hen would have absolutely nothing to say. There would be no possible retort. Even Caz would be impressed. It would be so gorgeously stage-managed that they'd only be able to sit there and marvel.

When she thought about it again, she *was* pretty chuffed with herself. After Hen had stormed off, Jules had turned and walked in the opposite direction. She'd gone into the news-agent and stood broodingly at the counter until the manager began to look as if there was something weird about her and she was forced to buy some fags just to show she wasn't a shoplifter or a psycho. Then she'd wandered up and down the main street for a while, not sure what she was supposed to do with herself. She didn't want to go back to the Manor just yet. It wasn't time, and she had things to sort out in her head. Finally, she had walked back into DiVinyl, gone over to the bloke Hen had been talking to, tapped him on the shoulder and said, 'Do you want to meet?' He hadn't laughed at her, he hadn't ignored her, and best of all he hadn't asked where Hen was. He'd just smiled and said yes, he'd meet them in the Cross Keys on Friday night. He said he'd bring some mates along as well. She'd walked back out of the shop in complete control of the situation. She was smart; no question, she was smart.

Somewhere behind her a church bell began to chime the hour. The road signs clanked in the wind. Down at the river, the water darkened, folding over itself, twisting into the sands. Jules saw the gates of the Manor and increased her speed.

+

By the time Ali came out, the shadows had stretched right across the little clearing. She stood on the edge of the cave for a minute, looking down at where she had been. The change in the light had altered the atmosphere. She had been thinking of using it as a starting point from which to run away, a refuge in moments of possible emergency. But now the thought made her feel foolish, as if she'd been caught playing with something she should long ago have outgrown.

She turned and began walking back towards the track. She could hear something banging rhythmically against the ground. Tap tap tip. Tap tap tip. Too regular to be a bird or an animal, but not regular enough to be a machine. It sounded quite far away, further down the track. Izzy. Of course. Izzy, heaving resentfully along beside her, Izzy, with whom she was supposed to have completed the walk. Ali felt remorse, not so much for having abandoned her but for having completely forgotten her.

She found the track and began walking. The wood was darkening now, and the undergrowth at the side of the track seemed more sharply green than at midday. The landscape which had seemed so beguiling earlier in the day now seemed shadowy and covert. She no longer liked the silence, or the way the shrubs at the side of the track kept up a steady rustle even without the wind. The colours seemed too sharp and the shadows too overwhelming. She hadn't really thought about it before, but there was something about the countryside in this part of England that didn't seem quite as domesticated as things in England should. She could sense the presence of animals somewhere. If she turned suddenly she might see something she didn't want to see. Perhaps there would be eyes shining in the darkness. Or teeth. Perhaps the forest had evolved differently to other parts of the country; perhaps wildlife flourished here that could not have survived outside this cavernous twilight. Perhaps there were giant beasts here: superrats and mutant cats, wolves slipping watchfully in between the tree trunks, invisible snakes shaded like stones. Perhaps the forest was a haven for a wilder kind of life where herbivores turned carnivores and preyed on passing fools. Maybe they were just lurking there, watching her go by, waiting until they were hungry enough. She pictured a rat as big as a dog leaping out at her, its scarlet eyes abstracted with blood. You cannot, she told herself firmly, get frightened by killer rats. There is no such thing as a killer rat. As she walked, she giggled, thinking about wild dogs and Izzy's huge pale face staring up at her.

She turned a corner in the track to where it forked three ways. 'Ali!' called a voice.

Jaws and Izzy had evidently been there for some time.

As she drew level, Izzy tipped her head to one side and squinted up at Ali. 'You OK?'

Ali nodded.

'Sure?'

Ali nodded again.

'*Really* sure? Look a bit . . .'

Ali looked down at her. Izzy looked as if she and the wood had come to some sort of agreement, and that she had found a place here now. There was an empty bottle of water and the remains of a chocolate packet beside her.

'You went off like that. Suddenly.'

'Mmmm.'

'Where did you go?'

Ali shrugged.

Jaws got up and brushed the bark off her trousers. 'We ought to be getting back.' She glanced once at Ali, a veiled look. Ali could not read what it meant.

'Where did you go? I looked for you. For ages,' said Izzy.

Ali shrugged.

'Like where? In that wood? Why? It's so *weird*, wandering off like that.'

'Mmmm'

'Oh, for God's sake. We've been waiting two hours for you. Two hours of boring sitting around in this place.'

'Sorry.'

Jaws sounded calmer than Izzy. 'It doesn't matter. She's here now, isn't she?' She inclined her head towards the track. 'Come on. Or all the shops will be shut.'

They walked on. Izzy began to wheeze a little.

Ali could still smell the coldness of the cave on her fingers. She wasn't sure what she'd found while she was there, only that it had helped her to make a decision, and that sooner or later she'd have to do something about that decision. Alone.

+

Hen stood in the loo with her back against the door, waiting. This place wasn't as private as she would have liked. It was halfway along the corridor, between one bedroom and the next. It had bright orange curtains and smelled of something industrial. Underneath the industrial smell was the smell of something nastier. Above her, a light bulb fizzed. Outside, she could hear the murmurings of conversation, Izzy's voice, the sound of the rooks coming home to roost. She leaned her head against the back of the door and closed her eyes. There was always the bathroom a little further down the corridor but that, she figured, was probably even more risky than this place.

Standing with her arms behind her, she began to feel faint. She stared for a moment at the toilet seat. It was black and she could see droplets of something on its surface. The toilet bowl itself was stained with age and unnameable dirt. There was a rim of brown scum just above the water level, and under the seat was a fine speckling of shit or blood or something. She could see wipe marks where someone had tried to clean it. It didn't look as if they had tried very hard.

When she had eventually returned to the Manor, Miss Naylor was standing in the hall, silhouetted against the evening sun. 'What time do you call this?'

'Sorry.'

'You were supposed to be back at five.'

'Yes. Sorry.'

'What were you doing?'

'Nothing.'

'Julia is already back. She said you walked off on your own.'

'Sorry.' Capitulation is always easier. Or, at least, capitulation is always quicker.

'Go on. Go and get your supper.'

After a few steps, Hen realized that Miss Naylor was following her. When they reached the canteen, Jules looked up from her food, a long, awkward stare. Hen went up to the serving hatch and picked out an apple, a stick of celery, and a bun with a thin strip of ham jammed inside. She began walking back, but Miss Naylor caught her arm.

'Over here,' she said, nodding to an empty table. 'You eat with me.'

'But everyone else—'

'Never mind everyone else. Over here.' Her fingers were squeezing Hen's forearm, not painfully, but hard enough that Hen could not pull away without making a scene. 'If you cannot be trusted to eat properly on your own, then you will have to be supervised.'

'Who says?'

'I say. Go on. The bun, please.'

Hen picked up the bun. It was white bread, with a hard lip of staleness beginning to form around the edge. It didn't seem to have any filling at all. Hen turned it round and round in her hands as if it were a new kind of gadget and she couldn't find the right buttons.

'Go on. It won't bite.'

Hen took a nibble. The bun was made of something weird

and light, like artificial pillow stuffing. Whoever had made it had barely bothered to include any ham, and the gap between the layers was filled with margarine slathered on so thickly it had crept into the pores of the bread. Hen thought about the slick of oily margarine, the globules of fat down her throat, all that yellow sewage seeping into her stomach. The thought was so nauseating she thought she was going to gag. A small chunk of ham fell out of one side and lay there on the table, its surface shimmering with grease. It was pink, with a flabby white rime of fat around the edge. Her throat felt blocked by something big, as if a stone had been rolled over it. I can't, she thought, I can't . . .

'Go on. It's not that bad. I'm eating it.' Miss Naylor took a cartoon bite of her own bun. Hen watched her lips working over the bread, the moist sliver of tongue.

'I can't,' she said miserably. 'I just can't. I just . . . It's . . .'

'Oh, for God's sake. Stop fussing. What do you expect? It's not great, but it's food, and we can't all be so precious about it.'

'I'm not . . . I'm not saying that. I don't mean that.'

'Well, just get on with it. And if you can't eat that, eat the apple or something. Or the celery.'

Hen put down the bun and pulled out the apple. It was a pale yellowish colour, bruised on one side and covered in a thin film of what looked like blackheads. If she looked at it for too long, she wouldn't be able to manage that either, so she closed her eyes and bit into it. The sensation of eating something unnatural came back to her again. The apple seemed to be made out of cotton fibre, with an odd false sweetness.

'There. See? You're eating that.'

Miss Naylor had a little red line, a burst vein or something, on the side of her nose. Her hair looked flat now, lifeless, as if she'd picked it up off the carpet that morning and plonked it on top of her head any old how. It was fixed into position with so much hairspray that it just sat there, immobile. It wasn't a wig; it was far too horrible to be a wig. It was also thinning a little, so that Hen could see the white skin of Miss Naylor's scalp through the strands. God, thought Hen, she's ugly. Who would have sex with her? She pictured Miss Naylor lying on a mattress like an upturned beetle, bits of her body moving, her legs trembling feebly. She would be making the kind of squeaky noises that people made on television. Up at the top, her hair would just crouch motionless, waiting till she'd finished.

Miss Naylor seemed discomfited by Hen's sudden interest. 'Right. That'll do. Off you go.'

When she got to the canteen doors, Hen turned. Miss Naylor was still watching her. She was too far away for Hen to see her expression.

She stood now with the door handle jabbing at her back, staring at the floor. The feeling of Miss Naylor's grip on her skin wouldn't go away. When she looked down at her arm, she was almost surprised not to see a neat line of fingerprints just above the wrist. It was odd, this new thing of being so aware of her bones. It seemed to coincide with a general loss of feeling in both arms. Sometimes they just went cold for no apparent reason, as if she was freezing from the inside out. When she touched the skin it felt like it always felt. If she put her wrist up to her face and sniffed her skin, she still smelled comfortingly of herself. But underneath the warmth, in the parts she couldn't see, something seemed awry.

She couldn't stop thinking about Miss Naylor's hair. Underneath all that hairspray, she thought, perhaps it's alive.

She remembered walking by the side of a burn in the country once, turning a corner, and seeing a rabbit right in front of her, just sitting quite still in the middle of the path. The rabbit didn't move when Hen came up to it. It just sat there, with its head hunkered down and its quick hot eyes sliding from side to side. Hen knew what a rabbit with myxomatosis looked like, but there seemed nothing wrong with this one. She had inspected it cautiously and then moved forwards to pick it up. As she did so, she saw why the rabbit wasn't moving. A thin dribble of blood was running down behind its ears. A stoat, perhaps, or a weasel; she'd obviously surprised it and the stoat must have run off. At the same instant she saw something else. The rabbit's fur moved oddly, not with the motion of its breathing but with a separate rhythm. The fur shifted in one place, irregularly, and then in another. Hen put her hand down to touch it, and as she did so she saw what was making its fur shiver. It was alive with fleas. Thousands of them. They lay in the soft folds between its haunches, burrowing and squabbling, making its fur convulse as they consumed it. The rabbit was being eaten from the inside out. Hen closed her eyes and the rabbit's shifting fur merged with Miss Naylor's hair. Hen saw insects and maggots crawling out from under Miss Naylor's hairline, running down her face, burrowing round her ears.

Hen leaned forward, lifted up the toilet seat and was sick.

THURSDAY

'Happy birthday,' said Miss Naylor, cocking her head to one side. 'We are getting old, aren't we? Fourteen. My goodness.'

Ali didn't reply, so Miss Naylor picked up one of the two small parcels by the side of her plate. 'Heavy. A book? We like books, don't we?'

No response.

'Aren't you going to open them?' She jabbed at Ali's shoulder. '*Look* at me when I'm speaking to you.'

Ali watched the floor.

'*Look at me*, Alison. Do you have no manners?'

'I'll open them later.'

'If you don't want to share your birthday with us . . .'

'Just prefer to open them upstairs.'

A rigid silence. 'Eat your breakfast. And be downstairs with your kit in half an hour.' They heard the squeal of her rubber soles against the lino.

'Stupid cow,' said Mel.

Jules picked up the water jug. 'She's a dictator, basically. She should work in a prison, not a school.'

'Thought school was prison.'

'Know what I mean. Mean like a place where sad twisted

fascists can kick the shit out of small people.' Jules stopped. 'Somewhere anyway where they put sexually frustrated old bitches like her.' She leaned over and shook one of Ali's parcels. 'Oh, go on. I want to see. What is it? Do you know what's in it?'

'You always get good presents,' said Mel balefully.

The way Jules was shaking the parcel made Ali nervous. 'I'll open it upstairs,' she said, swallowing a clot of toast so large it made her eyes water.

Presents from her parents were always fraught. Those from her father tended to be lavish, shameless, exuberantly over-generous. A Discman once, an electronic organizer the next time, a Dreamcast after that. They were lovely expensive things, but nothing about them suggested that her father knew who she was. He bought them because he liked them and assumed she would too. He liked them because they were expensive and because they were new. And, perhaps, because they came without any personality attached; just a nice shiny box with a nice shiny toy. He did not think about how they would look so many miles away in front of other people. He didn't think of other people's reactions. He didn't have to.

Presents from her mother, on the other hand, usually came with an invisible accusation attached. Two birthdays ago Ruth had sent her a cushion embroidered with a sampler her grandmother must have sewn many decades previously. It was made from some heavy, cool material and had 'My Presence Shall Go With Thee' embroidered in blue cross stitch over the front.

When she'd opened it in front of the others, Jules had stared at it for a second and then shouted with laughter. 'God, that's horrible.' She plucked the cushion out of Ali's hands and threw it over to Caz. 'Caz. *Caz.* Look. Stand up, stand up for Jesus . . .'

Caz held it out in front of her. 'Does your mother always give you stuff like that?'

Ali had tried to hold Caz's gaze and in the silence of that second felt a sadness much deeper than she could understand. She didn't like the cushion either and when she thought about the words stitched over and over so the linen had buckled underneath, they felt not reassuring but violent. She didn't want someone watching her all the time, particularly not God. Ruth had probably meant it as a compliment of sorts, albeit a confusing one. It seemed unlikely that she was meant to take religious comfort from it, since Ruth was as fiercely secular as she was fiercely everything else. But there was still some part of Ali that wished . . . well, wished at least that she could have swallowed her gall in private, kept it as something between the cushion and herself.

Now she sat on her bed with her back to the window. She had, she calculated, only about two minutes before the others arrived back upstairs. The parcel from her father had obviously been addressed by one of his assistants in the London office. She pulled the staples apart and gazed in. She could see the sort of wrapping paper favoured by cheap gift shops and a card with a joke she didn't get on the front.

Howdy! said her father's writing, *I bought this in London when I was last over. I hope you like it. So sorry I didn't get a chance to see you, but your mother said you were doing exams and I shouldn't disturb your studying!! How y'all doing, as they say here. Life in NY is fine and Mary-Anne sends her love. You must come over and visit sometime. The apartment is looking great and Mary-Anne has bought a puppy!!! He makes a mess, but we are both very fond of him. I hope school is nice. I'm sure you'll do well. Love and kisses, your loving Dad xxx.*

Ali undid the wrapping. A mobile phone, one of those international ones. What was she supposed to do with that? They weren't allowed mobiles. Ali jammed the phone under her pillow and considered the parcel from her mother.

Mel walked in and sat heavily on her bed. 'No post,' she wailed. 'No post, no emails, no phone, no parcels, no bloody anything. Bastards.'

'Expecting something?'

'Expecting my fucking useless parents and my fucking useless mates to remember that I'm stuck in this dump. Expecting them to bloody write.'

Strange, thought Ali, how right Mel always sounded when she moaned. Her voice was high-pitched and had a steady monotonal scrape to it, as if she'd been specially engineered for complaint. Ali couldn't remember a single instance of Mel ever sounding pleased about anything. Sometimes Ali found her whine comforting, but at other times – like now – it made her want to run to a faraway place without any voices at all.

'Let's see.' Mel picked up the empty packet.

Ali hesitated. 'It's a mobile.' She pulled it out from under her pillow.

'Fucking *outrageous*. One of those international ones. You could ring America or whatever. I want one of those. Fucking parents won't give me one.'

'Can't use it.'

'Course you can. Just hide it.'

'So what's the point in having it if no one can ring it?'

'God, you sound really ungrateful. My parents are so mean they'd never give me stuff like that. Fuckers.'

Jules and Caz came in. 'Look at this.' Mel wheeled round. 'Ali's birthday present.'

Jules busied herself by the sink. 'What's in the other parcel?' she said loudly. 'The one from your mother?'

'Saving it.'

'I bet. Bet you're dying for another Jesus cushion. Maybe you'll get a prayer book. Or one of those flouncy tissue-box covers with "I Love Baby Jesus" on it . . .' She turned back to the mirror. 'I know. A guitar. A guitar for singing "Kum ba yah" on.'

Ali closed her eyes. She thought of the cave and the darkness, and of silence.

+

Dear Jamie, wrote Hen, *This place is a dump. It is just as bad as school if not worse. It is a hostel place in the Forest of Dean and we are supposed to be walking or swimming or bicycling all day. We've got old Cow Naylor supervising us so no fun ever. Hopefully we will be able to sneek out sometime and get down to the pub. There is nothing like school to make me need a drink!!!*

How is stuff at home? How is Dad? Is he still being like an old woman about your music?! I am dying to get out of here and get back home. Send my love to the twins and tell them don't do anything I wouldn't do!! Lots of love. Lola xxx.

PS. Are you going to see Mum this holidays? Can we go together? I don't want to go on my own and it would be cool to hang around London with you.

She put the letter aside and started writing again.
Dear Mum,

Hello. How are you? Things are fine here. We have finished exams and we are now in the Forest of Dean which is very beautiful and senic. We are walking every day which is very good for my mussles. I hope you are well and it is nice weather in London. It will be nice to see you in the holidays but I think Dad wants to keep us in Edinburgh for most of it.

See you soon, lots of love, Lola xxx.'

She sealed the letters and whacked them down on the bedside chest. As she did so, she glanced at the photograph in its dull metal frame. It had been taken a long time ago when her parents were still together. It showed all of them, her mother and her father, Jamie, herself and her two sisters sitting on a boat at the harbour in Barra. The person who had taken the photograph had been standing on the dockside, and Hen remembered having to twist awkwardly in her seat so she could see his face. She had on an anorak borrowed from her aunt which had been too large for her, and the hood had flapped damply on her face. Her father was looking out towards the horizon, but Hen could still pick out the glow of pleasure in his eyes.

When she looked at the picture now, Hen didn't feel anything apart from a faint irritation at the dented frame and scratched glass. Two years ago it had seemed much more valuable. Then she had kept lots of photographs. They were visible proof that she wasn't merely Hen, she was Lola, with another life and a proper history. Now she just had one. People said that cameras didn't lie, but that was nonsense. Nothing in that photograph was true any more. Her parents were divorced, her father never looked as cheerful as the man in the picture did and it was only with an effort of will that she could remember her mother's face at all. Her brother had stopped looking like the old Jamie so long ago that she sometimes wondered if the boy in the photograph wasn't just someone she'd imagined.

The image had worn itself clean into anonymity and what Hen saw now was not *her* family but *a* family. She could have swapped around all the photographs in the room, Mel's for Izzy's, Caz's for hers, and it would have made no difference. They would all still have been false images and made-up stories.

When Hen had arrived at the school almost three years ago things had been different. Or rather, she had been different. She had come down to England from Edinburgh with long straight hair and a belief in things. She'd assumed that the lessons her father had taught her – that merit will out, that likeable people will get liked, that openness will take you to places that introspection will not – would hold true. They did not.

For a long time she'd just continued being herself. She hadn't been shy because nothing in life had taught her to be shy. She had been bossy because she was accustomed to bossiness. She wasn't the oldest child but she was the oldest daughter, and it had stood to reason that she should take a little of the care of her younger sisters upon herself. She didn't barge through life swinging and yelling like Jules did, she was just open. She was Lola. She told people about Scotland, about her parents, about the possible ways of doing things, because she thought they would like to know. She told Izzy not to play her music too loud because it made sense. She told Mel how best to prepare an assignment because Mel was doing it wrong. She attached herself to Jules and Caz's group because it was obvious that they were the most important people to know and since she had always been one of the most important people before, it stood to reason that she should be one of them now. She was not naturally cautious or mean-spirited, so she lent people her clothes or gave them her food quite happily, knowing it was the right thing to do.

She remembered explaining the right way to do something – ingratiate yourself with a teacher, wing your way through an essay, steal from the kitchens – and noticing the way people glanced at her and then turned away. She'd be walking along a corridor or sitting in her room and find herself caught on the outside of a murmur. In the past those murmurs had always involved her. She remembered standing in the playground with her shoulders braced against the outside air and her head inclined to catch each warm morsel of spite. She used to be the one standing in the huddle bending and glancing so that the person on the outside should know they were being discussed. Now, abruptly, she had become the excluded. Every time she walked out of the bedroom, she'd hear that same indrawn pause as the latch of the door clicked behind her, and then a rush like the sound of sparrows roosting.

And she told them about Scotland because they seemed to know so little about it. She remembered conversations at night, the kind of questions they would ask. 'Do Scottish people have telephones?' 'Do they have videos/mobiles/cars/computers/TV in Scotland?' 'Don't you have to show your passport at the border?' 'Don't Scottish people fuck sheep?' When she found that each of the questions would be accompanied by that hushed twittering laugh, she just assumed that her classmates were shy of their ignorance. So she explained, patiently and with a sense of benign superiority, that not all Scots had beards, that most of them had phones, and that only very rarely – to her knowledge anyway – did they ever interfere with live-stock. It became a regular thing once or twice a week for Hen to hold a kind of question-and-answer session about Scottish habits and practices. How reeling worked, what the weather was really like, why Glasgow was different from Edinburgh, who was permitted to wear tartan, the definition and pronunciation of certain words. They asked, so she told them.

It took a long time for Hen to understand. For months she went on believing that Jules and Caz turned their backs on her when she approached them not because they were hostile, but because they hadn't seen her. She believed that people asked about Scotland because they were interested. She believed that Mel's fat scowl was just because Mel was a bit slow to catch on. She believed that the pictures and books that she'd brought down from Edinburgh and which people seemed so interested in seeing must have been defaced through carelessness or accident. She believed that, though Mina's stepbrother came from Udaipur and Caz's father came from Singapore and Vicky had some sort of connection to Jamaica, they all found Scotland much more intriguing than any of these places.

It wasn't until one night near the end of the first term that she finally understood. They'd been asking her questions again – or rather, Hen had been offering to tell them things. She'd been talking about the west coast, about how beautiful it could be, the excitement of sailing and the thrill of pulling up lobster pots, like writing messages in bottles and finding their replies. She'd been caught up in her own explanation, remembering the trip to Barra, the five days of perfect weather, the last time her father and mother had looked at each other in that particular way they used to have before things went weird. Halfway through her explanation, Mel had interrupted.

'D'you get jet lag?'

Hen stopped mid-story. 'What?'

'D'you get jet lag?'

'What do you mean?'

'I mean, when people fly to Scotland they must get jet lag. It's so far away from England; they must get tired.'

Hen remembered thinking that she ought to be patient with Mel. Mel wasn't particularly bright, so it probably wasn't her fault if she couldn't tell the difference between 400 miles and 4,000. So she'd begun explaining. No, she said, there was no jet lag. It was less distance from London to Edinburgh than it was from Edinburgh to Orkney.

She had been confused at first by the laughter. Not the usual whispery rush, but full-on naked laughter this time. And not just Mel either. The whole room, all of them, even Izzy, sitting up in their beds, looking over at her and laughing. Her explanation faltered and then stopped. She saw Jules's mouth open wide, her shoulders twitching. They went on and on forever, looking at her, showing their teeth.

Caz wiped her eyes. 'We know. We were just taking the piss. We know what Scotland's like. We know it's just up the road. Most of us have been there.'

'Wh . . . why did you ask me?'

'Because you wouldn't shut up about it,' said Mel. 'Because you were always talking about it. Because you always think Scotland is the best thing ever invented.'

'I thought . . .' said Hen, but couldn't finish. She felt herself scalding and freezing at the same time, feverish with humiliation. The room ebbed and turned and she wondered if she fainted whether oblivion would be better than this. What had taken so long to become apparent now thundered into place. The stifled exchanges, the oblique turn of a shoulder as she entered the room, the silence as she left it, the things gone missing, the clothes returned damaged, the advances rebuffed.

She felt shame. She felt small and stupid. Worse than that, for the first time in her life, she felt wrong.

The Hen who rose the next morning was not the Hen of the previous day. After a sleepless night – she hadn't cried much, just lain there paralysed – she had taken everything she owned that had anything to do with Scotland and thrown it away: all the books her father had sent down from Edinburgh, the Hibs strip her brother had lent her, a T-shirt with the Festival logo, the warm Arran blanket, two jerseys she'd bought in Glasgow, most of her family photographs, and the collection of seashells and pebbles she'd gathered on Barra. The only things she kept were the little gold celtic cross she wore around her neck and the photograph of the boat trip.

When the others came back in and saw the spaces where her posters used to be, they said nothing. Something in Hen's downturned head and evasive gestures warned them not to. Mel made a couple of snippy comments until she was silenced by Caz, and then everyone got on with their lives. Hen stopped talking so much – every time she opened her mouth now she heard her own origins and felt ashamed – and she no longer tried to be part of other people's groups. When she thought of approaching Jules and Caz, she felt sick.

The worst thing of all was the whispering. Every time she left the room it would start up, every time she came back in it would stop. On and on, so often that the sound of doors opening and closing became the sound of fear. The most difficult bit was knowing that they knew she could hear, that the way they whispered was designed to be heard. She'd sit on her bed, paralysed, knowing that over in the corner Mel and Mina were absorbed in some elaborate new mockery, unable to leave, unable to move, unable to bear the shiver of release as the door clicked shut behind her.

Two weeks later, just before the end of term, she was called to Miss Naylor's office. 'Your father,' she said, holding out the telephone receiver. Hen took it but did not lift it to her ear immediately.

Down the line, her father coughed, small and unhappy. 'Lola . . . I thought I ought to tell you before you came home. Your mother . . . your mother and me, we're not together any more.'

Hen didn't say anything.

'I'm sorry. I'm very very sorry. Can we talk about it in the holidays?'

No reply.

'Lola? Are you there?'

'Right. Fine. Bye.' She handed the receiver back to Miss Naylor.

'Bad news?'

'Can I go now?'

'Lola. It's OK. We want to help.' Miss Naylor's voice was unexpectedly soft. For a wild moment, Hen thought of staying here, curling up in the warmth and allowing Miss Naylor to watch over her. It occurred to her that if she stayed much longer she would cry. She did not want Miss Naylor to see her cry.

'Can I go now?'

'Please . . . If you need . . .'

Hen flinched.

'Go, then.'

She didn't tell anyone about the phone call. There was no one she could have told. She had no allies, and besides, her father, her mother, her home, her brother and her sisters were irrevocably associated with Scotland and therefore with shame. She wanted no reminders of them and no associations. In fact, her father's phone call made it easier. Here – as if she needed it – was final proof that everything she had trusted was flawed. Her parent's marriage was an illusion, her family was an illusion, kindness and merit and honesty were illusions. By splitting the family apart, her father finished off the process her own stupidity had begun.

For a full year, Hen retreated. She stopped talking much. When she did speak she took care to mind the way it sounded. She hammered her vowels flat, shifted the rhythms, clipped away at her Os and Es, bullied her Rs into submission. The result wasn't much of a voice at all. At school she concentrated on being as unobtrusive as possible. At home she stayed in her room. No one talked much of divorce in that first holidays, although it was obvious that it was going to happen. They pretended that everything was as it should be. Her mother managed a vicious kind of gaiety, and her father worked more than usual. When she went back to school at the beginning of January, her mother was still in Edinburgh. When she returned home a few weeks later at half-term, her mother had gone.

And so Hen divided herself. One part of her was still – however reluctantly – bound up with Edinburgh and home. The other part crept through the school corridors, burrowed under the duvet at night, learned necessary adaptations. At the end of the process, she found she had become two different people. Each one spoke differently, dressed differently, ate different things, laughed at different jokes, had different interests. If one had met the other, they probably wouldn't have liked each other.

It was cigarettes that changed things. By the end of the second year, the group of those who smoked had acquired solidity and definition. When Hen sneaked out at lunchtime, she would often find Jules or Caz or someone sitting grumbling beneath one of the beech trees, sharing an over-used fag or a damp box of matches. Hen used to hate the walk into the little clearing, the distant self-conscious smile as she stood in her corner and they stood in theirs. Most of the time Jules and Caz talked to each other and – other than that initial smile – gave no sign that she existed at all. But towards the end of the second year, things began to change. Hen couldn't remember who had made the first move. She just remembered that one week she didn't exist, and the next week she did. She remembered offering Jules a couple of cigarettes and listening to her complain about how bored she was, or about plans for the holidays, or bitching about Izzy or Mel. None of it was particularly interesting or significant, but Hen was so astounded that Jules spoke to her at all that she wasn't sure how to respond. That same week Hen lent her an assignment to copy, and Jules seemed pleased. She spoke to Hen the next day, and the next. Despite herself, Hen found herself thawing, particularly when Caz joined her and began talking as well. Within a month or so the three of them were a unit. Hen never tried to understand why – when she thought about it, her mind seized up – but she was grateful for it.

Final confirmation of Hen's acceptance came in the summer term. They had been sitting in the clearing having a conversation about names. Caz took a long drag on her cigarette and leaned back against the tree.

'You shouldn't be Lola,' she said.

Hen looked puzzled.

'You should be Hen.'

'Why?'

'All Scottish girls are called Hen, and all the men are called Ken or Pal. So you're Hen.'

Hen held her breath and waited for the world to explode. It was the first time her origins had been mentioned since . . . She sat gazing at the fallen leaves, praying for whatever was going to happen to happen quickly.

But nothing did. Jules just laughed and said, 'Yeah. Right. Hen, definitely. Suits you.'

'Go on,' said Caz, watching interestedly. 'It's either that or Jock.'

She didn't say anything at all, just nodded, dumb with gratitude. It didn't occur to her until some time later that she didn't even like Hen.

+

Once they had stripped her of her real name, Hen's resurrection was complete. Now she was Hen for eight months of the year and Lola for four. When she went home at the end of term, she took the train from King's Cross to Waverley on her own, and as she listened to the sound of the cab's tyres peeling over the New Town cobbles she could feel herself shifting from one name to another.

At home, things had settled down. Or rather, she had become accustomed to things remaining unsettled. The twins didn't seem to mind that their mother wasn't there any more – as long as they had each other, and remained living in the same house, it was all the same to them. Her father never said much, just hurried from room to room with his usual air of panic-stricken absent-mindedness. And she couldn't tell what Jamie thought at all. He'd become increasingly crabbed lately, and tended to remain in his room with the volume on his stereo turned up so high it created a twenty-foot exclusion zone.

There had been only one occasion which suggested anyone noticed her mother's absence. The twins needed new uniforms: Fee had to have a jacket, Jen needed a shirt and both of them had outgrown their shoes. Worse than that – Hen had somehow to extract some money from her father to buy herself a bra. The evidence of her necessity swelled larger every passing month, but all of them – particularly Hen – had affected not to notice. Even Jamie, who would never normally have let her get away with something as girly as growing breasts, had said nothing.

They'd been standing in the shoe department of John Lewis in front of rack upon rack of sensible lace-ups and ugly trainers. Her father had been trying to attract the attention of one of the sales assistants. He was grumbling under his breath and kept adjusting the waistband of his trousers, which Hen recognized as a sign that he was ill-at-ease.

'Dad,' she said, speaking more to a nearby pot-plant than to him, 'Can I have some money?'

'What for?'

'I need to buy something.'

'What?'

'Something.'

'You know I'm not handing you out money unless you give me a good reason for it.'

Hen lost her nerve. 'Nothing. Doesn't matter.'

'You can have it as long as there's a good reason. I'm not going to deny you things if you need them.'

'Doesn't *matter.*'

'Tell me. Don't say you need things and then say you don't.'

'Never mind.'

He put out his hand to grab her wrist. 'Lola, don't be daft.'

Hen reeled round until she was close enough to see the stitching on his shirt. 'A bra,' she shouted. 'Right? A bra. I need a fucking *bra*.'

When she looked up, her father's expression was one of such horror, such embarrassment, that she felt as if she'd hit him. If he could have blushed at that moment in the soupy light of the shop, he would have done. Something in his eyes seemed so forsaken she felt almost intrusive.

'Jesus. I'm sorry, I'm sorry. Here.' He pulled out a wad of notes from his pocket and shoved them into her hand.

She leaned over and gave him a hug, stiffer than usual because there was too much feeling in it.

'I wish . . .' he was saying, '. . . Your mother . . .'

She took the money, gave his hand a squeeze and walked away. Upstairs, she walked through the racks of lacy underwear. Bras loomed at her, menacing as jellyfish. She grabbed a couple of the plainest ones, not looking at the sizes, and half ran towards the changing rooms.

Inside, she yanked her top off and stood watching herself in the angled mirrors. Her body looked back at her, pale and square. She hated it. She hated it for being itself, for being the same body she met every night when she took her clothes off, for being weak, for having sloped shoulders, no waist, clumpy feet, a face you'd never notice. She hated it for needing things, for having to be fed and dressed and maintained in ways that she didn't want and couldn't control. She hated it because it was hers and she couldn't escape from it. She hated it because behind the skin of her own face she could see the bones of her mother's. She hated it because it was stupid and disobedient and fat and horrible and profoundly, perpetually unlovable. Just at this moment, she also hated it for embarrassing her father.

'Want help in there?' The voice was more bellow than whisper. Hen wrapped half the cubicle curtain around herself and looked out. A middle-aged woman was looking back at her. She had powdery hair arranged in a curling bow wave above her forehead and a chest kept upstanding with the help of what looked like iron girders.

'No,' said Hen, pulling the curtain more tightly over her shoulders. 'No, thank you.'

'Will I measure you? If it's your first bra, you'll need measuring.'

'*No.*' Louder.

'Let's have a look at what you've got in there. We need to see if they fit you. You don't want to walk out of here with something which doesn't fit.'

'I'm fine. *Really.*'

'Incorrectly fitted brassieres can give you all sorts of problems.'

'I'm *OK.*'

The assistant pulled a measuring tape out of her top pocket and began unravelling it. 'Back problems, posture problems. You could end up with a permanent stoop. Osteoporosis.'

How could she make her go? 'My mother will be here in a second.'

The assistant looked dubious. 'You'll still need measuring.'

'*Please.* I'll be *fine.*'

Two or three other customers were signalling from the

doorway. The assistant turned reluctantly. 'When you need me, I'll be just over there.'

Hen yanked the curtain back across the rail. She saw herself in the mirror, round and round, hateful, inescapable. Then she bundled her top back on, picked up the horrible sea-creature bras and bolted out of the fitting room.

She kept the money. She couldn't bring herself to spend it; it felt like something spoiled. Afterwards, she wandered the streets of the New Town for a while and then went home. Her father didn't look up when she walked into the kitchen. 'Did you . . . ?' he said, stirring something round and round in big unnecessary circles.

'Yes,' she said. 'Fine.'

That night at supper she saw him glance, just once, at her chest. If she could have sacrificed herself at that moment, sawn her disobedient breasts off and served them up on a plate like St Agatha, she would have done.

+

Jules and Caz were conferring. There was something in Caz's murmur – the spurt of sibilants, the lispy constant whisper – which made concentration on anything else impossible. Ali was just about to find somewhere quieter to read when Caz got up and walked out of the room.

'Hi.'

Ali looked up. She couldn't remember the last time Jules had sought a conversation with her.

'How's your birthday been?'

Ali shrugged.

'Nice stuff from other people? Cards?'

No reply.

Jules looked sly. 'Jesus stuff?'

Silence.

'I won't be fourteen for another six months. Hate being thirteen. Thirteen's unlucky and crap and it's so sort of in the middle of things. It's so *not anything*.'

Ali couldn't immediately see how fourteen was any closer to being something, but didn't say so.

'Crap having a birthday near Christmas. Everybody always forgets or says that my Christmas present is extra-large or something.'

'Mmmm.'

'Would be nicer to have a summer birthday like you.'

'S' all right.'

'What's that you're reading?'

'Book.'

'Yes, but what?' She put a hand out to examine the cover.

'A book. Words. Stuff with pages.'

Jules made a visible effort not to appear irritated.

'You read masses.'

'Suppose so.'

'Wish I knew books. It's like, sometimes I really envy Izzy as well. Knowing music.'

'Nothing stopping you.'

'Tried. All the books in the library are crap. Twiddly stupid intellectual crap or complete retard shit. Nothing good.'

Ali shrugged.

'I liked your readings,' said Jules unexpectedly. 'They were good. You could read tonight.'

'Went through most of the books.'

'You like doing them, don't you?'

'Don't mind.'

'Can't ever be bothered to read the whole book. It's nice when you read them.'

Another shrug.

'Did you used to read a lot? Before here, I mean?'

Ali looked at Jules. She seemed quite guileless.

'Suppose so.'

'What stuff?'

'Everything. Just . . . whatever. Books my mother had.'

'Like intellectual stuff?'

'Sort of. Sort of anything. Whatever was there. My mother likes quite serious writers, lots of Jewish stuff, lots of stuff about war and other people's divorces. I didn't like them to begin with, but you get used to them. My dad didn't like books much. When he left, there were only five in his study. They were all called stuff like *Managing Arguments* or *Grow Big Shrubs.*'

'Do you ever see your dad?'

Despite herself, Ali felt a softening. 'Sometimes. In the holidays. I go over to America.'

'What's it like over there?'

'Weird. Big. Fast. It takes a while to get used to.'

'What's your stepmother like?'

'She's not my stepmother,' said Ali. 'She's just his new wife. She just talks about facelifts and make-up. Her idea of getting to know me is to take me for a pedicure. She talks about hair.'

Jules, it was clear, had difficulty in seeing why pedicures might be something to resent. She was also beginning to run out of questions. 'Ali? You know your mobile?'

Something in the centre of Ali's chest dropped away. Then she blushed, suddenly, fiercely. 'Yes?'

'Can we borrow it?'

Ali watched Jules's face. Jules, she noticed – not for the first time – had slightly prominent teeth. They made her look like a rodent. A sharp intentful rodent. 'Who's we?'

'Me. Caz. Just for a few minutes.'

'Why?'

'Because we want to ring someone.'

'Who?'

'Just someone.' Jules shifted. 'Does it matter? Five minutes.'

'Someone in this country? Or someone expensive?'

'Yes. This country.'

Ali crumpled. 'OK. Five minutes. You'll have to charge it.'

She took the mobile out of its packet and gave it to Jules. She felt sad that she wasn't allowed to be the first one to use it.

'Thanks. Give it back in five.' Jules galloped out of the room.

When she'd gone, Ali lay back on her bed again and started to read. But the words didn't seem to work any more.

+

Jules sat picking flakes of paper off the side of a large tin of cooking oil. She'd picked them off quite idly at first, but when the paper started to peel away and the clean tin shone out from beneath, she'd become interested. Now there was a whole pile of small ripped scraps fluttering round her feet, and she was wondering if it might be possible to spell her name out from three pieces of a 'Sunflower Best Value Low in Polyunsaturates' label and a couple of twigs.

It was evening, and the shade was slipping closer all the time. If she thought about it, she quite liked this part of the wood. It seemed to have an enterprising flourish to it. The plants corkscrewed their way to the light as if they were doing as they wanted instead of what someone else had ordered them to do. Further beyond, the older trees stood alone, each in its own soft clearing of leaves and shifting light. And the place was secure. Or secure-ish. Their usual smoking places were elsewhere, and neither Caz nor Hen would think to look in the mess at the back of the kitchens.

She had come out here to find a bit of silence and to get her head in some sort of order. She and Caz had phoned the boys – or rather, Caz had sat in the rhododendron bush smoking and giving instructions while Jules had done the ringing bit – and it was all sorted for Friday night. Tomorrow. Only twenty-four hours. How was she supposed to deal with that? She needed at least another week just to get a halfway decent suntan.

And there were other things. Relations with Hen were still strained. When she had returned to the room last night, her mind still half blinded with all the silent speeches she'd made, Hen had looked at her for a second and Jules had known that she couldn't open her mouth. She had explained – quite non-committally – about meeting the men in the music shop, but when it came to telling Hen all the important things, something happened. Or didn't happen. Jules wanted to speak, it was just that when confronted with Hen – that churchy face, the widow's peak, the air of unspecified suffering – she'd lost the knack. Or rather, she'd thought that she would wait until Mel left the room, and when Mel left the room she thought she'd wait until Hen had stopped fiddling with her make-up bag, and when she'd stopped fiddling with her make-up Jules had to go upstairs for a fag, and the moment had been bundled out of sight. When she had pulled her packet of cigarettes out of the drawer she hadn't suggested that Hen came with her to the roof. She had lain with her back to the tiles watching the clouds through half-closed eyes and parsing arguments in her mind.

When she got downstairs, Hen was folding clothes and placing them back in her drawer.

'Got anything I can borrow?'

'Sure.' Hen sat down on the edge of her bed and started picking the mud off her trainers.

Jules took everything out of her drawers, apologizing as she did so. 'Sorry. Sorry. Oh. Didn't mean . . .'

When everything was sprawled across the bed, she deliberated for a while.

'This.' She pointed to a T-shirt with a scarlet snake printed on the front. 'Cool. Borrow this?'

She could see in the hesitation that Hen had been wanting to wear it. Strange how difficult it seemed to hold her gaze, and how easily both of them swerved off to stare at other things.

'Go on. Pleeeease. I look much better in it than you do.'

'Course.'

She saw the second's tremor of hatred in Hen's eyes, and was pleased. 'Excellent.' She skipped off to the other side of the room, folded the T-shirt and laid it carefully into her own drawer. Small victory number one.

She stopped picking at the tin and kicked at it with one foot. It was clouding over, and this corner was beginning to turn grey. There must be other things she could do to prepare herself for tomorrow. If there was no way of doing anything about the roots of her hair perhaps she could steal a couple of lemons from the kitchen and use the juice to give herself highlights. But that depended on it being sunny. And besides, she was too fat. Too fat, too pale, too not-ready. Too spotty, as well. There was definitely one coming up on her forehead. If she squeezed it tonight, would she end up looking scabby tomorrow? These things needed thought. You couldn't just arrange to meet a bloke and turn up without preparation.

From somewhere behind her, she could hear movement: a rabbit, perhaps, or a bird. As she turned towards the sound she felt an arm slide round her neck. She jumped, but the arm stayed where it was.

'There you are.' Caz smiled.

'Oh!' She blushed as if she'd been caught doing something incriminating. How the hell had Caz found her?

'Just wanted . . .'

'Space?'

'Yup.'

'You OK?'

'Yes.'

'Sure?'

'Wanted to think.'

'About what?'

'Things.'

The way Caz was looking at her made Jules feel furtive. If she confessed her thoughts, then perhaps Caz would know that she wasn't doing anything wrong. There was always something about Caz's air of benevolent expectancy which made Jules want to start talking, to tell her everything right from the beginning, throw herself on Caz's mercy, pray for understanding. That look was somehow part of her mystery, the sense she gave of having come from a different place. She didn't talk much about her family. Her parents were divorced, her father worked in Singapore and her mother did something in interactive advertising. She wasn't close to them; she spent most holidays with her stepsister Elsa in Berlin. That was about as much as anyone knew. Caz didn't talk about home and by not talking about it she somehow made it seem even more glamorous. There was something in her silence which made Jules feel coy about her own adherence to home and family and parents, as if Caz had already shrugged off all the extraneous stuff of childhood and was occupied now by other concerns, by dreams and ambitions that had nothing to do with the smallness of other people's lives. Maybe, thought Jules, it was only that Caz was cool, and scariness was an essential part of cool.

'All right about tomorrow?'

'Yes.'

'Is it, then?'

Jules scuffed at the leaves with one foot. 'Promise you won't say anything?'

'Promise.'

'Hen. Had an argument yesterday.'

'About?'

'Don't know. Nothing, really.'

Caz waited.

Jules could feel warmth rising to her face. 'She was just being weird. Offish.'

'Why?'

'Don't know.'

'Do you like her?'

Jules was so confused by the question that she had to repeat it a couple of times. 'Like her? Do I *like* her? Yeah, course. She's my friend.'

Caz waited.

'She's my friend,' Jules repeated. The warmth was becoming heat. 'Course I *like* her. Why shouldn't I?'

'You just seem to have been arguing a lot recently,' said Caz reasonably.

'But that's normal. That's not bad. It's like she's gone funny at the moment and sometimes we argue.'

'How do you mean, funny?'

'You know. You said. You said it first.'

'Said what?'

'That she'd gone funny.'

Caz seemed puzzled. 'I didn't. Don't know what sort of funny you mean, anyway.'

'Yes you did.' The ground seemed to be slipping from under her. 'You said she was acting weird.'

'I don't remember that.'

'You did! You so did! The other day when we'd just got here. We were on the roof, and you said you were worried about her. I know you did.'

Caz got up. 'I don't remember it. Anyway, I only asked if you liked her.' She turned and walked back towards the kitchens.

Jules remained where she was, picking at the tin. Had she dreamed the previous conversation with Caz? And what did Caz mean, did she like Hen?

She stood up, kicked the shredded label into the wind and walked back to the Manor, hugging her arms round her waist.

+

'Do you want,' said Ali through the darkness, ' "Reclaiming the Uterus", "Clitoral Myths" or . . .' she paused, '. . . "Loving Thy Cunt"?'

Mel snuffled into the duvet. 'Had the cunt. Wasn't very good.'

'Give us something else. Dicks. Whatever. Not that shit,' said Caz.

'Why?' Jules sat up.

'Because it's boring.'

Ali turned the pages. It was a compendium of feminist writing. 'There isn't much about actual *dicks*.' She put the book down and removed a psychology textbook from the pile. 'You could have this. "When a male child's interest turns to his genitals he betrays the fact by manipulating them frequently . . ." '

Izzy tittered. 'Pu-uke.'

' ". . . and he then finds that the adults do not approve of this behaviour. More or less plainly, more or less brutally, a threat is pronounced that this part of him which he values so highly will be taken away from him. Usually it is from women that the threat emanates; very often they . . ." '

As she read, Ali felt the words flatten and blur. Reading aloud was different from ordinary reading. She found herself concentrating so hard on the style and manner of her delivery that the sense receded and became no more than a kind of lullaby recitation. It no longer mattered what she read – she could easily have gone through a couple of Spanish textbooks without it making much difference – and had become only about how she read.

It had taken until the end of the first year before it was discovered, almost by accident, that Ali had one useful attribute: she was good at reading aloud. She had therefore been unofficially appointed to read them all a passage of something as filthy as the frigid school library could provide. She had begun with fiction and worked her way through a number of important male writers. Most, she found, were either too coy or so painfully forthcoming she had to stop because the room had been reduced to shrieks of ridicule. Then she moved on to murders, historical, factual and fictional. Nilsen proved popular, as did Fred West, the Yorkshire Ripper and some American guy who'd been into boiling people. Finally, and most satisfactorily, she found the psychology and women's studies section. Miss Ewart, the Eng. lit. teacher, had gone through a brief but intense period of personal development during which she had persuaded her classes that talking about themselves for half an hour was as good a contribution to the study of literature as wading through Conrad would ever be. The phase lasted for as long as it took for Miss Ewart to restock half a shelf of the library and for Miss Naylor to announce a summary ban on anyone discounting themselves from class on grounds of developmental trauma.

Meanwhile Ali and the five other girls who shared her room had discovered empowerment in a big way, particularly the bits which discussed sado-masochism, the myth of the vaginal orgasm, and anything at all which involved the word clitoris, throbbing, or gusset. It had taken her two nights to read a short essay on female fantasies because every time she got to the word 'moist,' she had to stop for ten minutes. Discussion of rape or lesbianism, on the other hand, reduced the room to silence. Ali had never been able to work out whether that silence was borne of boredom, discomfort or longing. Eventually she'd had to stop those readings as well, after Izzy had gone without warning to Jaws and complained of nightmares involving blood and men with beards. Two days later, despite Miss Ewart's impassioned protests, the interesting bits of the psychology library had been moved to a locked cabinet. Two or three of the books had mysteriously been lost in transit, but the rest remained forever beyond their reach. For a while, Ali did no more readings.

' "He could put himself in his father's place in a masculine fashion and have intercourse with his mother as his father did, or he might want to take the position of his mother and be loved by his father, in which case his mother would become superfluous . . ." ' She drifted to a stop.

'Not interested in the woman stuff,' said Caz, plumping up her pillows with one hand. 'What's the point in listening to some woman going on about reclaiming the bloody menopause? It's the bloke stuff which is good.'

'Yeah,' said Jules weakly, 'But. It's funny. I think it's funny.'

'It's not funny. It's full of boring political shit.'

'Don't you believe any of that stuff?'

'About getting in touch with your menopause? Course not.'

'No. The other stuff.'

'Not really. It's old.'

'Not the stuff about women – girls – having jobs and things.'

'Yeah, that stuff. Of course you do that . . .'

'And stuff about people sticking together. We stick together, don't we?'

'Ye-es.' Caz was silent for a moment. When she spoke again, she spoke slowly. 'But what people – us, girls – really actually want is to make themselves up, put on their blind-ingest clothes, do the stuff with the heels and the hair and the lipstick. And then they want to walk into a room, looking as dead fuck-off gorgeous as they can ever look, and for every other girl in the room to look at them and think, "Bitch".'

A short silence. 'Who said that?'

'Me. I did.'

'No, you didn't.'

'OK, I didn't.' Caz smiled. 'Elsa did. It's still true.'

'Here,' said Ali. 'This might do.' She picked up her torch and began to read. ' "The classic sexual position – the one given as the position to those children who are taught, if they are taught at all, some form of sexual education – is that of the missionary position. The woman lies passive, the flattened receptacle for the penis, no more active or participatory than an insect on a dissecting board. The act of penetration is all; the penis's pleasure is the aim and goal of the act. The penis is thrust, weapon-like, into the wound of the vagina, whilst the woman, in order to escape the demeaning charge of frigidity, simulates the false promise of satiation. The woman is entered, sometimes violently, usually too early for her own pleasure. Sex becomes a form of midnight robbery; the ultimate form of breaking and entering. Our mother's generation were instructed to 'lie back and think of England.' The sexual act was regarded as a duty, a patriotic sacrifice, necessary but distasteful . . ." '

'Bo-ring,' said Caz. 'Told you.'

Ali put down the torch. 'There isn't anything else.'

'Are you sure?'

'Yes. It's all like that.'

Jules was sitting up. 'That stuff about walking into a room and people thinking "bitch". Do you think that?'

'No Of course not.'

'Yes, you do.' There was surprise in her voice.

'OK, yes I do. But not here.'

'When?'

'Outside. At parties. The world, where men are. Wherever.'

'Why?'

'Why? Because it's true. It just is. That's the way it works. Everybody pretends the other stuff, stuff about friendship and kindness and looking after each other and all the rest of it, but actually, really, what they're actually thinking is, she's got better legs than me or better tits than me or better hair than me or whatever. And then they're thinking, I want those tits or those legs or that hair, I want all that stuff that she's got and I haven't. I want it so badly I'll hang out with that person just so I can be close to it. And they know they'll never be six foot or a decent blonde or rich enough to slice their tits up and stick in implants, so they hate each other instead. That's how it works. That's how it is.'

Jules's voice had risen a full octave. 'And that's all? That's all there is?'

'Yep. That's all there is.'

'You really think that?'

'Not here. But outside, yeah.'

'Why?'

'Look.' Caz leaned forwards. 'Next time, in the holidays, come out with me in London. Like last holidays. Remember? You walk down the street, you go to a club, and you don't look at the men, you look at the girls. I saw you doing it. You look at the girls and you think, nice skirt, crap ankles, bad hair, face like a dog, wish I had a pair like that, God, those must be fake, cute nose, whatever. You walk down a street, and that's what you think, that's what you look for.'

'*Are you saying I'm a lesbian?!*'

'Stop shouting, for Christ's sake. No, I'm not. I'm saying you're competitive, like everyone else is.'

'My mother . . .' Hen stopped. 'My mother thinks that. I know she does. You can see it from the way she looks at people.'

Ali put down the book she was holding. 'My mother thinks that women are better than men. Fact, she thinks that men don't matter any more.'

'Well, who does she fuck then?' asked Caz rudely. 'Other women? Chickens?'

'But,' said Jules, unable to let go, 'aren't we supposed to stick together?'

'Yuh-huh. Yes, we stick together. Except when it counts.'

'D'you mean?'

'I mean except for when there's men or sex or important stuff involved.'

'That's bullshit! That's total bullshit! We stick together because of friendship. Because it does matter. You'd stick with me, wouldn't you? And Hen? And all of us?'

'Yes.'

'And women are better than men, right? We're special. We can do stuff that men can't, like babies. And we're kinder. We don't hit people.'

'We're not better. We're different, but we're not better. Just because we've got tits and lipstick and babies, it doesn't make us better nicer kinder friendlier people.'

'Yes it does.'

'Why?'

'It just *does*. We're nicer . . . We get pregnant. Men are stronger than us.' Jules stopped. 'And' – with the air of producing a conclusive argument, '*and* there aren't any paedophiles who're women. Or rapists. Paedophiles are all men.'

'So? There aren't many men who smother their babies, or batter them to death or leave them to die in doorways or all that stuff.' Caz sighed. 'Look, whose opinion do you really care about? Who does it really matter if they say you look good or you look crap or you're wearing the right shirt or you've got the right music?'

A complicated pause. 'Mine,' said Jules eventually. 'MINE' – again, louder – 'Doesn't matter what anyone else says.'

'Bull-*shit*.' Caz's eyes were suddenly alive. 'Don't believe you. You walk into a clothes shop and you don't buy the thing you like, you buy the thing that you think is going to piss off everybody else. You don't even *know* what you like; all you know is what's going to have the worst effect. You buy the T-shirt or the belt or the jacket that's so cute it's going to make everyone else think, "God, she looks good in that," or "how come when she wears that she looks great and how come when I wear it, it looks crap?" You buy stuff because you know it's going to get right up your sister's nose.'

'I don't!' Jules was shouting again. 'I DON'T!'

'Yes you—'

'How can you say I don't know what I like? How can you *say* that? I do know! I know *exactly* what I like! It's mine!'

Hen, who had been watching the two of them, spoke softly. 'Where did you get all this stuff, Caz? Is it you? Do you think it all?'

Caz subsided. 'Yes.' And then, afterthought, 'No. Some of it.'

'Did Elsa say all this stuff?'

'Some of it.'

'Is this what you do?' Silence.

Jules – shouting again – 'I don't buy things for other people! I buy them for me, right? Don't care what anyone else thinks!'

'OK.' Caz sounded tired. 'If you say so.'

'And girls don't hurt people. I don't hurt people. OK?'

'Whatever.'

'And I'm *not a fucking lezzie*, all right?'

'Sure.'

'God, Caz.' Jules straightened her pyjamas with quick ill-tempered movements. 'You talk so much shit sometimes.'

Silence. The ticking of Izzy's alarm clock became audible. All of them were still locked into position, sitting up in bed, tuned to the strains of discord. One by one they became self-conscious, twitched at the bedclothes and lay back. Nothing happened. The building cracked and murmured, the guttering dripped, and from somewhere downstairs they heard the sound of lights being turned on and off. All of them felt a curious sensitivity to the usual noises; all of them rehearsed sentences in their heads which none of them felt able to speak.

Finally, after half an hour of turning in circles, Jules sat up and looked over towards Caz's form under the bedclothes. 'Caz?' Her voice was tentative. 'You . . . me . . . I mean, we do sort of matter, don't we?'

'Of course, babe.' Caz unmuffled her voice. 'Of course you do.' And she smiled.

FRIDAY

The gym. Again. Jules had not bothered protesting. If she didn't get irritated by it, maybe it couldn't touch her. If she stayed here, scissoring one leg slowly through the air, perhaps the time would pass, and she would find herself on the other side.

Outside, the sound of a car came and went. The last time they'd been here, there had been music, but the machine had broken. This time they were doing it all in silence. Jules realized that the music had been useful not just for providing something to get irritated with but for concealing the discomfort of gym's exposure. It felt weird, flinging her leg up and down with nothing but the sound of cloth on skin as an accompaniment.

'Fifty sit-ups.'

Jules levered herself into position. She'd been careful this time not to choose a mat too near to Caz. She didn't want to spend the entire afternoon reminding herself of Caz's marvellousness. They were facing a whole evening of that, anyway. She'd been worrying about meeting the boys tonight. Would it be cool? Would it end up like most other things did, with Caz

116

shining like a floodlight while the rest of them remained in darkness?

When she thought about it, she'd been away from male company for so long – nine weeks, for God's sake – that she could barely remember how they worked. Blokes, she knew, came with a different set of instructions to girls. It wasn't only that their interests were different, it was other, more subtle things as well – an obscure humour, a habit of filling silence with more silence, a weird obsession with quite boring bits of other people's bodies. The closer the time came to seeing them, the more she remembered how complicated things could be. She felt the first flutterings of excitement shorten her breath.

'Hen. Mina. Up the ropes.'

Izzy, decoding this as tacit criticism for being too heavy to go first, glanced with anguish at the window. Jules came out of her reverie and looked up. She'd forgotten how high the ropes were. The ceiling seemed dingy from here, as if distorted by the immensity of the distance. They couldn't climb those. They were so high she could barely see the tops of them. Naylor must be taking the piss. She was about to turn and say something to Hen, but to her astonishment she was already walking towards the left-hand rope. She couldn't seriously think it was possible to climb something that long.

Hen took her time. In places the hemp was smooth from use, and in others Jules could see it jabbing roughly at her hands. She heaved herself upwards, driven more by the desire to be out of reach of Mina and Miss Naylor than any particular compulsion to do well. She reached the mid-point and looked down. Her arms were weakening, and she looked tired. Miss Naylor gave a reluctant nod, and Hen slithered back down.

'Vicky and Mel.'

Vicky, taking the line of least resistance, made a joke of it. Hauled herself up once, dropped back down to the floor. Hauled herself up again, dropped back down. Hauled again, sprawled on her back. The others laughed.

Miss Naylor strode over to the empty rope and held it still. 'Very funny. Could we put a little effort in this time, missy?'

Vicky plucked wanly at the knot near the bottom, looked round to gauge the sympathies of her audience and began to climb. She got no further than two or three feet off the ground before sliding back to earth. Mel, not much higher, took Vicky's effort as a signal that she too could give up.

Miss Naylor turned. 'Seems we don't quite understand, do we? We can either put some effort into this and behave like adults, or we can carry on clowning around until midnight.' She held out the rope. 'Now. Julia, Catherine, shall we see if we can do this properly?'

Jules walked over to the ropes. The day's irritations carried her up the rope with surprising speed. If she felt the strain on her body then she ignored it, fighting to get higher. Opposite her, Caz climbed steadily. Jules battled, tightening her legs round the base of the rope and hauling herself upwards. Just this once, perhaps she would outdo the laws of physics, transcend her own faults, go further than any of them.

'Well,' said Miss Naylor, turning her face to the light, 'looks like Julia's finally decided to show us.' Jules hung from the middle of the rope, one hand gripping the prickly hemp and the other extended in what she felt was a casual flourish. She pulled idly at the collar of her T-shirt to prove to all of them down below that this required no more than grace and self-possession. Caz, watching her, smiled and then dropped downwards.

'Very fancy,' said Miss Naylor. 'Perhaps we can start the stopwatch and have a bit of a race.'

Jules, triumphantly overriding the pain in her arm muscles, slid back to earth. As her foot touched the mat, she stumbled slightly. Caz, standing close, felt Jules push against her and turned. They gazed at each other for a second. Jules took in Caz's easy calmness, the new blush on her cheeks, the blackness in her shining eyes. In that one moment, seeing Caz clearly for the first time in years, Jules knew exactly what she wanted. She smiled back at her, hard and passionate, and as she did so, she could feel a fresh resolution building in her limbs. OK, if that was what Naylor wanted, she'd race Caz. She'd be glad to.

The two of them stood side by side, watching the others struggle upwards. Izzy made a hash of things. Her tracksuit got tangled up with the rope, her legs dangled to one side or the other and the rope swung out abruptly, almost hitting Vicky. Her face darkened with every inch that she climbed. Ali, sturdy and silent, got up and down with neither fuss nor glory. Mel, as usual, seeemed to be on the verge of complaint, but kept it to herself.

'That wasn't too hard, was it, missies? Take it two by two again.' Miss Naylor held up a hand, waiting for the seconds to tick round. 'Right. You two. Go.'

Rage and hope propelled Jules as far as the mid-point. Her muscles no longer felt rusty as they had the first time; they felt clean and ready. Beside her, she could hear Caz giving thoughtful little huffing noises as she pulled hand over hand up the rope. Jules could hear chanting in her head, the chanting of some absurd internal coach yelling, *Go, go, get on, get beyond, get higher. Go on, go on.* She twisted her legs a little more tightly around the rope. This was all she wanted, this one single thing

– just, for once, to beat Caz. The thought made her smile with fury. And still Caz was there almost beside her, making tiny exhalations to mark her tiny efforts. About halfway up, Jules could feel her muscles start to scald. She'd put too much effort into climbing the rope the first time, and to do it again after such a short break seemed too much. But her own physical shortcomings only made her fiercer. Caz wasn't feeling this, Caz was still climbing the rope as swiftly as she climbed stairs. And now her fucking body was sabotaging her only chance of getting ahead, giving her one more bitter proof that Caz's body, Caz's muscles, Caz's bloody everything were better. Always better. Jules put her hand up a few more inches, gripped and pulled. The hemp rasped at her palm. She could feel her own weight dragging her back, and the ache in her shoulders sharpened. Her legs didn't seem to be holding on to the rope so well, and she was sure she was losing speed. *Go, go, go, get on, get up, get going. Beat her, beat her, beat her.*

'Well,' said a voice below her, 'Julia does seem to have livened up.'

Jules was conscious of Miss Naylor and the others only as an irritant, another reason to climb the rope and get as much distance as she could between her and the ground. She was hauling herself up automatically now, half snarling with effort. All of it, the chafing rope, the consciousness of Caz beside her, the stupid normal people down there on the floor, were goading her onwards. Her muscles hurt, her heart thumped so hard it made her ribs hurt, and she didn't give a fuck if Caz could hear how loudly she was breathing any more; she had no choice. But just as she felt herself beginning to fail, she saw the little white band of tape at the top of the rope. She was almost there. She had almost arrived. She put her hand up and heaved once, twice, feeling her tracksuit drag and yanking it up in frustration. Her palm closed around the white band and she was there. The rope swung triumphantly out behind her.

'Two minutes forty-eight seconds,' said a voice far, far below. 'Well done, Julia.'

Jules swung round slightly and saw Caz reaching for the white band. Her eyes were half closed and there was a blush of colour on both cheeks. Her ribs kept appearing and then disappearing through the sides of her T-shirt as she breathed. Her hair had come loose and swung over her neck. Which, thought Jules savagely, only made her look more bloody attractive. Caz stabilized herself and then swung round to look at Jules. Neither of them could speak.

'Two minutes fifty-three seconds.'

Jules looked down at all the upturned faces on the mats below. They seemed so far away, so unnecessary. And the view from up here was amazing. If she turned the rope a bit she could see out of the window towards the lawns and the river. It all looked so blithe and peaceful, as if it didn't even realize the incredibleness of Jules at the top of a rope before Caz. She could still feel the blood thundering through her body, but her pulse had slowed and she was beginning to feel a little dreamy. Caz smiled again. This time something in Jules softened and she smiled back. The envy which had pushed her up here had gone and in its place was a different feeling: the feeling, for once, of equality. She laughed, and Caz laughed back, and it felt as if part of her which had been stuck had suddenly expanded.

'Come on then. Down we get.'

Jules ignored Miss Naylor. She looked tiny anyway down there on the ground, small and petty and unnecessary. She'd climbed this bloody rope, she'd beaten Caz, and now she was going to enjoy being here. But Caz began to slide downwards, unfurling her legs, going hand over hand. Jules stayed where she was, watching the top of Caz's head as it slipped southwards. She took one hand off and waved it out behind her, twirling the rope round and round like a circus gymnast. This was the best feeling she'd had in bloody ages.

'Very nice,' said Miss Naylor drily. 'Could we get down now?'

Jules was still feeling serene, gracious, unexpectedly benevolent. Her heart had stopped thudding so loudly now and she could feel warmth sliding pleasantly through her skin. But as she moved downwards, both hands still gripped tight to the rope and both legs twisted round as securely as possible, she felt something – something to do with the fading adrenaline and her muscles relaxing after all that effort. Suddenly, out of nowhere, there was a rush of sensation. Not in her heart or her lungs or her hands, but in the bit of her which she usually associated with nothing much except period pain and euphemism. Her muscles had lost it. They were doing things to her insides that she couldn't understand, going into spasm or cramp or something. But this didn't feel like cramp; this felt warm and gorgeous, like sensual electric shocks. She was so startled that she stopped moving down and just hung there on the rope, her eyes wide, paralysed. The aftershocks faded, and she was just there with the darkest part of herself doing something that it had never done before.

'Come on,' said Miss Naylor. 'We're waiting.'

Jules couldn't do anything. She just stayed suspended, trying to push the feeling away. She knew suddenly, appallingly, what had happened. The worst, most embarrassing thing that could possibly have occurred. She'd come. She'd had a bloody orgasm. On a rope. In a gym. With everyone staring at her. Every conversation she'd ever had in the safety of the night, every magazine she'd ever flicked through to find the filthy bits, every 'parental guidance' bit of music she'd ever listened to confirmed it. That feeling, like a lovely version of cramp, was what it was.

She slid floorwards so fast that the rope ripped the skin from her thumbs. She crashed onto to the mat and sat there, half stunned. Miss Naylor put a hand out. Jules ignored it, still oblivious to everything except that warm appalling feeling.

'Shows what you can do when you try.'

'Your hands OK?' Hen bent over.

Jules didn't reply.

'Oi. Jules. Your hands all right?'

Jules looked down. Half the skin had come off her heart line, and they both looked painfully burned. She didn't feel anything. 'Y . . . yes'

'You were really fast.'

Jules turned again. She didn't want Hen to look at her; Hen might somehow see it in her face. *Oh my God.* She'd been here, in a gym, thinking about Caz, all twisted with desire and hate, and her innards had suddenly exploded. She'd had an orgasm, surrounded by girls. She was a lesbian. It showed. They'd see it in her; they'd know she wanted to have sex with girls. She had been turned on by Caz. Girls made her come. It was too hideous, too appalling to think about. She *wasn't.* She *didn't* like girls, they *didn't* turn her on. Caz must have done something to her. It was Caz's revenge for having been beaten to the top of the rope. It was the worst thing that could possibly happen.

Jules didn't notice that Hen was speaking to her. She didn't hear the words and she was only dimly aware of the movement around her, people pulling things around, shifting the mats, tugging the wooden horse across the room. She only noticed that anything was happening at all when Caz loomed towards her.

'Not more,' she was saying. 'Can't do more.'

Jules stared at her.

'Could do with a fag.'

A couple of days ago she'd said all that stuff about Naylor; how she just liked getting them to do gym because she fancied them. She just wanted to see them half undressed, prancing around, doing things that made their tits wobble, hoping for a glimpse of knicker. Before, it was Naylor who was the sad sordid lesbian. Now it was her. There was something wrong with her.

She couldn't look at Caz, or Hen, or any of them. 'The . . . I . . . I might . . .'

She walked over to Miss Naylor. She couldn't look at her straight, either.

Miss Naylor, busy with the horse and the mats, turned. 'Yes?'

'I'm just . . . I'll be . . .'

And Jules fled from the room.

+

Caz put her fingers to her lips. 'Got something. Check this out.' She slid open her top drawer and took out a magazine. It showed a woman with her back arched and her breasts looming like party balloons. The woman's nipples were covered by a flimsy veil of text.

They were upstairs an hour later, waiting for supper. Jules had still not reappeared. Hen had asked a couple of times where she was, but Caz had shrugged. 'Who cares? Look at this. This will put us in the party mood.'

'Ohmygod!' said Mel. 'Where did you get that?'

'Elsa sent it. Nicked it off her boyfriend and sent it for a laugh.'

Mel stared at the woman's nipples. 'Gross. Let's see.'

'It's hysterical,' said Caz. 'The stories . . .' She began flicking through the magazine. Photographs of women with their legs open, arses waggling at the camera, glittering with something that wasn't sweat.

'Crap tits,' said Mel softly.

Caz kept flicking. A woman in a bath, being licked by another woman.

Hen did not know what to say. The pictures were fascinating, but somehow scary as well. She stared at the women's sculpted pubes. Hers didn't look anything like that. Was that how they were supposed to be? And all that raw ugly mess between their legs. How could men find that sexy?

Caz thrust the magazine at her. 'Go on, look.'

'Why didn't you get the bloke one?'

'Told you. Got sent it by Elsa. She just took what she could.' She dropped the magazine onto Hen's lap.

Hen turned the pages. She didn't like it. She couldn't stop the feeling that by touching it, she was also touching the torn flesh.

'The ads,' breathed Mel. 'What are the ads like?'

Quickie Blonde Whore, All Hole Fucking, Dirty Fucking Cunt of a Bitch, Cock-Sucking Slut . . . Hen turned the pages faster and faster.

Caz grabbed the magazine. ' "Tied and whipped by strict bitch, feel my throbbing shaft, busty nurse, big twat fetish . . ." ' She laughed. 'Go on, Hen. Might help you with Adey.'

The magazine fell open at a picture of a woman smeared from head to toe in baked beans. The beans were the same vicious orange colour as the woman's skin. They dripped down her stomach, over her thighs, between her open legs. The beans looked like white slugs. The woman's eyes were half shut and her mouth was open, as if she'd just eaten something she couldn't chew.

'Oh my *god*,' said Mel. 'That is *vile*.'

Hen kept turning, trying to find an image she could look at without feeling weird. The same woman, with her back turned and her hips waggling at the camera, beans sliding down the crack between her legs, oozing onto one of her legs. Then two women, one of them lying back and the other licking beans off her stomach. Another woman, dark-haired this time, in what looked like a child's bedroom, full of soft toys. The woman had a small frilly nightie on that barely covered her shoulders and was doing something to herself with a Barbie doll. There was another woman beside her, bending over. Hen thought of the dolls in her sisters' room at home all lined up in a row on the dresser, and of them being used for such grown-up corruption.

Another woman, licking a dribble of cream being poured onto her tits by some unseen hands. The cream had splashed all over her neck and waist. She too had her legs open, and the liquid dribbled over her pubic hair down onto the sheets. Hen was beginning to feel hysterical. The mess, she thought frantically, think of the mess it would make. All that richness, reeking over the bedclothes. It would be impossible to clear up. It would stink, it would lie there and rot on the bed, and every night, in her dreams, she would smell it again . . .

She shoved the magazine back into Mel's lap. 'Just . . .' she said, and ran out of the room. She heard Mel shriek, and the flutter of the pages as the magazine fell to the floor. Then she heard Caz laughing. '*Hen!* Come back.'

She bolted into the toilet, slammed the door shut and leaned against the wall. It felt cool and a little dank. She closed her eyes, and the world swung from side to side. Her heart was kicking so hard against her ribs that she wondered briefly if she might have a heart attack. She slid down the wall until she was crouching on the floor, staring at the side of the bath.

Mel's voice outside. 'Hen. *Hen.* You OK?'

No reply.

'Hen?'

'Fine,' said Hen eventually. 'Be fine in a second. Don't worry.'

Mel giggled. 'Sure?'

'Yes.' Vehemently. 'Yes. Promise. *Fine.*'

The footsteps receded.

Hen crouched there on the floor and closed her eyes again. The images swam back towards her, the creeping baked beans, the cream, the raw hideous slits like wounds. The images wouldn't stop crawling into her mind. Even when she opened her eyes again, they stayed, oozing over her vision until it felt like the side of the bath was covered in thighs and lips and sluggish white bodies.

Stop, she thought, *please, please, please stop.* Stop it. Go away. She tried to think of something else, something kind, like home on a sunny day or the dog they'd had which died, or the road towards the sea. It didn't work. When she thought about the road, she remembered the woman in her Valentine's hat and the glimpse of something far outside her understanding of the solid world.

Hen stood up. She had to stop this somehow. There was a mirror on the wall by the sink, and she wobbled slightly as she walked over to it. All she could see was this face, this little monkeyish face with the bones standing out. Her skin looked green and the shine on it looked like the sweat on the women's bodies. The sockets of her eyes seemed huge, as if her face was melting back into her head.

When she looked at her eyelashes, they began to move. They crawled down her face, over her cheeks. They moved with the stealth of insects, slowly, jerkily. Hen couldn't stop staring at them. Her eyes were huge and black, and out of them came the insects, moving down her face, over her forehead.

Quite slowly, Hen ran her fingernails down her arm. The nails bit into her skin, leaving little red lines in their wake. Hen pulled one of her longer nails off so it left a ragged edge. Then she raked deeper. Where the sharp edge of her nail bit into the skin, she could feel pain. She looked down at her arm. The rake marks looked sharper now, almost through the skin into the flesh. Someone would see this. It was too obvious. She scrabbled in a pocket and found her penknife. It was just a little one, rather blunted. It had been in a cracker she'd got a couple of Christmases ago and had proved useful once in a while for cleaning her nails.

She pulled out the long blade and ran her finger down the blade. It was so blunt that all it left was a red mark like a fold on her skin. She shoved the knife into the side of her hip, the fat bit she hated but no one else ever saw. It didn't connect;

the cloth of her trousers was gettting in the way. She pulled them down and picked up the knife again, gripping it in a proper stabbing motion like murderers were supposed to do. She raked it deep and hard into her hip.

The pain made her eyes water. She looked down. The knife had been too blunt to go to the bone, but blood was beginning to seep out of the cut. *Wimp*, she thought. *Can't even do that properly. Fucking wimp. Coward. Can't even give yourself what you deserve. Stupid fucking cow.* All the frustration, all the weariness at bullying herself into how she ought to be, all the wormish tedium of her hate, all of it went into the knife. She shoved it back into her skin again and again down and down, plunging at herself.

The pain was immediate, a pure, straightforward kind of hurt. It felt right. It felt better.

... FRIDAY

There was whispering in the dusk and a high-pitched squeak. The light from a torch wavered over the ceiling.

'Lipstick,' someone was saying. '*Lipstick*. Over here.'

Ali rolled over and pulled the covers over her head. Underneath the bedclothes she had a book. If they would just shut up, she might actually be able to get some reading done. Someone shuffled past her on the way to the bathroom, clutching a bag of make-up.

Ali turned on her side and watched Caz applying mascara. Her hair was pinched back in a blue headband and her lips rumpled awkwardly as she concentrated. Ali found herself riveted by the delicacy of the little brushstrokes, their gentleness and patience, when all she knew of Caz was not gentle or patient.

Caz clipped the mirror compact closed and ran a finger over each eyelid. She caught Ali's gaze and smiled before Ali could look away. 'Does that look OK?'

'Amazing.' With the torchlight shining sideways on her face, Caz seemed transformed: darker, older, elegantly menacing. 'You look about eighteen.'

'Excellent.'

Jules came back into the room. She had spent over an hour making herself up, but the mascara and the lipstick against her pale ungrown face seemed more garish than Caz's efforts. Jules looked like a simulated woman, thought Ali, not like a real one. The dress she was wearing fitted so closely it looked as if it had been painted onto her.

'Shit.' She bent over and waved her hips in Caz's direction. 'Can you see my knickers in this?'

'Yes. Never bothered you before.'

Jules straightened up fast. 'You ready?'

Hen reappeared in the doorway. She had done what she could to wake up her face and had put on a pair of tight black satin trousers. She alone seemed unsure, neither as nervy as Jules nor as purposeful as Caz. Standing there by the door she hesitated, as if she might have been about to say something.

Jules gave her a quick visual strip, no more than a split-second up-and-down movement of the eyes. In that one glance she took in Hen's attempts at eyeshadow, the earrings knocking diffidently at her cheek, the curveless hips, the way she kept jamming her hands in and out of her pockets. Hen's legs were better than hers and her face – though white with nicotine and fright – was perhaps a little prettier. But her clothes were reassuringly terrible, and what should have been a cleavage was now no more than a sallow breastplate. Her hand trembled as she lifted it to the cross around her neck.

'You look nice,' Jules said smugly.

Hen stared at the floor. 'So do you.'

Izzy was under the bedclothes again. Ali could hear the faint hiss of her Discman.

'Iz? *Iz?*' Jules prodded at Izzy's foot. The hissing stopped and Izzy surfaced. 'Will you look out for us?'

'Yup.' She plunged back under the duvet.

'Ready?'

Hen shrugged deeper into her jacket and nodded.

Jules opened the window and swung one leg out.

'Go,' said Caz. 'Hurry up.'

Jules slid out of view.

Caz followed her, reversing out of the window, catching her foothold on the brickwork below. 'Cover for us,' she whispered, slipping down beyond the window ledge and out of sight. Ali heard a faint crump as she hit the roof of a car. She waited for a minute, listening to the darkness, and then pulled the covers back over her head.

+

'Shit,' Jules was saying. 'Heels.'

Caz flapped at her. 'Shut up.' Both of them crouched down low and ran over to the plywood fencing at the edge of the lawn. Caz found a gap between the posts and wriggled through. Jules came through after her, and the two crouched down. The wood felt scratchy and precarious on their spines.

'*Hen.* Where are you?'

A figure appeared from behind one of the shrubs, tottered through the darkness towards them and squatted next to Jules. 'D'you think anyone heard us?'

'Too late now.'

Jules pulled out a small metal tin painted with the face of Bart Simpson. She took out cigarette papers and a small lump of something wrapped in cling film. 'God. Been dying for a spliff.' She peeled open a cigarette and began arranging the tobacco along one of the papers. The wind scurried over her legs, picking at her hem.

'C'mon. Haven't got that long.'

'It's windy. Hang on.' She was fussing longer than was necessary, she knew. Even in darkness she didn't want to look at Caz. She held the joint up for inspection, covering the gaps in the paper with her thumb. A few stray flakes of tobacco fluttered onto the grass.

'So.' Caz turned to Hen, 'who you planning to snog, then?'

Hen looked appalled. 'Don't know. Haven't thought yet.'

'What about Mutant Albino Freak?'

'No way. God. No *way*.'

'Go on. Must have fancied him just a bit.'

'She did,' said Jules nastily, lighting the joint and spitting bits of tobacco out the side of her mouth. 'She was talking to him for ages.'

'So? That doesn't mean anything.'

'And?'

'He's horrible. He's albino, for fuck's sake. If he had babies, they'd come out like little white rat things.'

'Sweetheart, maybe think about babies a bit later. How about just thinking about snogging him for now?'

'Didn't like him.'

'You don't have to fucking *like* him, retard. You just have to *snog* him.'

'This,' said Caz, holding up the joint and glaring at it, 'is pure Oxo.'

'No, it's not. It's OK, that stuff.'

'Smells like Sunday lunch.'

'It does not.'

'It does. Where d'you get it from?'

'Sister. Said it was good stuff.'

'How much did you pay her?'

'Nothing,' said Jules, lying.

'Try.' Hen took a drag and coughed theatrically. '*Eeeuwrgh!* Vile. That's dried dogshit or something. You been had.'

'Anyway,' said Caz, 'what about you? What was he called?'

Jules shrugged. 'Bill. He was OK.'

'Snog him?'

'Course not. Were in the middle of a music shop, God's sake.'

'But you fancied him?'

'He was OK.'

'D'you like to fuck him?'

'Might do. Not sure.' Jules curled a strand of hair around one ear. 'Bit bored of sex at the moment.'

'*Bored?*' Caz stared. 'How are you *bored?*'

'Just bored. All that snogging and spit and stuff.'

'*I* don't get bored of sex. *I* don't find it boring.'

'He looked hairy to me,' said Hen. 'Like he'd probably have chest hair.'

Caz laughed. 'He got a hairy back, Jules?'

Jules curled her hair faster and faster. 'Don't know.'

'Hairy men it's like sleeping with a shag-pile carpet.'

Jules shrugged. 'He's OK. Not like I only fancy him, though. And he's not as bad as Mutant Albino Freak.'

'He wasn't that vile,' said Hen.

'You do fancy him, don't you?'

'I *don't.*'

'Yes, you do. You just said you did.'

'I *didn't.* I just said he wasn't that horrible.'

'So you fancy him. Obvious.'

'I *don't.* I just *talked* to him.'

'Don't fight it, pet,' said Caz.

'God's sake.' Hen got up abruptly and stamped on the joint. 'Let's go.'

The three of them stumbled off into the darkness, down to the road. They stood for a while on the grass verge a little way down from the driveway. Cars came past in clumps, driving fast, their headlights flicking past the three girls.

'Stick your thumb out.' Jules poked Hen in the back. 'Can't see you properly.'

'I am. They can see fine. Hate hitching.'

'Golden rule of hitching—' said Caz. 'Soon as you light a fag, a car comes along. Works every time. And buses. And taxis.' They stood in silence for a while, sticking their hands out when a car approached and swearing softly when it swished on past. Finally, they heard the sound of gears changing down and turned round. A dirty red Ford van was stopping in the lay-by a few yards ahead. All three of them ran towards it.

'Probably a rapist,' said Jules.

'Or a mad axe-murderer,' Hen said, out of breath and giggling.

The driver wound down the passenger window. Jules saw glasses, a scrappy beard, a neglected sort of face. Can't get raped by someone wearing glasses, she thought. She had a sudden image of a staring-eyed maniac pausing to remove his spectacles midway through a psychotic axe-attack. Maybe rapists wear dentures, she thought. Or braces. Or hernia trusses. Maybe rapists have blond pubes. She started snickering, tight, in the back of her throat.

'You wanting a lift?'

Jules nodded. 'Just to Stokeley.'

The man shovelled a layer of tabloids and spanners onto the floor. 'Get in.'

All three of them squashed into the passenger seat. It was uncomfortable; Caz had Jules's elbow digging into her hip, and Hen's foot was crushed by Caz's shin. None of them, it was clear, could think of anything to say. The driver seemed as discomfited by the three girls, with their thick feral reek of perfume and their naked clothing, as they were by him.

'I'm Steve,' he said, fingering the side of his neck. 'Hi.'

'Hi,' they said simultaneously.

'Where are you going?'

'Pub.' Caz spoke into the back of Jules's jacket. 'Cross Keys.'

Hen giggled. They drove the rest of the road in silence.

Steve let them out by the side of the road. Jules watched him drive off. 'Fuck. Weirdo.'

'You kept laughing,' said Hen. 'You set me off. Was fine until you started.'

'Had the weirdest beard.'

'He was just a bloke. The only reason he was weird is we never see blokes.'

'People with beards are child-molesters. He was going to kill us.'

'Oh yeah? Why?'

'The spanners. Definitely. For hitting people with. And he had rope too.'

Hen stared. 'You have a sad, twisted imagination. So why didn't he axe-murder us, then?'

'No time. Come on.' She set off at a run, giggling.

Caz pushed open the door of the pub. It had recently been refurbished and was now decorated in a pragmatic shade of nicotine-yellow, while the comfortable chairs had been taken away and replaced with uncomfortable ones. On the walls were a selection of chain-store hunting prints and three blurred instamatic snaps of the landlord laughing at a party a long time ago. When they walked in, two women sitting by the bar turned to glance at them. One of them put her hand up to her mouth; Jules watched her fingers, barnacled with gold rings, flick just once in her direction. The barman was watching a sitcom and did not turn round.

Caz placed a proprietorial arm on the bar. 'D'you want?'

'Vodka and Red Bull,' said Jules.

'You?'

'Get it in a sec.' Hen was watching the room at the back of the bar. 'Just go and see if they're there.' She darted into the darkness.

Jules felt the half-turned glances of the women, saw the whited glimmer of their eyes. She stared straight ahead. The way they were looking at her, she knew what they were thinking: *little tart, silly little slut, all done up like a party trick.* She picked up the drinks and walked past their table with her head up high and her hips waggling from side to side, perfectly brazen. *Fuck you,* she thought, half drunk on nerves. *Fuckyoufuckyoufuckyoufuckyou.*

In the gloom of the back room she could see a huddle of men in the corner. Hen was standing in the doorway, twiddling one of her earrings and smiling fixedly at a spot just above their heads. The boys had their arms folded and were watching her.

When Caz walked in, one of them laughed softly. 'Things are looking up.'

'Hi.' Caz pulled out a stool.

The one who had laughed leaned forward. 'I'm Higgs.'

'Sorry. Took ages to get here,' said Caz, bumping her chin against his. 'This is Jules, and that's Hen.'

Higgs gestured to the others. 'Adey.'

Mutant Albino Freak inclined his head and smiled.

'Yves.' A thickset boy with poky eyes and a stringy neck. 'And me.' He gave a little bow.

Higgs was the best looking, no question. Hen glanced at them all from under her hair and sat speechless, swinging her earrings to and fro. The one Jules had met in the music shop wasn't there. She felt disappointed; she hadn't liked him, but at least he was familiar.

'Eve?' she said. 'Thought that was a girl's name.'

Yves rolled his eyes and looked up at the ceiling. 'Bo-ring. French, actually. Y-V-E-S, like Yves St Laurent.'

Jules examined him. 'You don't sound French.'

'Mother comes from France. Parents have an apartment in Paris.'

'WooOOoh. Ve-ry fancy.' She took a heavy swig of her drink. 'I've never been to Paris.'

'Like London, except the women are better-looking.'

'Yeah,' said Higgs, 'like you really know.'

Yves shoved at him with his free hand. 'Fuck off. Tosser.'

Jules looked down at the pattern on the carpet. It was sticky in places, and her shoe came away with a faint ripping sound. She remembered being in her father's car last holidays. He'd just finished giving her older sister Claire a driving lesson and had offered to show Jules how the controls worked. Jules had sat in the driving seat holding tight to the steering wheel, unable to move either forwards or backwards. Her feet had trembled above the pedals for so long she got cramp. The view from the windscreen seemed so huge, the potential so overwhelming. She'd had to lose her temper just to keep from crying. It felt the same now. She couldn't remember – if indeed she had ever known – which instruments might keep her safe and which might cause her harm. She couldn't remember how boys worked. And yet she had to do this just to prove she wasn't a lesbian; she had to do this because it felt so wrong. She took a gulp of her drink, and some of the liquid spilled down her top. She dabbed at it surreptitiously, hoping they hadn't seen.

Caz put down her drink and took off her jacket. The boys admired her chest.

'You look . . .' Higgs stopped, 'um . . . very well.'

'This?' Caz looked down at her red top as if seeing it for the first time. 'Ancient.'

'Lovely pair—'

'Fuck off. Don't suppose any of you boys might have any drugs on you?'

'*Caz!*' said Jules hoarsely, '*Shut up.*' She glanced at Hen for support, but Hen was busy gazing away into the middle distance, twitching her foot against the table leg and swinging her cross from side to side. Adey seemed equally dumbstruck.

'Nah. Ran out ages ago. Sorry, mate. You could always go and ask out there.'

'A man's job, I think.'

Higgsy laughed. It sounded forced.

'Adey?'

'Not really in the mood.'

'Balls. Never not in the mood.'

'God,' said Jules, 'we got so stoned before we got here.' She jabbed at Caz for support. 'Didn't we? Wasted.'

A silence.

'Amazing. So needed to get stoned, that fucking exercise stuff . . .' She tailed off.

She remembered, too late, that Caz was different in the presence of men. She held a glass differently, her nails clasping the neck in an elegant diagonal. She swivelled her foot differently, so the boys could see her cut-throat heels. She laughed differently, not as she did when alone with Jules, but low and sweet and disturbingly suggestive. Jules had seen her with men three or four times, and every time it was the same. Every time it made Jules feel younger, and more lonely.

Hen wasn't helping at all. She was just sitting there gazing sometimes at the carpet and sometimes at Adey, too anxious to commit to speech.

'What you doing round here?' asked Higgs.

Jules shrugged. 'Some stupid activity thing. 'We've finished exams and they don't know what to do with us till the end of term so they make us walk halfway round the country. Boring.'

'What were the exams?'

'GCSEs.' She hoped it sounded guileless.

'How many?'

'Ten. Mathsfrenchphysicsgeographychemistrybiologyenglit englangfood'n'nutcomputing.'

'What's food'n'nut?'

'Food and nutrition. How to bake a lemon meringue pie for a retard's tea party.'

He turned to Caz. 'What did you do?'

'Twelve. Minus food'n'nut, plus Spanish and German.'

'Right spod, you are.'

'I can do other things.'

'So they say.'

Jules looked down at her empty glass and wondered if she

had to pay for the whole table or if it would be possible just to get a refill for herself.

'Oy, babe.' Caz gave her what looked like an affectionate nudge and was in fact a jab in the ribs. 'Your round.'

'Only got seven quid.'

'I bought the last ones.'

Adey raised himself off the bench. 'I'll get them.'

'I'll help.' Hen leapt up.

'Made for each other, those two,' said Caz, watching them. 'The world's first completely mute couple.'

Hen and Adey stood by the bar. Hen had one ankle wrapped round the other and was staring upwards at the bottles of electric-green liquid above the till. She leaned over. 'She's not doing GCSEs for another two years. None of us are.'

Adey looked at her, noticing the little beige scab on her chin where she'd put too much concealer over a spot, the raw unwoken complexion, the clotted mascara. He shrugged. 'Course. Obvious. How old are you?'

'Um.' Hen swung her cross. 'Fifteen.'

'So how come you're not doing exams this year, then?'

'Alright, fourteen, then. Thirteen. Sort of. Don't tell the others. Please.'

'Won't. Promise.' He gathered a cluster of glasses and walked back to the table.

+

It got later. Jules looked at her watch and was surprised to see that they'd been there for over an hour. The noises from the bar rose and flowed. People came and went, banging the door. Jules felt herself beginning to drift with the motion of the drink, slipping deeper into the evening. The details of how they were to get back and what might happen if they were caught seemed very far away. She thought of Ali, Mel and Izzy still lying there in the darkened bedroom, Izzy scratching, Mel whining. She was puzzled by how little it all seemed to matter. The vodka settled agreeably in her head, tugging at her senses.

Higgs and Adey were whispering together. It seemed to Jules that there was some secret understanding which was bestowed on all men at birth. They knew things that she never would, they could negotiate the world and its complexities in a way that she could not. She looked down at the hairs on Higgs's wrist. His arm was tanned, and his fingers were unexpectedly graceful. She felt a sudden impulse to fold his wrist inside her own hand, to feel that human solidity against her own skin. Under his shirt, with his clothes off, what did he look like? Where his arm disappeared into the sleeve, where his neck was hidden by the collar, what did he feel like? The skin on his shoulder, what did it smell like? What would he be like when he was naked? How would he feel if he was next to her?

Yves was watching her. He saw the introspection cloud her face and the look – part wistfulness, part avarice – she was giving Higgs. He saw the faint blush shading her ears and followed the wander of her thoughts.

Jules stood up abruptly and stumbled towards the ladies' toilets. She got tangled up in a stool at a nearby table and took a second to stand upright again. As she walked, her legs stammered against the floor. Yves heard the peel of her shoes on the sticky carpet and saw her look round, just once, at Caz. He waited for a minute, half listening to Adey's laughter and the placid grumble of the bar. Then he got up and followed Jules towards the corridor. He stood outside the ladies' loo, plucking at the flaky paint by the phone.

When Jules re-emerged, there was a fine sheen of sweat on her forehead and her face had lost its glow. She leaned against the doorpost, trying to look casual, feeling for her balance.

Yves loomed. 'Fancy a snog?'

Jules opened her mouth to say something. There was a clatter of teeth. She felt the snail's trail of his saliva down her chin and the sweet reek of beer on his breath. When she shut her eyes, the world shifted sideways, so she opened them again. She caught a glimpse of raspberry-pip acne scars and the scab of an old spot at the side of his nose, closed her eyes again and moved her tongue around in what she hoped was the right way. She had never been sure about kissing, never been sure that this weird damp writhing was what she was supposed to want. Yves shoved his pelvis hard up against her so Jules's hip cracked painfully against the doorpost. She reached for his arm to steady herself and felt a jolt of suprise at his touch. Men were like snakes; though everything told her that their skin should be as dry and human as her own, some part of her still expected them to be slithery, almost alien, to the touch.

'Here,' he said. His voice had clotted. He shoved her further down the corridor towards a fire exit, pushed down the bar and suddenly they were out at the back of the pub, and the wind whacked hard against Jules's legs.

'Over here.' Yves half led, half dragged her through the darkness towards the shadows of the beer garden. Jules tripped against something and squeaked in fright. At the same moment, there was a faint click and a light came on far above them.

'Fuck,' muttered Yves, clutching at a handful of her dress. 'Come on.' He pulled her along, past the summer picnic tables and the murmuring trees.

At the back of the garden there was a children's play area: a see-saw, a climbing frame and a sandpit. Jules started giggling. She was beginning to feel sick. Yves clamped one hand on her hip and the other one around the back of her neck so she was pressed up close to his face. Some of her hair was tugging painfully between his fingers as he shoved his tongue between her lips again. She could hear his breath speeding up, smell the fag smoke on his mouth. It sounded as if there was something blocking the back of his throat. Yves shoved himself hard up against her again so Jules felt his erection for a second before she overbalanced and fell backwards into the sandpit, catching her ankles against the wooden sides.

The sand rasped against Jules's back as she pushed herself away from the edge. Yves was grappling at his jeans. She could hear him breathing faster and faster, and saw his face congeal in the sodium glow of the street lights. His gaze was not focussed on her, but on some distant place.

He knelt down, squashing Jules's shin. 'Move. Up.'

He felt for her thigh, pushed her dress upwards so it bagged around her breasts, and snapped at the waistband of her knickers. He knelt upright again for a second and pulled down his boxer shorts.

She stopped watching his face and stared at his dick instead. It looked unnatural, as if someone had pinned a big stupid coat-hook on him for a joke. Jules, accustomed only to the surreptitious geography of other girl's bodies, the sneaky changing-room glimpses of thigh or cleavage or waist, could not understand this squared-off gout of flesh glowering above her: no curves, no shape, just this doggish tangle of hair and muscle. She began to giggle. Yves grappled in the darkness and pulled something out of the pocket of his jeans.

Jules lay in the sand and just for a second remembered how she had imagined it would be, all her life swelling towards one moment of inevitable desire. This seemed to be nothing like that. All this disjointed groping and prodding, all this noise. She heard snapping, like the sound of someone flicking rubber bands, and the tight whine of Yves's breathing. What's he doing? What's he need a condom for? She couldn't stop giggling now. It sounded foreign, as if it wasn't actually her who was laughing.

Yves plunged abruptly down on top of her, pushing his face into hers. She wanted to put her hand up to rub away the pain, but she was squeezed underneath him, his flesh wrenching against hers. His hand floundered around down by her hips, catching at her clothes, plucking at the gap between her legs. When he shoved his finger up inside her, it was covered in grains of sand. It felt to Jules like someone was trying to strip away her insides, like someone was scraping her to death. She tensed with the pain, banging her ankle against the side of the pit and making a small noise way down low in the back of her throat. Each grain of sand, each scrape of his nail, became a separate agony. Yves, far away on some private journey, did not hear her, even when she started to cry quietly. He pulled his finger out, hauled himself further up her body and groped around for his dick. Then he pushed inside her, rasping through sand and hair and flesh, until Jules could feel nothing but a kind of white-hot ache. She was saying something, although she had no memory of starting to speak. As he rubbed himself up and down her, crushing her into the sand, the ache got worse, until every other thought – the fear, the self-consciousness, the loss – dwindled away, and all she could feel was the hope that the pain would stop soon.

When he came, she felt no different. The scraping stopped, and she could smell a hot metallic scent, like wild garlic. He did not move, just lay on top of her, so Jules's thinly upholstered bones screeched with the pressure of his weight. She lay there, staring up at the clouds and the sad lustre of the street lights.

Finally Yves rolled off her. 'You a virgin?' His voice was muffled.

'No.'

He turned his face away from her. 'You're not now.'

Jules stayed where she was, staring upwards. She felt the bile rise up through her throat, leaned over away from him and was sick in the sand. Then she lay back and passed out.

Yves got out of the pit, pulled up his trousers and stuffed something into his pocket. He looked down at Jules, curled absurdly, smeared in muck and prickling leaves, her dress still rolled up around her chest, hips and arms pale against the darkness of the pit and the grass beyond. Then he dusted himself down, shook the leaves out of his hair and walked back to the bar.

+

In the back room, Hen had gone for more drinks. Adey was having a half-heated argument with Higgs, and Caz was silently examining her ankles. She seemed aware that the argument was partly theatre, a sideshow dialogue performed for her benefit.

When Yves came back into the room, she did not look up.

Adey gave him a watery glare. 'J'ou get to?'

'Piss.'

Higgs raised one enquiring eyebrow. Yves winked. Neither

of them noticed Caz intercept the look. Neither of them saw her get up and walk across the room.

She went into the ladies' and said softly, 'Jules?' No answer. Behind her, she could feel the draught from the fire exit on the back of her legs. Outside, the wind was shoving paper bags at the dustbins, and an incomplete moon was rising. Caz walked out on to the grass, moving slowly until her eyes adjusted to the dark. The dew cooled the toes of her shoes.

The security light came on, blinding her, so she turned back towards the pub and skittered out of the spotlight's range. When the spotlight went off again, she walked up to the corner, past the shadowy swings and the see-saw.

She looked down at Jules, still lying curled asleep in the sandpit. There was sand dabbled all the way down her calves, her tits and bum were naked to the world, and one shoe was lost in the dark. Beside Jules, just to the right of her head, was a splatter of vomit.

She stepped back a pace, pulled a cigarette out of her pocket and lit it. She could hear the faint shushing of the traffic on the road beyond and the scream of a rabbit in a nearby field. The sound the trees made seemed like the sound of the sea. Caz stood there, listening to the trees and the road and staring down at her friend. She smoked the cigarette to the end, and then stamped it out by the edge of the sandpit. Then she turned and walked back to the pub.

✦

Hen was tipping her chair back and forth and glaring at Higgs. 'Drink any you under table. No problem. Nooo prob-lem-o.'

Someone had placed three small glasses of clear liquid on the table next to the half-full pint glasses.

'Slammers, then,' said Higgs. 'Go on.'

Hen giggled. 'Race.'

Caz bent down and whispered something in her ear. Hen flapped a hand. 'Naaaw. No' now. Later.'

Caz whispered again. Adey looked up. 'What is it?' His voice had blurred and his eyelids had a sleepy angle to them.

'Got to go. They'll check up on us.'

Hen leaned over unevenly and tried to pull out the spare stool. 'Siddown. In a minute.'

Caz plucked at her arm. 'Now. Come *on.*'

'Piss *off.*'

Higgs stretched his arms out, mock-pleading. 'Don't go,' he said. 'Don't leave us. Not nearly drunk enough yet.'

Caz smiled and began dragging Hen towards the door. 'Gotta *go.*'

'Wait!' said Hen, lunging for the table. 'Moment.'

Caz stood by the doorway, waiting.

'Bag.' Hen groped around on the floor, giggling. Higgs caught her eye and nodded slightly. 'Go on.'

Hen picked up the glass of tequila, tipped her head back and swallowed it down in one. Liquid dribbled down the corners of her mouth. When she slammed the glass back down on the table top, her eyes were wild. She was drunk, triumphant, gorgeous. The men were watching her. She was perfect.

'*Hen!*' shouted Caz, 'Come on! We're going.'

Hen shrugged her jacket on, walked to the door and gave the watching men a little wave. 'Byeeee. Byeeeeeeee.' Then she stopped again, raised one finger at the staring boys, and shouted, '*Kiss my slit.*' Spun round and tripped out after Caz.

The boys heard her laughter – high, jerky, almost mad – all the way through the next room.

+

In the minicab on the way back, Hen's head flopped down on Caz's shoulder. Caz stared out of the window. Two or three groups of people wavered down the road, shouting companionably at each other.

Hen sat upright suddenly. 'Where's Jules?'

'Dunno. Probably gone back already.'

Hen slumped back again. 'Oh,' she said, and went to sleep.

EARLY SATURDAY

Jules woke up.

Whatever she was lying on was uncomfortable. Things kept poking into her skin, and she had a memory of being cold in the night. Her sleep had been unusually dark, and when she woke it seemed as if some extreme noise had been abruptly switched off. The light was tentative; it was not quite dawn. The trees moved above her, and she could feel the damp sand scratching at her back. The dress was still wrinkled around her ribs and her skin was mottled with cold. Somewhere, she could hear the sound of a tractor in a nearby field.

She pulled herself up far enough to wriggle the dress down over her hips, and then lay back again, staring up at the cold sky. She remembered the drink, the sandpit, the weight of Yves on her bones. When she stood up, her body didn't seem anchored properly to the ground, and the sand seemed to stare back at her from a long way away. She could see a splatter of something liquid, and realized she must have been sick. Her mouth felt full of some unpleasant furry stuff like the sticky carpet in the pub last night. She could also detect an unspecified ache somewhere up in what might have been her womb. It felt hot and indignant and when she moved or bent over it got worse. This was not like any pain she'd known before; this wasn't like period pain or stomach ache, it was a deeper hurt. The consideration of her innards and the thought of how the ache had got there made her feel sick again.

One shoe was upside down at the end of the sandpit and the other one was way off to the right, by the trunk of a tree. The ground was soggy with dew, and the shoes felt damp when she picked them up. Jules shook the muck out and began searching for her knickers. She had expected a glimpse of white poking shamefully out of the long grass or under one of the benches, but there was nothing more than the skirl of yesterday's litter in the wind and the fading glow of roses. She scuffed through the grass and examined the small patches of shrubbery bordering the beer garden. They weren't there. As she searched, she felt a new panic rising. What if someone from the pub saw her searching through the grass, looking for a pair of incriminating knickers? The thought of anyone having seen her, stripped and raw and all smeary with sick, made her feel ashamed. She ripped up a hank of grass and pushed the sand off her legs, anxious to get away as fast as she possibly could. She could feel the panic in her throat now, and the push of tears against the back of her tongue.

The beer garden rustled around her. The pub had long ago been locked up, and Jules looked round for some kind of exit. The only way out that she could see was the tall iron gate leading on to the car park, which had been closed and pad-locked sometime yesterday evening. The gate had a vicious set of iron spikes along the top designed to deter intruders. The bars were too close together to wriggle through, and the base too close to the ground to slide under. She was going to have to climb it. She kicked off her shoes again, dropped them over to the other side, and began searching for a foothold. The fear that someone might see her, knickerless and filthy, halfway over a pub gate, made her scrabble and yank. Three times she lost her footing and slid back down to the ground, banging her shins against the metal. She heard footsteps on the pavement beyond the car park and sank back into the shadows. The walker passed by and she tried climbing again, desperate now. The fourth time she pulled herself up she kept her foothold and began gingerly levering her right leg over the spikes. She could feel the clammy dawn cold on her hips and the spikes digging into her thighs. She was sobbing now, panicky with shame, acutely aware of how stupid she must look. She balanced for a second on the top cross bar, yanked her left leg over, found the foothold and dropped down onto the ground. Then she started walking.

Please God, she thought, please God, let nobody I know see me. *Please. Please.* She was crying now, but she had nothing to wipe the tears away. Two or three cars passed by, so she swung her hair over her face and stared down at the pavement. Once out in the country again the pavement disappeared abruptly. Every few steps, she sank back into the verge, half-hobbled by the little heels of her shoes.

As she walked, she remembered the night. Nothing seemed a complete memory any more, only a series of images and impressions – the rasp of the sand, the expression in Yves's eyes, the trees watching her from above. The experience seemed wrong somehow. She felt angry, not with Yves, but with herself. She had obviously done something wrong: moved in the wrong way, held him the wrong way, had the wrong sort of anatomy. She'd spent so long – so unbelievably long – waiting to cast off her virginity, and when it finally happened she had flunked it. Half her life had been spent waiting for last night, and when last night actually happened she'd been so drunk she could barely remember it. When Caz had done it, she'd lain on the grass when they got back to school and talked about it all with such perfect assurance that Jules had been unable to sleep that night for fear. According to Caz, it had all been gorgeous – a man who'd fancied her for ages, a reluctant (but not too reluctant) wooing, a room lit with candles, a silent space without intrusions. Jules had imagined it to herself again and again, the honeyed light, the liquid glances, the heroic union. In her mind, it was all so smooth, so quiet, so *right*. It was nothing like the clankings and grabbings of last night.

And when it occurred to her that she too was now part of the invisible sisterhood of non-virgins, the thought did not seem as consoling as it might have been. A man had finally wanted her – not Caz or Hen, but her – and she should have felt triumphant. She should have felt vindicated, safely on the side of the straights, cleared of all possible lesbian fear. But all she felt was tangled up and sad.

As she walked, the last of the darkness faded. The day was bright, and even the houses along the route seemed briefly charming. A marmalade cat ran across the road and she watched its ticking gait as it disappeared into the hedge.

Three miles on, when the dawn had gone and it was properly day, Jules saw the driveway of the Manor. She crossed the road and walked up it, skulking close to the sides. She had no idea what time it was, only some vague notion that midsummer dawns come early, and that she had a few hours of grace before the rest of the world woke up. The place looked peaceful, a summery place on a summery day. The house could have drifted here from any age, with its lawns and roses and lichened brick. It looked, thought Jules, as if nothing had changed. It looked exactly like it had looked yesterday before Yves and the pub and the ache. The sight of all this busy English indifference seemed reassuring. Perhaps, she thought, perhaps I'll get away with it.

She skirted round the front of the building and off to the side, down to the back door by the kitchens. The back door would be risky, but worth it for a short cut. She snuck up the steps and pulled as quietly as possible at the handle. It was locked, so she slipped down the steps again and headed over towards the car park. Someone – Caz, perhaps – had left the window wide open. The car they had jumped down on to last night was still parked where it had been, and Jules could see the little cavity where her heel had dented the metal. The one next to it was a high 4X4 with a roof rack. Jules clambered onto the bonnet, positioned herself on the edge of the rack and gripped the window ledge.

Just before she climbed, some small movement off to the left caught her attention. Through the window of the room below theirs was a face, staring up at her. The reflections on the glass made it impossible to see if the face was male or female; it was just a face with white cheekbones. Jules stood where she was, trembling. The face shifted and became one of the men staying in the hostel. She had seen him in the kitchens a few days previously. Jules stared back at him, waiting for hell to break loose, for him to start yelling, or to fetch Miss Naylor, or to ask her where she'd been. But he didn't. He just stood gazing up at her, expressionless. Finally he drew the curtain back into place and disappeared. Jules began to climb again. Maybe he was going to report her. Maybe he was going to come out and ask what she was doing shinning up a wall in a small dress at dawn. But there was nothing, no noise at all, except for the faint click of a light switch. The man's face had made her tremble so hard that her legs had gone wobbly. She couldn't hear anything from inside until she paused and picked out the sound of snoring.

She scrambled up the wall and over the ledge. The watery light in the room gave it a limpid feel, as if the five lumpy mounds of bedclothes were shapes at the bottom of the ocean. She slipped down onto the reassuring floor, heard the sound of Izzy snoring and felt, for the first time, a deep relief at being back among familiar things. Two minutes later, with the remains of her make-up still leaking down her face, Jules slept.

SATURDAY

Hen felt terrible. Truly, profoundly sick. The worst of it was not the headache or the way her stomach kept wandering from one place to another, it was the sleepiness. If her head touched a pillow now, she might plummet into such faraway unconsciousness that she'd never wake again. Perhaps the drink had been spiked. She'd been drinking vodka all night, vodka and fizzy mineral water. Wine and tonic and all the other stuff had too much sugar in it: vodka was pure. Or it had seemed pure last night. But now there seemed something stealthy about it, as if the scentless, tasteless, silent liquid had deceived her. Perhaps someone had dropped some invisible toxin into it while she'd been away in the toilets. And then – oh God – there had been the tequila. That stupid bloody final tequila. The only thing she could remember about it was how revolting it had tasted.

Hen looked at her bowl of cereal and clutched one arm protectively over her stomach. Once every few minutes, she arranged a few twigs of bran on her spoon, raised them up and then let them fall again.

Last night seemed a long time ago. She had no memory of how she had got back to the Manor, or of how she had got to bed. That hole in her memory was the one advantage to the drink – it cancelled out time, rendered part of her life blessedly absent.

Jules had only made it downstairs with difficulty. She'd held on to the banisters all the way, and crept into the canteen like an old person. Caz seemed the least damaged of the three of them. Her face was pale, but she could just about meet the eyes of the others.

'When did you get back?'

'Before you,' said Jules, after thought. 'Dunno. Elevenish? Found a bus.'

Hen nodded. She couldn't remember seeing Jules when they'd got back, but then she couldn't remember getting back.

Caz was watching Jules. 'You enjoy yourself?'

'Mmmm.'

'Must have left very early.'

'Mmmm.'

'Yves liked you.'

Jules blushed.

Caz leaned across the table. 'Are you sure—' she began.

'Good morning, missies.' Miss Naylor.

'Good morning, Miss Naylor,' said Jules, slightly louder than necessary.

'Bit peaky, are we?' She reached across the table, pushing her face up close. '*Bit peaky*, I said.'

Jules nodded fractionally.

'Well, then. A good day's swimming should sort you out, shouldn't it, missy?'

Hen put her hand up to her mouth, shoved her chair back and almost ran towards the door. Upstairs both the bathroom and the loo doors were locked. Hen rattled them a couple of times. Whoever was in there wasn't moving. She walked a few panicky steps up and down the corridor and banged on the doors again. Nothing. She could feel the desperation rising through her throat. She had no choice. She never seemed to have a choice any more.

+

The swimming pool was tucked into the back of a mid-eighties leisure centre. It didn't look very different from all the other flat-packed warehouses round Stokeley, but someone had evidently thought that the addition of a corrugated roof and a little coloured paint would give the necessary impression of municipal goodwill. The centre had yellow doors, blue pipes and green window frames. It was unquestionably one of the ugliest buildings Jules had ever seen. Even the plants in the car park were ugly – big fleshy things with serrated leaves and an air of organized hostility. When they walked through the entrance doors, the tired air surged out, momentarily choking.

They had left Hen behind at the Manor after she had pleaded successfully with Jaws that she had her period and was on the verge of death. 'Oh yeah?' Caz had muttered. 'That girl no more gets periods than Higgs gets periods.' As they walked along the road, Jules had been surprised at how peaceful everything looked. The light had a buttery morning warmth to it, and if it hadn't been for the unnameable ache, last night might never have happened.

Downstairs, the women's changing rooms were empty. Jules stood in the doorway. There were three long aisles with grey metal lockers on either side and benches below: no privacy, just this dense air full of sweat and unidentified exhalations.

Mina jostled at her from behind. 'What are you doing?'

'Thinking,' said Jules crossly.

'Why?'

She stepped away from the door so it swung back accident-ally on purpose onto Mina's foot. 'Just felt like it,' she said, and walked over to the furthest locker.

Swimming itself was all right, but the stuff which sur-rounded it was not. Wasn't there a single swimming pool in England which offered an individual changing room? There was nowhere in this place that she could look with safety. Wherever she rested her gaze there would be a stretch of naked flesh, a new discomfort waiting in ambush. All these people trying to look casual about something which wasn't casual at all, trying to see without being seen, trying to thieve a few scraps of information about someone else's body while trying equally hard not to be seen looking. All of it involved trying, and today she didn't feel like trying at all. She didn't want to look at other people's skin today, didn't want to be reminded of the bits of her body which ought to be corrected or emphasized or removed or chastised. She sat down on the bench and pulled slowly at the legs of her trousers.

Caz, already changed, walked over to Jules. 'Coming?'

Jules couldn't look at Caz's face, so she looked at her ankles instead. They were thin, much thinner than Jules's, and they had a long pale grace which had somehow managed to with-stand a fetid room and a regulation swimsuit. She couldn't explain why, but there was something very grown-up about Caz's legs.

She spoke without thinking, honest and unhappy. 'You look amazing.'

'So do you, babe.'

'I don't. Not like you.'

'You'll be fine. It's just a bit of puppy fat, that's all.'

Jules recoiled. *'Puppy fat?'*

'It goes. Don't worry.'

'Wh-when?'

'Whenever. Soon. Couple of years, you'll be gorgeous.'

Puppy fat? Jules felt something begin to ache behind her eyes. Oh my God. Caz thought she was fat. Worse than that, Caz had always thought she was fat. Day after day, watching each other, monitoring the faintest motion of an eyebrow, the lightest shift of hair or ankle or hand, and this was the concluding truth.

She pushed her hands under her legs so they were squeezed into the smallest space possible and hunched low, hoping that no one would see her face. She felt a sudden overwhelming hopelessness, a sense that however far or high or long she tried, nothing was attainable. *Nothing.* She'd lost her virginity, but she'd lost it wrong. She'd beaten Caz in gym, and then she'd been shamed. There was going to be no redemption, no improvement, and no one to lift her up. This is how it was, this is how it was going to continue. Things didn't get better, people didn't suddenly discover the lost treasures in each other, the world didn't stop tweaking and pinching just because she asked it to. She'd spent her whole life trying not to be herself, and it hadn't made any difference at all. All she'd ever wanted was to be special, to be – even temporarily – astonishing. But she wasn't special. She wasn't even right.

'Don't wait.' She plucked at the strap of her swimsuit, not looking up.

'OK.'

The changing room was silent by the time she was finished,

and as she walked towards the entrance to the pool she caught sight of herself in the mirror. Her hair was sticking up in places and looked greasy. The heat had turned her cheeks an unbecoming shade of pink, and her eyes were still half closed with sleepiness and alcohol. She looked monstrous: sad and useless and monstrous. If there had been any use in crying, she would have done.

She stepped out into the violence of sound and water. The strip lighting above the pool gave the place a gauzy feeling, as if it occupied a space a little separate from reality. One side of the pool had been roped off for the use of the public, and a group of women with toddlers squealed at the shallow end. It was still early, and there were no other school groups, just these children in their jellybean colours and their mothers stretched out by the steps of the shallow end.

She stood for a while by the edge of the pool, staring down. There was something in the water's instability and its pretty, sinister colours which made her wonder for a second if it would support her. Perhaps, she thought, one day, you could jump in and the water wouldn't let you float any longer. Perhaps you'd sink, go straight to the bottom, like you'd fallen through air.

Jaws was surprised to see Jules raise her arms above her head when she put the whistle to her lips. And even more surprised to see that when she blew one quick note, it was Jules who dived deepest and furthest, and Jules who took longest of all to surface.

+

Hen looked at the envelope in front of her. She didn't want to think about it, not with all the other complicated stuff as well. She could feel the letter's contents leaking through the envelope even before she opened it. She knew, more or less, what it would contain; a list of parties grapeshotted with exclamation marks, two or three indecipherable passages where the writing had been smudged by tears or drink, and then a couple of lines about dear sweetheart children. Those lines always carried a hint of malevolence with them, a threat of something just out of view. Sometimes her mother would enclose a packet of stamps or a pre-addressed envelope. 'Remember, no excuse now for not writing back!! I LOVE YOU, darling. Hugs and Kisses always.'

If Hen held the pages up, she could smell something on them. Perfume, and something sweeter. Before her parents divorced, her mother always smelt of herself, of cooking and cotton and Scotland. When she came to hug Hen goodnight, Hen could smell reassurance on the backs of her hands. Now she smelt of other things, of emotions in packages: Romance or Desire. She had lots of little bottles by the mirror in her bedroom now, and each day, depending on her mood, she'd pick one out and become someone else. Some of the perfumes were obscure, but others were well known; Hen had come up behind a woman on the escalator in the underground one day and realized with a shock that she could smell one of her mother's perfumes seeping out from a stranger.

Hen didn't see her mother that often any more. Maybe at half-term sometimes, when the journey up to Edinburgh would have swallowed up too much time. She was living in London now, in a big smug stucco flat near the Westway. The last time they'd seen each other it was an unexpectedly sunny day. They'd been to Harvey Nichols and bought Hen a small black satin dress and her mother a Wonderbra. In the afternoon, they'd sat in one of the pavement cafes, watching the people passing by.

A waitress came over and asked if they'd like to eat. Her mother shook her head. 'Terrible skin,' she said, pointing the tip of her cigarette at the waitress's retreating back, 'Can't do anything with skin like that.'

'Mum?' said Hen, 'D'you want to see my report?'

Her mother was wearing sunglasses so Hen couldn't see her eyes. 'Might as well.'

'I came top in French and physics,' said Hen hurriedly. 'And haha God you'll never believe this maths too. Unbelievable. Maybe they swapped the papers round or something and I got someone else's result.' She was beginning to feel self-conscious. 'But Miss Phillips is so stupid it's not surprising. They're going to put me in a year early for GCSE geog and Eng lit. Caz is doing it too, and so's Ali. Be good to get some of them out of the way. Done masses of assessments. They say I'll probably do about maybe ten next . . .'

She tailed off. Her mother sniffed.

'Mum,' said Hen desperately, 'Don't cry. Please don't cry.'

Her mother removed a tissue from her bag.

'Muuumm. Mum, *please*. Mum, it's embarrassing.'

Her mother didn't cry like Hen did. When Hen cried, it hurt. Her whole face dissolved, and she'd end up with tooth marks on her lower lip from biting it too hard. Her mother cried elegantly, as if crying wasn't a messy, humiliating business. When she put her fingers up to her face, she brushed the tears away with her fingertips so she wouldn't smudge her make-up. 'Oh my darling. Oh my *darling*.'

Hen looked around for the waitress. 'Maybe we should go

back home. Maybe we could get a couple of videos and I could go and find supper . . .'

'My darling, my sweet child. What are we going to do?'

Hen could smell the sweet sick scent of alcohol on her mother's breath. 'Are you upset about the report?'

Abruptly, her mother slipped the sunglasses back over her eyes. 'Where's that bloody waitress?' she said, and turned away.

Later that night, after they'd gone back to the flat, Hen crept into her mother's room. When her parents had still been together, their bedroom had not looked anything like this. Then, it had a worn kind of tidiness with pictures of the four of them on the bedside table and a scrawl of wifeish clothes on the sofa in the corner. In this room, clothes covered every available surface, oozing out of drawers, over the chairs, round the bedlegs. They weren't the same kind of clothes her mother used to wear. These were light and silky, pretty pink velvet things, tiny skirts and cute cardigans like Caz sometimes wore. And the colours were different. In Scotland, all her mother's clothes looked as though they'd been rinsed in rainclouds. These were bright as billboards: buttery yellow, shocking pink, scarlet. The empty cups of a red satin bra gaped at her from an open drawer.

There was a picture of the twins on the window ledge which hadn't been dusted for a while, and one of Jamie with his arm around her that Hen had never liked. There was also a photograph she hadn't seen before: a man, smiling into the camera, suntanned, wearing a bright yellow baseball cap. The man was young; he wasn't her father. As Hen shifted some of the clothes aside, a faint aroma of cigarette smoke and perfume drifted from them.

By the bedside were a pile of books, a tissue box and a tub

of vaseline. Hen looked at them for a long time and then moved them aside, trying not to touch them too much. She dialled her father's number. And lied and lied and lied until he said she could come home.

+

They were gathered around Jules's bed in a tight semicircle, listening. It was just before supper, and the sunlight was catching on the pockmarked walls. A row of damp swimming costumes were laid out on the radiators to dry. For a brief moment, the warm light softened a little of the institutional bleakness and the clutter of belongings made the room seem almost homely.

'So,' Caz was saying, 'last night. When did you get back?'

'Told you.' Jules's voice was muffled. 'Sort of elevenish.'

'How come you weren't here when we got in?'

'Probably in the loo.'

'Took you ages.'

'Had to take off my make-up.'

Caz stared at the grey rings of kohl under her eyes. 'Right. How strange. Yves said . . .' she paused, '. . . Yves said that you . . .'

'What?' said Mel, leaning over. 'What?'

'Yves said that you were out in the back garden with him.'

'What? Oh my God! You didn't *do* it with him?'

Jules was silent for a long, complicated minute, tangled between truth and untruth. She started plucking at the duvet cover, gathering it up between her fingers in little pleats.

Caz bent over and peered through her hair. 'What's wrong?'

No response.

'Go on,' said Mel. '*Please.* What was it like?'

'It was nice,' Jules said eventually.

'And?'

Her lips worked, but nothing came out.

'Don't be so unfair. I've told you all about when I've done it,' said Caz.

Silence.

'Did he have a hard body?'

Izzy, sitting on the next-door bed, giggled. 'Was he special? Was he tender? Was he *creamy*?'

Mel's voice got louder, more mannered. 'Did he gaze deep into your eyes and say he'd be yours forever? How long did it last? What was his cock like?' When she said 'cock' it sounded so absurd she had to say it in a deep, mock-husky sort of voice. 'He have a big cock? You suck him off?'

'It was nice,' said Jules suddenly. The words came rushing out as if she couldn't get rid of them fast enough. 'Just nice. Kissedmeandthenwewereoutsideandwejustsortofdiditandthen Icamebackhere.' She stopped. 'He was nice.'

Caz prodded her. 'Stop saying he's so fucking *nice*. Nice is *nothing*.'

'What sort of "did it"?'

Jules looked down again. 'Just did it. You know. Got his thingy out—'

'*Omygod!* What was it *like*?'

'It was just . . . just a thingy,' said Jules desperately. 'It was just a normal, *average* sort of thingy.'

'Yes, but what *sort* of thingy? Was it big? Small? Did it hurt?' Mel paused, and then whispered, 'Was he moist?'

'You were out there for ages,' said Caz.

'Pub was making me feel sick.'

'Did it last long?' asked Mel.

'Dunno. Wasn't timing him, was I?'

'You must have noticed. Was he one of those ferry types?'

'Ferry types?'

'Roll on, roll off. Like those ferries.'

'I don't know.' Jules looked cross. 'I haven't slept with a ferry, have I?'

'*No.* Not that, retard. I mean like he's too quick, just bang on and bang off. Was he too quick?'

'I don't *know.* Told you. I wasn't timing him.'

'How long did you spend snogging?'

'A while.'

'You go down on him?'

Jules began plucking at the bedclothes again. 'N-no.'

'Did he do any foreplay stuff?'

Silence.

'Did he get out his long throbbing knob and twirl it like a lasso in the moonlight? Did he cover you in chocolate and lick it all off? Did he stick live goldfishes up your giblets? Did he make you dress up like a policewoman and play nurses and doctors? That kind of thing.'

Jules laughed uneasily. 'No.'

'So no foreplay.'

'Not like that.'

'So he just stuck his thing up you?'

'Um . . .'

'Did it hurt?'

'No. Not at all.'

'What did it feel like?'

Jules left the bedclothes alone and started fiddling with a

strand of hair instead. 'It felt normal,' she said. 'Just sort of . . . nice.'

'D'you think he's done it lots?'

'Don't know.'

'Did he make noises?'

'What sort of noises?'

'*I* don't know. Noises. Like men are supposed to make when they're doing it.'

Jules looked at her and then looked away again.

'He did, didn't he?' said Mel triumphantly. 'What sort of noises? Did he . . . Did he shout? Did he call you darling? Did he . . . did he gurgle? He *moaned*, didn't he? He moaned. Moaned, like, *passionately*.'

'Not really. He just sort of did it.'

'Was it big?'

'D-don't know.'

'Show us. Was it like this?' Mel put up her hands like a fisherman showing the size of his salmon. 'Or like this?' She spread her hands wide apart. Jules stared at her long pale nails. 'Go on. Go on, tell.'

Silence.

'Must have been like this.' Mel pinched her finger and thumb together and squinted between them. 'Tiny. Minuscule. An eeny weeny needledick. Needledick, needledickneedle dickneedledickneeeedleneedle-neeedneedneed . . .' She tailed off, coughing with laughter.

'No. No.' Jules stopped again. 'Just sort of . . . average size. Don't know. Sort of like a . . .' – she searched for an honourable comparison – 'Sort of like an extra large sausage.'

'Ohmy*god!* A *sausage!* What kind of sausage? Like one of those fat banger things or like a floppy hot dog thing?'

'No,' said Jules. 'No.'

'Did it squelch?'

'No.'

'Did it flop?'

'*No.* It was just . . . nice.'

'Did you come?'

For a second, it seemed as if Jules might start crying. 'Sort of.'

'Ohmy*god!*' shrieked Mel. 'You came! What was it *like?*'

Jules thought of the gym, the rope and the sandpit. She felt tears pushing hard at the back of her throat.

Caz leaned back. 'Go on,' she said.

Mel snickered. 'Did it feel like?'

'Like nice. Good . . .' Jules tailed off.

'Yeah, but what *sort* of nice? Like long nice or short nice or big creamy romantic nice or what?'

'Like just really . . . good.' Jules sounded tired.

'So go on then.' Caz nudged her. There was something carnivorous in her eyes. 'How many times?'

'How many times what?'

'How many times d'you come?'

'D-don't know.'

'You *don't know?* How can you *not know?*'

'I mean I . . . was lots of things . . . maybe once or twice.'

'That's crap,' said Mel decisively. 'Once or twice is shit.'

'Oh yeah?' said Caz, turning. 'The fuck do *you* know?'

''Cause it says. In all the mags and films and stuff. You should come like thousands of times, otherwise he's got a small dick or you're frigid or something. He must be stunted.'

'You frigid then, Jules?' said Caz playfully.

'No!'

'You said you'd got bored with sex. Said you'd got bored of it earlier.'

'Well, yeah . . . Just bored of it with other people.'

'Like which other people?'

'Just other people.' Jules picked up a comb and began yanking at her hair.

'Like who?'

'I *don't know*. It's private, OK?'

'Go on,' said Mel, bouncing up and down on the bed, 'Tell more. Tell more. What happened? Was he a good snogger?'

'OK. Average. Normal.'

'You going to see him again?'

'Dunno. Might do. Might not.'

'Don't you want to do it again?'

'Maybe. Perhaps.'

'I was going to call them anyway,' said Caz casually. 'Maybe see them tomorrow. Maybe next week.'

Jules picked at the teeth of the comb.

'You'd be up for that,' said Caz, prodding at her with an elbow. 'Wouldn't you, babe?'

Jules didn't respond.

'Oh, go on, Don't be such a wimp. What you scared of?'

'I'm not scared,' said Jules, plucking harder now. 'I'm just . . .'

'Hen's coming. Aren't you?'

Hen looked confused. 'Give us a chance. Still got a hangover from last night.'

'Oh, for God's sake,' said Caz, standing up so suddenly that Izzy had to lurch out of her way. 'All such fucking wimps here. Pathetic. I'll just go on my own then.'

Jules looked up at her. 'Caz . . .' she said. 'CAZ.'

Izzy got there before her. 'Wait,' she said, scrambling off the bed. 'Wait for me.'

Caz was standing in the passageway with her arms folded. 'Yes?'

'I'll come,' said Izzy, 'I'll come with you. I'm not worried about going. Like to go. Godsoboredofthisplace. Dowithadrink.' She laughed, though she hadn't said anything funny.

As Caz watched, a thin trickle of dampness slid from under Izzy's hairline and down her face. Izzy lowered her eyes.

Caz saw the small cringing gesture, the submission behind the bravado. She unfolded her arms. 'No,' she said, and walked downstairs.

+

It was long past midnight. From far away, Hen could hear a tap dripping somewhere and then a sound like a scream, high and forlorn. Some nocturnal bird of prey, she supposed. It sounded a little like the creaking of the seagulls at home. Sometimes they would wake her in the mornings. When she banged on the window they would stare at her with bright malicious eyes. Home seemed very far away now.

She was in the toilet again, sitting on the floor with her legs tucked up, and the line of the parting in her hair shone pale against her head. She had brought her book, but it lay untouched beside her on the floor. She should have been in bed, but there was no question of sleep. Every time she lay down on the mattress she'd get about five minutes rest and then something would start prodding at her. There would be a lump or the shape of a spring poking out of the end or – more usually – just the scrape of her own bones.

She was cold again. She'd got up and put on whatever she

could find nearest to hand, but it never seemed to be enough any more. She hated all these layers, hated the necessity of pulling herself in and out of clothes designed to conceal and to falsify. The thinner she got, the more clothes seemed encumbrances: huge hairy jerseys that scraped at her neck, a fleece the size of a small duvet, endless T-shirts which had fitted her at the beginning of term and now – despite the shrivellings of the school wash – seemed to be a couple of sizes too large. She supposed she should have been pleased. It was at least evidence that she was finally losing weight. But it irritated her having to flap around in all this stuff, even at night. She hated the constant metallic ache of the wind on her skin, the way the mildest of draughts sent her scurrying for another layer of woollen armour. Most of all she hated the way she had to think about it so much: worrying about the food, worrying about her clothes, worrying about the weather, worrying about her bones, worrying about other people's worry.

After about five minutes, she stood up, walked over to the sink and stared at herself in the mirror. She wondered what she would look like when she was older and then – without much interest – if she'd actually get to be older. She couldn't think of anything particular to look forward to. She was dreading the holidays, she was dreading tomorrow, she was dreading everything, really, except perhaps the chance of a comfortable bed and an endless night's sleep. She couldn't think of anything she didn't feel guilty about. If she started thinking about her father, she felt guilty about him because he was good and because she'd forgotten the shape of his face. She felt guilty about her sisters because she hadn't written to them. She felt guilty about Jamie because she'd lost the trick of talking to him. She felt guilty about her mother because her mother frightened her.

She felt guilty about here, and Caz, and Jules. Most of all, she felt guilty about standing here in a cold toilet in the middle of a forest staring at her own bones.

She crossed her arms and looked at her own face. She stood like that for a long time, not moving. Then she pulled something out of the pocket of her fleece, feeling its edges with one finger. She rolled one leg of her pyjamas up, balancing her foot on the lid of the toilet. Outside, the night bird screamed again. Perhaps it was catching rabbits or mice. She knew the sound of a rabbit's fear. Surprisingly penetrating, like a child's scream.

She thrust the broken glass into the side of her thigh. Once, twice, stabbing hard at her skin. Again and again. The motion made her head shake slightly from side to side. Through the corner of her eye, she could see the sluggish glimmer of blood. She felt only a soft tickle as the blood began to run down her leg. It took a while for it to begin hurting. Even when it did it seemed like a distant kind of hurt. Hen reached over and picked up a piece of white cloth from the side of the bath; a pillowslip which she'd ripped up a couple of days ago. She put it over the cut and held it there. Then, very slowly, almost lovingly, she tied the strip of cloth around her thigh. She could feel the blood soaking through, see it blooming out from between the layers of soft cotton. She watched it for a minute or two, interested by the way it spread so silently, sliding in between the folds of the material, leaking softly over the skin beneath.

She rolled the leg of her pyjamas back down, pulled the fleece tighter around herself, unlocked the door and walked back into the bedroom. It took a while for her eyes to adjust to the darkness. She could see the outline of each sleeper under the sheets and hear the rhythm of their breathing. There was a strange smell in the room, high and slightly sweet, like perfume corrupted in the bottle. She sat on her own bed for a while, feeling the blood creep under the bandage. She'd have to stick on another layer, otherwise the cut would start bleeding onto her pyjamas and she'd have to explain things to people in the morning. She pulled another strip of cotton out of her pocket, rolled her pyjamas up again and pulled the material around her thigh, almost tight enough to stop the circulation. She could feel the rhythm of her heart and the jagged edge of the glass in her pocket. When she'd finished, she lay back, resting her head on the pillow, staring sightlessly at the ceiling. Her leg thundered at her now. She turned on her side and closed her eyes.

In the bed opposite, Caz settled deeper, breathing slow and regular. It was only up close that it would have been possible to see the flicker of her eyelids and the faint glitter of one eye as she watched Hen tighten the bandage.

SUNDAY

The church was cold. Stone-deep never-ending Sunday cold. Not for the first time, Jules wondered why freezingness was next to godliness while sin was supposed to allow you some kind of decent central heating. What was it about God, or Jesus, or whoever he was? Did he really think that hypothermia was a sign of devotion? Could he really be that clever if he thought that people would want to follow him into the hereafter for a bad case of gangrene and a lot of lectures about never having any fun? Come unto me and thou shalt receive eternal frostbite? Hang out in my House and spend your time wondering why I'm such a penny-pinching mingy old bastard?

All churches were like this, or all the churches she had been in, anyway. There was something about them – the mean, stabby wood, the stones exhaling dead breath all over you – that always made her think wistfully of the flames of hell. She wondered if it might be worth announcing herself a convert to Catholicism or Islam. Catholics had a thing for candles; perhaps that warmed their churches up a bit. And at least Muslims got to hang around on bits of carpet instead of these sadistic pews.

She was sitting in the fifth row, Caz on one side and Hen

on the other. Izzy, two pews in front, was dreamily scratching her thigh. Apart from them, there were only a handful of others in the congregation: two or three young mothers with bland creamy faces, a guy with white-boy dreadlocks and a man at the back who Jules considered surprisingly good looking for someone who believed in God.

The church had evidently once been beautiful in a bare sort of way, but then the Victorians had come along and started fussing it up with glum mahogany pulpits and disapproving windows. In recent years a glass screen had been built dividing the choir from the nave, and a strip of sick green carpet now ran down the central aisle. To relieve the boredom, she'd tried reading the inscriptions on the memorial stones, but most of them were quite dull: quotations from scripture and lists of ailments. Then she'd sat reading the Bible for a while, but it was difficult to stay interested in a book with characters named Muppim, Huppim and Ard who all seemed to live for seven hundred years and did nothing much except hang around in the desert endlessly smiting and begetting.

The vicar was a thick-lipped youngish man with defeated hair and a mimsy voice. Jules knew that if she met him in the street, he would talk completely differently from the way he talked in here. His diction was odd, and he kept punctuating things in the wrong places. When he'd been leading the creed a little earlier, they had all kept getting out of rhythm despite knowing the words off by heart. 'We believe in one. God the Father the. Almighty maker of heaven. And earth. And of all that is. Seen. And unseen we believe. In one Lord Jesus. Christ the only. Son of God eternally. Begotten of the Father. God from God light. From light . . .' He was telling a long story which had begun with his being unable to find his Honda in the Safeway car park but which suddenly seemed to be about the parable of the lost sheep. Jules found the story irritating, not because she cared about its outcome, but because his voice wasn't quite dull enough for her to ignore.

She sat back again and cast around for something else to stare at. It seemed the vicar was coming to the end of this particular story, though since none of his anecdotes so far had produced anything approaching a punchline, it was difficult to be sure. She fixed on his flabby lips. They were pink and slightly moist, and reminded her of an occasion when she had been intentfully mounted by a labrador whilst staying at her aunt's. Jules had been lying on the lawn and her little cousins had been arguing over possession of a plastic tractor lying nearby. The labrador had given one of her cheeks a desultory slobber and then started shoving at her leg. When she looked down, all she remembered seeing was this horrible glistening pink dick thing. The vicar's lips looked like that. And the longer she looked at them, the more they looked like bits of randy labrador. Or – worse – what Yves might have looked like if she'd been able to see him properly.

'One more. *Thought*,' the vicar was saying. 'As my melancholy experience. In the car park illustrates, there. Are things in this life which we cannot. Sadly alter. Though the Lord is good, I am afraid I shall never. Acquire an adequate sense of direction' – he paused for a second, but no one reacted – 'But I say to you. If you allow. *Christ Jesus.*' Another pause. 'To be your guide through this. Life you will find yourself in safe hands. Perhaps you will recall the. Following prayer which. I *myself* find unexpectedly useful. In supermarkets.'

Jules cracked her spine against the pew and swore quietly. 'God grant me the. Serenity to *accept* the things I cannot change. The courage. To change the *things* I can. And the *wisdom*. To know the difference. Amen.' He made a slight pecking motion and moved aside. The congregation stood up and began searching for the next hymn.

Jules nudged Hen violently in the ribs. 'That's like AA.'

'What?'

'Like Alcoholics Anonymous. That's like the drunk people's prayer.'

'Which?'

'That one, the one the vicar just said. It's the alky prayer. Like with your mother.'

'*What?*'

'Your mother.' Jules gazed at Hen, and then began cautiously back-pedalling. 'They use that prayer thing in AA.'

'What's that got to do with my mother?'

'It's just . . . nothing.'

'What do you mean?'

'Nothing. Really.'

Caz leaned over, interested. ''Tis it?'

'My mother doesn't go to AA,' Hen said furiously.

Jaws leaned over and tapped her on one knee with the prayer book. 'Shhhhh.'

'She *doesn't*.'

'OK, OK. Whatever.'

They raised the hymn books and began to sing.

+

Outside, they waited in the graveyard as Jaws paused to thank the vicar. It was warmer out here than it had been inside, and many of the graves closest to the church leaned aside at a nonchalant angle. Beside the more recent stones someone had placed pots of bright flowers, and the place now had an air of comforting untidiness.

Hen took off her jacket and spread it out on the grass. 'What were you saying in there?'

'Never mind.'

'No. Tell me.'

'Forget it.'

Caz was watching them both. 'I think she was saying that they use that thing about the serenity to change or whatever in Alcoholics Anonymous.'

'And?'

Jules seemed discomfited. 'Nothing.' Pause. 'You're always going on about your mother being a . . . being whatever.'

'An alky? No she's fucking *not*.'

'You did sort of say so.'

'She's got *nothing to do* with that prayer.'

Caz sat down next to Hen. 'You said sometimes she drank a bit.' Her voice was gentle, cajoling.

'Not like that.'

'AA's fine. Elsa goes all the time to NA. She's got lots of friends who were junkies. Fact, she probably sold them the stuff. AA's just the same. They're just places where you hang around and talk a lot.'

'Yeah.' Jules nodded, encouraged. 'Couple of really good mates have been. They said it was cool. You have to stand up in front of other people and say you drink like six pints of vodka every night. But it's all nice. They all just shag each other and stuff.'

'She just meant,' – Caz gazed into the bushes – 'that from what you said, you'd meant that your mother sometimes drank a bit too much. It doesn't matter. So does everyone, for God's sake. *We* do.'

'She does, I suppose,' said Hen slowly. 'She does drink.'

'Too much?'

She nodded. 'Sometimes. She drinks when I'm there because she says it's a celebration. Every night, she says the same thing: "Go on. It's a celebration." '

'And it isn't?'

'I just wish . . . she starts shouting. About us, about Dad.'

Jules frowned. 'Don't you stop her?'

'It's not like that,' said Caz. 'You can't stop someone drinking if they want to.'

'I poured her wine down the sink once. Three bottles of it. She was so angry she made me go out in the middle of the night, find an offie and get her three more. I walked for miles. Miles and miles. And she made me use my own money. All of it.'

'Cow,' said Jules.

Hen sighed. 'She's just . . . she says she misses us. She rings Dad in the middle of the night. I can hear her. She shouts.'

Caz's voice was soft. 'Is it always like that?'

'Only since they got divorced. Only since . . .' Hen thought for a minute. 'I think sometimes it's London that makes her like that.'

Jules smirked. 'London makes her drink? London gets like this whole huge bottle of drink and sticks it down her throat?'

Hen did not reply. As she turned her head away, some subtle shift in her face made her a stranger again, the best friend Jules had never met.

Caz looked up. 'Oh, shut up. You're useless.'

Jules walked much of the way back on her own. For a while

she tried to make herself believe that walking alone was what she had chosen to do, but with the other two talking just out of earshot, she felt only a solitary defiance. She did not like being on her own, walking down the main road, aware of every footstep. She didn't like the sense that the people in the passing cars would see her a little separate from all the rest. As they flicked by, on their way to work or beaches or significant lives, this would be the only image of her they'd ever have: the girl on her own.

She was having difficulty working out what she had done wrong. She had evidently said something offensive to Hen in church, but since Hen often talked about her mother, the champagne, the drooling midnight promises, Jules couldn't see what she'd got so upset about. Or why Hen was furious with her for mentioning it but perfectly forthcoming when Caz picked up the subject.

Jules had always wished that her family would summon up some sort of exotic crisis. Not anything too terrible – no deaths, no disfiguring ailments; just something other people would be envious of. Drugs would do. Addiction of most kinds was cool because it was reversible, and because it seemed to offer more anecdotal value than illness. Perhaps it would be good to have a mother who smashed up washing machines with an axe or a crazed great-aunt locked in an attic. Divorce was boring because everyone was divorced, but affairs were interesting and unwanted pregnancies even more so. Just something. Even a relatively minor tragedy would do. But there was nothing. Her parents were still together, her sisters were evolved and functional members of society and she had only to look at herself to be reminded that she was not the product of some twisted genetic legacy. Instead, she was condemned to listen forever to other people's stories, to Hen discussing her mother, to Caz talking about Elsa, to Izzy whining on about her allergies. She'd been lying when she said she had friends who went to AA – she only wished she had. Everything she knew about it had been gleaned from a couple of magazine articles and an eavesdropped conversation on a London bus.

Jules was the middle one. Middle in age, middle in position, middle in temperament, middling pretty, middling intelligent, middling fun. Her older sister was the clever one, reading law at university and already possessed of a lawyer's claw-fingered mind. And her younger sister was the beautiful one: sweet brown eyes, a welcoming face, and a body in which everything good came together to make something better. Jules remembered watching other mothers at parties when she was younger, the way they'd gaze so fixedly at Anna and murmur, 'She'll be a looker, that one. Fighting them off.' She didn't remember anyone ever looking that way at her.

The understanding that her sisters were *something*, that they had somehow been born to an identity which Jules lacked, made her unusually alert to injustice. She felt bookended between two people whose solidity and intent had never been in question. Jules's main hope of being noticed was simply to be louder than the other two. Even now she lay awake at night brooding savagely over hidden meanings. Why did Anna look better than her in short skirts? Why had Claire been given the best bedroom? Why, for God's sake, did the family dog always bark at her and no one else? There was some some basic inequality in her family, recognized but unacknowledged, which it seemed only Jules resented. It made her feel small and mean and bitter. Sometimes it made her hate her parents. Most of the time it made her hate herself.

She recalled Christmas when she'd been about seven. Christmas was always the same; they'd have a long boring breakfast and then a long boring lunch round at her grandmother's house and then – when it was late and dark and they were all exhausted – they'd be allowed to open their presents. Claire and Anna always took ages opening theirs. Claire would sit there fondling each new package, spinning out the ritual for hours. Anna would open about three and then lose interest. There would be something in one of them – a game or a toy – and that would be it: she'd put all the unopened packages aside and play with that for the next three weeks. Only Jules would race through them all and then sit disconsolately on her haunches wondering why it was that despite getting exactly the same number of presents as her sisters, hers always seemed to amount to so much less.

This particular year Claire, in deference to her seniority, had been given several uninteresting books and a new pair of trousers. Jules and Anna had been given pencil cases. Inside the cases there were ten separate compartments, each with something in it; a ruler, a set of felt pens, a pencil sharpener in the shape of a mouse. Anna's case was gold and Jules's was silver.

Jules stared at her case in disbelief. The silver top shone dully at her: second prize. She didn't want to pick it up just in case picking it up meant that she'd accepted possession.

'That's not fair,' she said quietly. 'That's *not fair.*'

Her father was folding wrapping paper. 'What's not fair?'

'She got a gold one.'

'And you got a silver one.'

Not for the first time, Jules felt herself overwhelmed by the idiocy of her parents. 'It's. *Not. Fair.* Hers is gold.'

'And yours is silver. It's got exactly the same things in it, in exactly the same places. What's the problem?'

'Hers is *gold*. Gold is *my* colour! I *always* liked gold. You gave the gold one to her!'

Anna looked up. 'I like gold too, sometimes.'

Her father crouched down beside her. 'Julia, gold isn't yours. Gold is a colour.'

Jules burst into tears. 'You gave the gold one to her,' she sobbed. 'Gold is mine! Gold is *always* mine!'

'Julia . . .'

'Gold is *my* colour! It's *mine!*' How could they be so stupid? How could they not understand? 'I hate you!' she shouted. 'I *hate* you! I hate you *all*! You're all *horrible!*'

She hurtled out of the room. Upstairs in her room she banged the door shut, pulled the large suitcase out from under the wardrobe and began flinging things into it.

Her father banged on the door. 'Julia. *Julia.* Don't be so silly. Come down. What about your presents?'

Jules ignored him. After she'd put in all her clothes, all her toys and dolls, and the special pillow she took everywhere with her, she closed the case. When she tried to lift it, she found that it was almost too heavy to carry. She crashed the case furiously against the bedside table, hating it, hating them, hating Christmas, hating everything. When she opened the door the case clouted her ankle, making her sob with pain.

Her father was still standing outside. Jules bumped past him with her head down, tears blinding her, not speaking. Downstairs, her sisters and her mother had come out to watch. As she walked past them, she could hear them cupping their hands round their mouths, trying to muffle the laughter. Jules opened the door, and stepped out into the freezing rain.

It was the silence that she found weirdest. The street was deserted. She could see the warm glow from the other houses, hear the whispers of conversation and music. Above her, the empty blue light of a television screen flickered against the walls of someone's flat. It took her a couple of seconds to remember that it was Christmas and that it was normal for the roads to be so quiet. She'd forgotten to bring her coat, and the rain soaked through her jersey down the back of her neck. The case got heavier and heavier. She walked unsteadily to the end of the road and wondered if there might be a bus she could take. Not far, but far enough to show them all.

She watched the rain sleeking down the pavements. It was lonely out here, lonely and wet and cold. Up above, she could hear laughter and the sound of someone stacking plates. She turned back and, as she walked along the road, she saw her mother watching her from behind the kitchen curtains, smiling.

That night she lay awake for a long time, staring at the ceiling, sad in a way that she couldn't understand. She wondered if Claire and Anna really were her sisters, or if she belonged to another invisible family who had discarded her. Maybe she was adopted. Maybe she was a second-hand child picked up cheap in a sale. Maybe she was a discount sister, an unwanted remainder. Maybe she wasn't meant to be here at all.

Several months later and as a direct consequence of the pencil-case incident, Jules tried to poison her sisters. Her mother had a migraine and had retired early to bed, telling Claire to prepare the tea for all three of them. Claire was watching television and did not seem much interested in feeding anyone. Jules pleaded to be allowed to make tea instead. Claire didn't bother looking away from the screen. 'All right,' she said. 'Burgers or something. Don't make a mess.'

Jules ignored the burgers. Instead, she made biscuits. They contained butter, sugar, eggs, flour, cocoa and icing. They also contained compost, slug pellets, a spray for cleaning ovens, and a can of something called Doom for killing insects. As she'd mixed it she'd thought about how good life would be without sisters. Once they were gone her parents would have no choice; they'd have to love her.

When the biscuits were cooked, she sprayed on a thick gloop of oven cleaner with a squirt of Doom underneath, slathered chocolate icing all over and stood back to admire her handiwork. If it wasn't for the odd smell, no one would know the difference. Then she put all the cleaning stuff back under the sink, arranged the biscuits onto a plate, and took them through.

Claire was still engrossed in the programme, but Anna, younger and greedier, fingered the biscuits hungrily. 'They smell weird,' she said, inspecting each biscuit to find the one with the most icing.

'No they don't,' said Jules, chewing a fingernail. 'They're fine.'

Claire picked up one of the biscuits and took a bite. 'Phtheeurgh! Eeurghth!' She spat it back onto the plate. 'That's *vile*. What did you put in them?'

'Chocolate. Normal stuff you put in biscuits.'

Undeterred, Anna bit hard into hers. 'Tastes funny.' She chewed thoughtfully.

'Aren't you going to have any?'

'I licked the bowl.'

'I'm not eating those,' said Claire. 'They're disgusting.'

That night, Anna was sick, copiously and for a long time. Jules lay in bed, listening to the sounds from the bathroom and her father's footsteps going to and fro. Anna might die, she thought, staring up at the ceiling, Anna might die. She pictured herself at Anna's funeral, sobbing prettily into her hymn book, listening to her aunts and uncles nudging and murmuring behind her: 'Poor little thing, with her sister dead. So young. Poor lamb.' By the time Jules eventually fell asleep, the fantasy had grown and Anna now lay cold in a satin-covered casket with Jules standing over her, pale and invincible.

Anna did not die. In the morning, she sat at breakfast looking tired but eating her cereal with her usual appetite. And no one ever did find out that Jules had been responsible. Claire said something about having to fetch her own tea, but their father was too distracted to listen properly. And, since Jules had cleared and washed up quite obediently, it was just assumed that Anna must have picked up a stomach bug from school.

Jules no longer wished her sisters dead. They still annoyed her and they were still unfair, but Jules had learned that unfairness was to be expected of life. She no longer believed that she belonged to a different family. Diligent study of her own face in the mirror told her all she needed to know. The pencil-case incident, meanwhile, had been turned into family lore, anaesthetised by overfamiliarity. Once in a while, it would be taken out and retold by her father or Claire – the argument, the suitcase, the rain. All that incoherent fury had worn away and seemed almost comforting now. When the others laughed, Jules had learned to laugh too, although some private corner of her did not think it was funny. She had not forgotten how it had felt then. She had not forgotten how she used to think of them, and the deep corroding ache of that old hatred. She had not forgotten the joy she'd felt as she added poison to the bowl.

+

A mile on, and she heard footsteps quickening behind her.

Hen huffed up alongside. 'Hi. How's it going?'

Jules didn't turn, just watched Hen's trainers padding along the pathway. The way Hen was acting – her evasive gait, her arms pressed in close to her sides – told Jules exactly what she'd come to say.

'Best if it's just us,' said Hen eventually. 'Me and Caz. I mean, you're definitely coming the next time. Probably actually be quite boring. Just Sunday afternoon.'

Silence.

'We thought you'd probably not enjoy it much . . .'

'Did Caz send you?'

'No. Not really.'

'Are you taking Izzy?'

'No.'

'Well,' Jules said, 'I hope you have a *lovely* time.' She knew Hen was pleading, but she wasn't interested in being nice to her just now. In fact, she hoped that Hen would feel terrible for a long time.

When she thought about it, she didn't particularly want to go with them. She didn't want to see Yves again or talk to him or even remember him. Jules felt a new, complicated sort of rage at not being invited to a party that she didn't want to go to. The knowledge that she was relieved just made it worse. Somehow, in some unspecified way, it was all Hen's fault. Jules walked on, brooding, violent, hoping now that the passing cars would see her and notice that there was purpose in her rage.

. . . SUNDAY

'The secret,' Caz was saying, 'Is just to look as if you're meant to be here. Look as if there's no reason in the world why you shouldn't be walking along this road. Elsa taught me that. It's like lying. If you believe the lie yourself, then other people will believe it too.' She fiddled with the buttons of her jacket. 'Works, too. Really does.'

'Yeah,' said Hen, 'But if Naylor or Jaws come along, they'll know we're not supposed to be here, whatever we say.'

'They won't.'

'They might.'

'They won't, right? It's going to be fine.'

Hen did have to admire Caz's panache. She'd borrowed Ali's mobile and arranged a date as coolly as if she'd been fixing a date in the centre of London. Then she'd rung one of the local cab firms and told the driver to wait for them outside the gates. They had four hours before anyone would check up on them. Naylor was off on some private mission in Bristol, and Jaws was marking exam papers in her room. And now here they were, walking the last half-mile to Stokeley as if they had every right to be there.

Hen wrestled with her sleeve. The weather had cooled

slightly and it was windier than the past few days. She was glad about the breeze. The previous week's sun hadn't touched her – when they'd been walking through the forest she'd felt only bone-deep cold – but she had hated walking around in a couple of jerseys and thick jeans when everyone else was glowing through their T-shirts.

The college was bordered by a long, high brick wall stretching for a mile or so. Behind it, Hen could see the drift of smoke from one of the kitchen chimneys. Once in a while she heard the sound of male voices and the impact of a football.

Caz, a little further on, turned. 'Mon. Got to hurry.'

Hen should have found Caz's assurance comforting. But this wasn't like Friday, when they'd all felt that surreptitious thrill. This was different. Caz seemed uninterested in Hen as an accomplice. Hen felt more of a cumbersome accessory than a true partner in crime. It would have felt better with Jules here. Jules would have been as jumpy as she was. And Izzy, she thought. She'd promised Izzy she would ask on her behalf. Perhaps she should ask now. Then again, perhaps not.

They rounded a bend in the road and felt the forest frown over them. As they passed the main entrance, Hen saw a broad expanse of pockmarked tarmac, two lime trees fetlocked with old growth and a notice with 'Stokeley Institute of Higher Education Please Drive Slowly' written on it in red. Her heart walloped against her ribs. They would be seen, surely.

When they rounded the bend and found the tree Higgs had told them to look for, Caz barely hesitated. The beech had been worn smooth and obvious by generations of students using it as a ladder, and she swung herself up into the lower branches easily. 'OK,' she said, 'They're there.'

On the other side of the wall were Higgs and Adey, looking

up at them, pale-faced. There was something disorientating about their presence. Hen realized that she had not seen either of them in daylight. She'd only seen Higgs under a twilight smirr of drink, and Adey she still associated with the shadows of the music shop. Seeing them in naked sunlight seemed wrong somehow. Boys were something she associated with midnight, not with a docile Sunday afternoon.

Higgs motioned to a log shed directly underneath the wall. 'Onto that,' he whispered. Caz did not bother to check that Hen was following her. As she jumped, she put out an arm for Higgs to support.

The climb had made Hen feel faint. She leaned against one of the branches and closed her eyes. If she stayed here, she'd never move again. She hauled a foot over the wall and jumped.

+

'Pity about the music,' said Adey, twitching at the volume dial.

Hen nodded. 'Sorry about that. I would have brought them . . .'

She was struggling to remember what Izzy had told her yesterday. It felt like cramming formulae in physics: drum and bass equals volume squared, heavy dub plus history of hard house equals forward motion. If you can't remember the names, Izzy had said, just talk about remixes.

'What do you mainly like?'

'Oh, masses.' *The secret of lying is to believe in the lie.* 'Some hardcore, early house, trance . . .'

'What was the last thing you bought?'

'Compilation. A UK garage thing. You probably wouldn't know it.' No it hadn't. It had been *The Legendary Jimmy Shand*

and his White Heather Band as a reluctant present for her grandmother nearly two years ago. 'Kind of stuff do you like?'

Where his white hair parted she could see the thin pink line of his scalp. He'd put some sort of sticky gel on his hair to make it look as if he had more of it. The sticky stuff hadn't worked; it just looked as if he'd glued all the strands together. 'Early stuff. Soul, R&B, whatever. All the money I get goes on music. Spent all last summer working for a joiner so I could buy stuff. Makes this place bearable.'

The room was small, not much more than a cubicle. It was part of a modern block built in haste in the early nineties to house a new influx of students and to boost the Institute's revenue from the holiday conference trade. There were three floors, all part of a squared-off U shape. Each floor had a central corridor with row upon row of small uniform rooms just like this one. The doors were hollow hardboard and the walls trembled like a stage set every time someone ran down the corridor. Adey's room was on the right side of the U and looked out over a log hut and an expanse of decrepit concrete. A bed, a sink, a desk, a chair. A few posters, presumably put up by the regular occupant – billings for gigs, an *Evening Standard* hoarding, a notice with nothing on it but the words, *I love the smell of napalm in the morning.*

On the table lay a clutter of books, a heavily-doodled A4 pad and a scatter of pens. Above it was a timetable and a few photographs. Hen got up and inspected them. A woman, a man, and a red-haired girl laughing in a garden. Pale male faces taken too close, swigging bottles of beer, the liquid dribbling down their necks, teeth bared at the camera. A spaniel with its black nose shining.

'These yours?'

He nodded.

'Who's she?' Hen pointed at the red-haired girl.

'Ex. Deborah.'

'When d'you split up?'

'Christmas.'

'Why?'

He looked out of the window. 'I decided that we ought to split up. But she actually said it, you know? So she thinks she chucked me, when really it was the other way round.'

'Did you like her?'

He sniffed. 'Why are you asking all these questions?'

'Just interested.'

'You all do that. Girls. Ask questions.'

'Is that bad?'

'You all do it.'

A silence. Adey stared up at her. His eyes were a dilute blue and ringed with pinkish lids, as if someone had forgotten to fill all his colours in. She found she could only look at him when he wasn't looking at her.

'Want tea?'

'Yes, please,' said Hen, suddenly formal. 'Very kind.'

In the corner next to the sink there was a small shelf with a kettle, several used teabags and three or four open mini-cartons of milk. Adey got up and switched the kettle on. 'Out of sugar,' he said, stepping over Hen towards the door. 'Hang on. Back in a sec.'

Hen got up and stared at the photographs again. All the faces, the men with the beer sliding down their mouths, the whited-out skin, the teeth standing out like punctuation. All those people are his friends, she thought. All those people.

She didn't have those people. She had Caz and Jules, a

couple of old Edinburgh friends, and two or three girls in London who her mother had insisted (wrongly) that she would love. Otherwise, her wall would just have been relatives and inventions: a bug-eyed cousin palmed off as a mate, silent friends of her brother's who looked at her from under their eyebrows and laughed when she glanced back at them, a defiantly handsome colleague of her father's whom she'd once had to occupy for ten minutes while her father took a call.

She wondered how Caz was doing. She'd disappeared with Higgs, smiling up at him. He'd stroked her hair casually, as if he had stroked the hair of many girls and knew how it should be done. Somewhere in these anonymous miles of rooms, perhaps they were having sex. Hen thought of Caz's body next to his, her face shaping expressions that no one else would see. She neither envied Caz, nor did she feel any particular curiosity. The thought of someone touching her own body made her feel only a kind of abstract pity. Sex now seemed like something which she ought to want rather than actually did want. She ought to because Caz did, and Jules had. And besides, the point wasn't to like it. The point was just to prove that you wanted it, and someone wanted you.

Adey was taking ages. Hen roamed the room, shuffling through the papers on his desk, looking out of the window. The door of his cupboard was standing ajar, so she opened it and peered in. A dishevelled lump of shirts and trainers, a pair of trousers hanging by one leg. On the door was a poster of a woman with the same expression of greedy boredom as the ones in Caz's porn mag. At the back of the cupboard there was something pinned to the wall. Hen parted the clothes and looked at it. It was a dartboard, with different coloured darts sticking out of it: green, red, blue and yellow. From the darts were hanging things that looked like handkerchiefs or little flags. Most were white, some were pink or blue or black. Then she saw the shape of them and realized they weren't flags at all; they were knickers. Women's knickers. The green dart was stabbed through two pairs, the red dart through three. Blue had two and yellow – the one closest to the bullseye – had four. As Hen had parted the hangers to look, the clothes brushed against the knickers and moved them round. Impaled on the red dart were one black pair and two white. The one at the top had a name tape sewn on the seam. '-minter,' Hen read. She didn't want to touch them so she shifted the clothes again and the knickers moved round. She saw a name tape on the yellow dart and angled her head so she could read it. 'Julia Pr-' she read. She put her hand out gingerly and touched the tape so she could see it properly. Julia Prentice. Jules. *Jules?* What were a pair of Jules's knickers doing here, pinned to a dartboard at the back of Adey's cupboard?

She shuffled the clothes back over the board and closed the cupboard doors. She could hear footsteps in the corridor, the sound of men shouting to each other outside. The breeze plucked at the curtains and at the hems of Adey's posters. Hen sat on the edge of his bed, staring at a large black and white poster of two soldiers beating a man with the butt of a rifle. *Peace?* said the lettering above the picture, *I Hate The Word.*

When Adey came back in with two sugar lumps and a dripping teaspoon, she got up and walked over to the window. 'Adey?'

'Yeah?'

'Um. You know your cupboard?'

'Shit.' He put the spoons down on the sideboard. 'Were you looking in there? It's a slum.'

'N-no. Not that.'

'They come round and check up once a week, but—

'No,' said Hen again. 'It's . . . a . . . there's this board at the back, and the door was sort of open, so I was looking at it.'

Several expressions tangled on his face at once. Guilt and laughter, mostly. 'That. I'd forgotten about that.'

'What are all those things hanging from it?'

He switched the kettle on. 'Nothing.'

'Say. Please say.'

'Can't. It's . . . it's just a private thing.'

'What sort of private thing?'

'A joke. Doesn't matter.'

'Go on. Tell me. Won't tell anyone else.'

He considered. 'Promise? Really promise?'

'Yes. Promise. Absolutely.' Hen put one hand behind her back and crossed her fingers.

'It's a game. There's four of us. One for each dart. I'm green, Higgs is red, Yves is yellow, Bill is blue.'

'And?'

'And it works on a points system, You get points for each pair.'

'How do you get them?'

'You have to . . .' – he coughed – '. . . you have to have sex with someone. You have to . . .'

Hen watched the carpet. It had a coffee-coloured splodge shaped a bit like Italy.

'You get ten points for proper full-on sex. Twenty if you pop their cherry. Don't get anything if you don't have the knickers to prove it.' He grinned, more self-deprecation than embarrassment.

'Wow,' said Hen politely. 'How many points have you got?'

'Thirty. One shag, one cherry.'

'And Higgs?'

'Higgs only got a couple of shags. And a blow job. Five points for a blow job.'

'What about the one with four?'

'Yves. Don't know what it is about that guy. He gets lucky all the time. He's way ahead of the rest of us.'

Hen looked down. 'He did it with Jules, didn't he?'

'Yeah. Second cherry.'

'But Jules . . .' Hen stopped. 'But Jules is . . . isn't . . .'

Adey got up and began pouring out the tea. 'You're not offended by all of this?'

'N-no,' said Hen. 'Not at all. It's amazing.'

'Thought you might find it . . . bad.'

'No. Really.' Hen laughed. 'Makes sense, kind of.'

The way he looked at her made her want to turn away. 'Told you because I thought you'd be cool about it. Higgs said we shouldn't tell anyone.'

'Not like we don't do the same thing.' She got up again and went over to the window. All the need and all the lies were starting to make her head hurt. She stared out of the window. A couple of boys were walking round the corner, holding tennis racquets and a canister of balls. One of them was bouncing the mesh of the racquet up and down on the palm of his hand.

'Wonder how Higgs is doing,' Adey said idly.

'D'you think he's really into Caz?'

Adey smirked. 'Probably. All pathetic one inch.'

'No. Not that. I mean does he like her?'

'Don't know. If she sleeps with him, sure he'll like her a lot.' He picked the two sugar lumps off the side and sat down next to Hen. 'I'm not bothered about getting laid. Higgs cops off with anyone, but I'm more . . . selective, know what I mean?'

'Yep,' said Hen, watching the Italy-shaped coffee splodge. As she watched it, it seemed to swell at one corner.

'You got to really like the person. Like, I've been with lots of girls I didn't really rate. Doesn't mean anything like that.'

'Mmmm.'

'Higgs is obsessed with it, all the time. You're not into that stuff, are you?'

Hen could feel the heat of his arm against her shirt. She said, 'You got a girlfriend at the moment?'

'No. Taking a rest, right? After Deborah, I just thought, fuck it, who needs it?' He turned towards her. 'You're not like that, are you? You're not going out with someone?'

'Hrmmm,' said Hen.

He leaned over until he was almost at a forty-five degree angle to her. Then his hand shot out from nowhere, slid round her shoulder and clamped itself over her chest. Hen leapt up so fast the tea slopped over the side of the mug. 'God. So hot in here, ha ha.' A fraught silence. 'Amazing view out your window. So weird being here in this place. We still have to share and there's another girl in the room Izzy I'm in at the moment she snores like unbelievably. Holidays soon. Going to be doing amazing things this holidays working for this mate who does stuff at the Festival the Edinburgh Festival you know and I'll be kind of helping her and I'm really looking forward to it. Just dying to get back I'm going to stay with my Dad he's up in Scotland be really good to be away from here England's such a sort of funny place sometimes. Really. I had a sort of a um boyfriend.' It came out quick and high. 'And sometimes I'm a you know a lesbian thing. Occasionally.'

Adey stared up at her. 'A lesbian? No *way*.'

Hen nodded. 'Just got into it recently. Girls are great because they're totally different from men and . . .'

'So you like *do it* at night at school?'

'No. Not with them. With people at home.'

'What's it like?'

'Um,' said Hen. *Believe in the lie.* 'Very sexy. Girl's bodies . . . they can be really different.'

He watched the floor. 'Did you think I was hitting on you?'

'No, no way. Ha ha. Not at all' – a pause – 'I mean, you're really nice, but I'm kind of . . . not . . . not so much into . . .'

'Sure,' said Adey hurriedly. 'Right.' He stared down into his mug.

Through the window, Hen heard the sound of a door slamming shut and saw a figure with a denim jacket running out towards the back wall. For a long couple of seconds, she saw only a girl, running. Then the figure turned slightly and she saw her face. Caz. Familiar but completely unfamiliar. One hand was up by her eyes, and the other was holding the jacket tight around her waist. Her skirt had lurched over to one side and the collar of her shirt kept stabbing at her ear. Her hair had fallen out of its clip and now twisted in the wind. Hen thought stupidly, Caz never doesn't brush her hair. She could hear the sound of her shoes clacking against the tarmac, and the etherish squeak of some noise that Hen didn't associate with Caz. Sorrow. Hen stared. It couldn't be Caz. Caz never looked like that, so unkempt, so unstudied. And Caz never cried. The image seemed so alien, so incorrect, that Hen found

it difficult to trust the evidence of her own eyes. She turned.
'Got to go. Now.'

'What?'

'Just got to.' She picked up her jersey from the bed.

Adey stretched out a hand. 'You're offended.'

'I'm not. I'm really not. Just got to go.'

'You can't. There'll be people all over the place.'

'I've *got to go*.' She opened the door and glanced down the
corridor. 'How do you get back outside?'

Adey's expression had changed. 'Not my problem.'

'*Please*. You've been really nice. I promise.'

'Like I said. Not my problem.'

Hen glared at him. 'Fuck you,' she said softly, and closed
the door.

+

Ali was sitting in a tree, reading. The perch was not particularly
comfortable – two or three small branches stabbed at her back
and her view was obscured by a blind of leaves – but the
branch was wide and allowed her to swivel round occasionally.
She'd brought her packed supper out here and was munching
on a small stick of sweaty cheese. She didn't like cheese, but
there was nothing else to eat.

Jules had been out trying to sun herself on the grassy bank
just below the terrace, but the wind had grown frisky and she
had disappeared back inside. Izzy and the others were upstairs.
There was something about Sunday evenings – the hours
drizzling by, the aimless waiting for something dull to arrive –
that depressed Ali. Sundays had some separate dread attached
which never quite disappeared, even in the holidays.

She had been thinking about home. The kitchen, with its

bright crockery and the fridge divided into separate shelves, top for her mother, middle for the office, bottom for her mother's assistant Denise. The table around which her mother debated, plunging her arms through the air as if she wanted physically to push each point across. The hallway, which was always dark even in the early morning when the light shone through the little window. Her bedroom, which never felt like hers. When she wasn't there it got used as the office storeroom and stationery cupboard. She'd return home to find that she was sharing her nights with box files and redundant computer parts. Something about all this accumulation made Ali feel as if she represented nothing more than another storage problem.

Ali didn't know why she felt so wan about the holidays. Perhaps it was the certainty of their sameness: the cold damp beds at her uncle's house, her mother's snappishness, the sense of guilt both of them seemed to feel in each other's presence. After the first few days, things would go back to normal. Her mother would start giving her instructions. Ali would look at her in the wrong way, her mother would shout at her, Ali would go upstairs, Ali would come back downstairs three hours later, her mother would apologize whilst looking at a spot just to the left of her shoulder, they'd have a tight, over-emotional supper, they would both go to bed full of talk and good intentions, and the next day the whole thing would be repeated. Ali wondered sometimes – often, in fact – if her mother's conscience wouldn't be easier if she wasn't there at all.

Perhaps this time it would be different. Yesterday, she'd got a letter from America, addressed in her father's handwriting and containing £500 in beautiful new notes. He said he'd spoken to Ruth and that it was unlikely that Ali would be allowed to come to America over the summer, so here, by way of apology and consolation, was some money to make the holidays more enjoyable. He seemed neither downcast nor relieved to be without his daughter for a further six months. It sounded like this was the situation and this was how the situation would continue. Ali also understood that he did not want her to tell Ruth about the money.

She saw movement to her left and looked up. One of the men who was staying in the hostel. Maybe he was the psycho who had been peering into the gym. He had a tin of tobacco and was rolling a cigarette as he walked.

Ali watched him. Nondescript dark hair cut short, clothes that indicated no particular style or opinion. His legs were long but slightly bowed, which made his walk seem a little effortful. Young, or youngish. She was hopeless at judging people's age, but he didn't have wrinkles so he must be in his twenties or thirties. His hands – or what she could see of his hands from here – were long, with blunt fingertips and elegant, almost girlish wrists. Despite the breeze, he seemed able to roll the cigarette almost without looking, pinching just the right amount between finger and thumb, holding the paper between two fingers so it didn't blow away.

It wasn't until he sat down beneath the tree that she realized the problem. She had seen him, but he had not seen her. She must be too high to be visible, and the leaves probably obscured her from further away. Should she say something? Should she already have said something? If she didn't say something would he think she'd been spying on him? She put a hand out to reposition herself and the book which she had been reading fell to the ground with a splatter of pages.

He looked up.

'Sorry.'

'How long have you been there?' From the bluntness at the edges of his words, he sounded northern.

'I was reading.'

'Do you always read in trees?'

'No. Sometimes. I'm very sorry.'

'Stop saying sorry. It didn't hit me.'

She examined his face. From this angle he looked older than when she'd seen him walking. He leaned over and picked up the book. 'Is this one of your textbooks?'

'No.'

'Are you enjoying it?'

'No.'

He smiled.

Ali, emboldened, said, 'Are you the one who was watching us? In gym?'

'Watching you?'

'Through the window.'

'I don't think so. When was that?'

'Couple of days ago. Miss Naylor – our teacher – chased him away.'

'Must have been exciting.'

She couldn't tell if he was taking the piss. She felt uneasy again, abruptly aware that she had no idea how to judge him. She was better at reading girls; she hadn't had much choice. She'd spent her life in the company of women and had acquired a certain fluency in their translation. She did not know what to make of this man's easiness, the way he turned his face towards her with such assurance even though he was looking up and she was looking down. She would have stayed silent, but she supposed that it would be rude. 'Why are you here?'

'Here underneath this tree or here at the Manor?'

'Here at the Manor.'

'It's a holiday. A kind of holiday, anyway. I wanted to do a bit of research.'

'About what?'

'About the area. Industrial history. All very boring.'

'Is it boring?'

'Sometimes. Not at the moment.' A silence. 'Why are you here?'

'They don't know what to do with us. We're supposed to be doing activity things: exercises, biking, swimming. It's just a way of filling the time between exams and the end of term.'

'Why do you climb trees? Is that part of the exercise?'

'No.'

He waited.

'I like it. It's private. I like being private.' She sounded ridiculous, as if she was about eight. She slithered downwards onto a lower branch and sat warily surveying the crown of his head.

He picked up the book and handed it to her. 'I'm Rob,' he said. 'And you?'

'Ali. Are you with those other . . .'

'Yes. We're from the same university in London.'

'The others think you've been watching them. Spying.'

He watched her. 'What do you think?'

Ali shrugged.

'Did it ever occur to you that some people might find a pack of semi-house-trained schoolgirls quite alarming?'

It was Ali's turn to laugh. 'No. How?'

'That pack mentality, that power, the imagination . . .' He

205

drifted off. Ali wasn't sure if he had finished. 'I think some of my colleagues do find you frightening.'

'A whole bunch of men are scared of a few girls?'

He nodded. She was beginning to think that perhaps he was all right after all. He dropped the roll-up and ground it under one foot. 'So. I still want to know. What were you thinking about up in your tree?'

She shook her head. 'Stuff. The holidays.'

'Are you going somewhere nice?

'Home.'

'Home isn't nice?'

'It's normal.'

'What's wrong with normal?' He squinted up into the branches, and as he did so Ali looked properly into his eyes for the first time. His eyes looked older than the rest of him. There was something in them that she felt she could recognize. It was at that moment that she decided to trust him. She began to talk.

+

As a special Sunday dispensation, the television was on. The television was old and the picture looked garish no matter how sober the programme. The reds were redder and the greens greyer than they should have been. A woman in a maroon skirt walked across the screen, scattering a halo of emerald rays as she went.

Jules was lying back in one of the armchairs, her eyes half closed. Mel and Mina were squelched together on a chair, and Caz had lain down flat on the sofa.

None of them looked up as Ali walked in an hour later. 'What's on?'

Mel jerked her head against the back of the chair. 'Ow. Get . . . fucking . . . move.' Mina giggled. 'Move yourself, fat cow.'

Ali sat down in one of the empty chairs and stared at the psychedelic people. 'What's this?'

'Fuck knows.' Jules didn't move her eyes.

'Anything else on?'

'Can look.'

Ali picked the newspaper up. Nothing. Nothing for hours and hours.

Time passed. The picture did not improve, but after a while she began to adjust to these strange people with their reversible colours and their phosphorescent limbs. Mina and Mel heaved and giggled until Caz looked over at them and they stopped. Ali felt the tension in the room, the way both Jules and Caz sat so still, staring so determinedly at the damaged images.

None of them heard Miss Naylor behind them. She must have been standing in the doorway for several minutes. All Ali heard was her voice, electrifyingly ominous. 'Catherine. Out here. Now.' No one had bothered to turn the lights on, so all that they could see of her was an outline: a blurred nose, the empty planes of her face, the stripe on her tracksuit top. She looked almost frightening for a second. 'I don't know how you can stand that thing.' She flicked the lights on, making them blink.

Caz did not look at Jules – did not look at anyone – as she followed Miss Naylor out of the room.

✦

Far away, over by the river, they could hear a siren. Not an ordinary police siren, but a long hoarse swoop of sound like the air-raid sirens in old war films. There was something disturbing about the desolation contained in that single note as it rose and fell. It gave the night a strange feeling, as if they had lurched abruptly backwards and were sitting out here smoking in a darker time altogether. The birds didn't like it either. Every few seconds, they'd startle from the trees, whirring and calling.

All they could see of the water were the reflections of a long slick skein of lights. From here, it looked creepy, as if the river's blackness was more than just the reflection of the night and was its true colour, solid as oil. As she watched it slide along the valley, it occured to Hen that there was something odd about a river that never seemed to have any boats on it.

'Here', said Vicky. 'Give us one.'

Hen inspected the contents of her cigarette packet. She had seven left, enough to last her for most of tomorrow. 'Running low.' She did something urgent with her laces. 'Have to share one.'

Vicky didn't usually bother coming up here, but when Hen and Caz had climbed out through the little window a couple of minutes ago, they'd found her crouched with her back to the tiles, staring into the darkness. 'So?' said Vicky. 'What'd she give you?'

Caz took a while to answer. 'Twenty years' hard labour. Compulsory buggery every Tuesday.'

Vicky giggled. 'Lucky you.'

'And regular knicker inspections.'

'Have to have the knicker inspections. Old lezzie.' She smiled up at Caz.

Hen, watching her, was irritated. She'd forgotten that

Vicky had a thing about Caz. Always had done, right from the beginning. Doting on her, always laughing at her jokes, always there to appreciate when necessary. Caz seemed neither to mind nor to notice particularly. Hen supposed that she was probably used to people behaving like that now. Maybe she even thought it was normal. But still, something in Vicky's willing simper irritated her. She had a life, didn't she? Couldn't she just go and live her stuff instead of picking up someone else's scraps?

'How'd she bust you?'

'Dunno,' said Hen, swinging her Celtic cross from side to side. 'Someone must have grassed.'

'Grassed? Who?'

'She didn't say. Just that "it had been brought to her attention." She's told our parents, and gated us for the first three days of the holidays. Detention.'

'*What?*'

'Yep. First three days. We have to stay back at the end of term. She'll find us work: gardening, laundry.'

'But she can't do that.'

'She can, apparently. It's in the rules, she says. Some cretaceous by-law; "ye olde woade pupilles can be helde and torturrèd at ye olde schoole's pleasure. Ye olde woade pupilles must wear sackclothe and have ye no funne for ye fucking ages." She asked my father. He' – a note of bitterness – 'seems to think it's a great idea.'

Vicky looked over at Caz. 'Who told her?'

Silence.

'Yeah, well,' said Hen. 'Exactly.'

'Did anyone see you going?'

'Don't think so.'

'Who knew you were going?'

'Everyone. Jules, Izzy, Mel, you, Mina, everyone.'

Silence again. Caz seemed to have lost interest. She just sat there, smoking slowly and looking out to sea. Hen wondered if she had done something wrong, but nothing came to mind. She had been careful not to say anything to Miss Naylor about getting back to the Manor after Caz, or to imply that she thought it a little peculiar that Caz had just disappeared without doing anything to fetch her. If it hadn't been for seeing her out of Adey's window, she might still have been stuck there, picking her nails and staring at a dartboard covered in other people's knickers.

Vicky looked up. 'No one would grass, would they?'

'They might do,' said Hen, 'if they had reason to.'

'Who?'

She hesitated. 'Suppose Jules. She wanted to come.' It seemed wrong to mention Jules in front of Vicky. It wasn't as if she and Jules were supposed to be joined at the hip, but she knew the admission of vulnerability would be exploited. It always happened. As soon as anyone else sensed injury they'd find the sore and then pick until it bled dry. They weren't necessarily malicious, just bored and curious.

'Jules? Why?'

'Because . . . Don't know. It's kind of complicated.'

'But you two . . .' Vicky watched her, considering '—She wouldn't grass on you.'

'Maybe.' She stamped her feet uneasily. It was evident that Vicky thought all this new dissent was wonderful.

Caz sounded tired. 'Izzy wanted to come. I said no.'

Vicky laughed. 'God. That would have really killed things. Izzy with a bunch of men. Imagine.'

'Yeah,' said Hen, 'right.'

'Must have been her,' said Vicky with satisfaction. 'Must be. She's so insecure.'

Hen, caught between condemning either Jules or Izzy, drew deeply on her cigarette and condemned both. 'Could have been either. Probably was. Point is, what do we do about it?'

Caz stared upwards. 'Usual rules. Hit where it hurts.'

'You going to hit them?' said Vicky covetously. '*Really?*'

'Not really hit. Hit in other ways.'

'I understand.' Hen nodded. 'I know what you're saying.'

Vicky was frowning. 'Does that mean like you're supposed to take something? Do stuff to stuff they care about?'

'Yeah,' said Hen. 'What kind of thing should we do?'

But Caz seemed to have lost interest again. She was staring up at the first pale scattering of stars, and the cigarette flared briefly between her disembodied fingers.

Hen extended a hand. 'Caz . . . Caz. Tell.'

Caz gave no sign of having heard her.

'What should we do?'

Vicky watched them both, her gaze flicking back and forth.

'Look,' said Hen, discomfited, 'I'm really sorry about whatever happened today, I'm really sorry I—'

Caz whirled round. 'It's none of your *fucking* business. You have *no idea*. Just. Fuck. Off.' She stepped across the roof and back through the window before Hen could reply.

Vicky giggled. When she turned back to face Hen, her eyes were shining. 'Oh dear. What's with her?'

Hen didn't reply. The sound of the siren looped around their heads, enclosing them, pulling tighter. It took a conscious effort of will for Hen to stop herself from screaming.

MONDAY

Miss Naylor put the whistle to her lips. The pool was almost deserted. It was too early and too grizzly outside for most people to think of swimming. And it was Monday. Which, she said, was precisely why it was such a fine idea to get to the pool early. Jules, recognizing someone who had long ago stepped way beyond the forces of logic or humanity, hadn't bothered arguing. Argument only encouraged the sadist in Miss Naylor.

'Okey-dokey. Ten lengths. Warm up. All of you. Crawl, no butterfly or breaststroke. And I'm looking for best times, so no shirking, missies.'

Hen stood slightly to one side, but gave no sign of having heard the whistle. Jules, looking at her clearly for the first time in months, was shocked. Her swimming costume could not conceal the deep shadowed cavities round her collarbones, or her lumpy knees. Across her ribs and hips, the skin had buckled inwards like plastic vacuum packing, and Jules could count every knuckle of her spine from neck to hip. Even her face looked different. Her cheekbones now had deep shadows beneath them, and the pale hair on her jaw was more noticeable than usual. Her skin seemed almost luminous, like the liverish pallor on a corpse.

There was no good reason why the sight of Hen should so disconcerting, but it was. Despite the dressings and undressings they all had to negotiate in full view of each other, Hen had somehow managed to cover herself up. She, like Jules, had perfected the art of removing her clothes without ever quite being naked. Now, torn between envy and repulsion, Jules realized how much Hen had changed, and what that change meant. Though there was no question that Hen looked freakish, there was something compelling about her, something that hadn't been evident when she'd just been herself. Starvation had separated her. It had made her shine.

I want . . ., thought Jules, and stopped. Something in the thought seemed too confusing to go forward. I want to look like that? I want to be that thin? No. Even she could see that Hen had stepped many miles past the point of pretty-thin and become something different now, become freaky-thin, ugly-thin. But she did want something that Hen now possessed. That separateness, that pared-down bony glow. She saw the mothers at the other end of the pool lazily watching the line they made along the side. Jules could see their gaze move from left to right and the way they'd stop when they got to Hen. Something in their eyes would sharpen and they'd lean over and murmur to each other, making the water glimmer as they moved. That was what she wanted. She wanted to be the one that they saw.

Miss Naylor blew the whistle.

Nobody jumped. Izzy tested the water with one foot and then withdrew it.

'Come on. In. All of you.'

'Cold,' grumbled Mel.

Miss Naylor stepped up behind her.

'OK, OK, I'm *going*. Just *wait*.'

Jules raised her arms above her head and closed her eyes. When she dived, the overwhelming water stopped her from thinking about anything except remaining afloat. She wasn't a bad swimmer, but she wasn't fast, and therefore rarely attracted attention. Usually she took pleasure in the stroke of the water against her skin and the sense of a new, but not hostile, element. But this pool was so full of chlorine and her head was so full of Hen that she couldn't concentrate properly.

Halfway through Jules's seventh length, she parted the water and looked up. Miss Naylor was talking to the guard, a girl of not much more than eighteen with muscular shoulders and the corn-fed sheen of someone who had spent too long in a gym. She had on a light blue T-shirt with 'Detroit Athletics' written across it.

When they had finished, they flopped back onto the side. Miss Naylor walked back towards them. 'Bad luck. The life-guard needed to speak to me so I didn't manage to time you. You'll have to do those lengths again.'

'No *way*,' said Mel.

'Five minutes to catch our breath. Then another ten.'

Mel wailed. 'So *unfair*.'

'Burns those nasty little calories, swimming.'

Hen lay with her legs still dangling into the pool and her arms behind her head. Jules noticed the way the water gathered in a little pool where her rib cage ended and her stomach – or what was left of her stomach – began. She seemed indifferent to Miss Naylor, to them all.

'Lola. Up. Come on.'

Hen turned her head and said something Jules couldn't catch.

'Tough. You had enough energy to go chasing boys, didn't you?'

Hen turned her head away. Miss Naylor, standing above her, crouched down suddenly and put out her hand as if to grab one of Hen's arms. 'Get up. *Up.*'

Hen took a long time to sit upright.

'Go,' hissed Miss Naylor. And then to them all, standing on the side. 'Go. Go on. Get in. Swim, the lot of you.'

Jules just had time to see Hen's knees collapse underneath her, and the crashing trajectory as she half jumped, half fell over the side and into the pool. Then the water covered her.

✦

By the time Hen had been rescued, propped up on the side next to Izzy, wrapped in towels and given a lukewarm cup of tea (which she ignored), it was evident that there was no point in continuing with the swimming. When she saw Hen fall, Jules changed direction in mid-dive away from the deep end and towards the lifeguard. But the girl in the T-shirt had been watching and had already started out of her chair. Together she, Miss Naylor and Jules had levered Hen out of the water and dumped her, dripping and gasping, on the side of the pool. The lifeguard spoke to Hen softly, bent low near her head. Jules could see from the way she smiled that she was consoling Hen, and that Hen, however silent, was helped by the kindness.

Slack with staring, the others padded off to the changing rooms and changed in silence. They sat outside on the grass, picking through the contents of their backpacks. When Hen and Miss Naylor emerged, they looked up, not speaking.

Miss Naylor strode towards them. 'Come on.'

Jules fell into step beside Hen. 'What happened?'

Hen gave no sign of having heard.

'Did you feel ill?'

Nothing.

Jules tried again. 'God, Naylor's a cow. She ought to be sacked.'

Still nothing.

Jules didn't know how to speak any more. She wanted to tell Hen that when she had fallen, it had felt almost as if it was Jules herself crashing through the air. She wanted to say that things had gone too far, that Hen was too thin, that everything was wrong. She wanted to say that everything about Hen felt like an accusation now. She wanted to say she was sorry, even if she didn't know what she was sorry for. She wanted acknowledgement that Hen felt as sad and as weird as she did. She wanted Hen to say thank you for not quite rescuing her. She walked a little further, concentrating on the rhythm of their feet. Why was Hen staying so silent? What was the problem?

It took about half a mile before Jules lost her temper. Half a mile of hurrying to keep up, and half a mile of thinking about things so that they turned sour and annoying. Yves, the sandpit, the drink, the interrogation, the stuff in the church, the boys, Hen falling, Miss Naylor – all of it becoming one big furious stew. She felt wild all of a sudden, spoiling for . . . not a fight exactly, but a small bad-tempered victory, proof that if she felt bad, she could at least ensure that someone else felt worse.

She took off her jacket and swung it around her waist. 'You going up to Scotland for the holidays?'

Hen's back stiffened as if Jules had poked it. 'Yes.'

'With your dad?'

'Yes.'

'How come,' said Jules thoughtfully, 'nobody's ever met your dad? Everyone else's parents hang around. Your family – it's like they don't exist. Like to meet him.'

'No point.'

'Doesn't he ever come out of Scotland?'

'Sometimes.'

'Don't you want him to come and fetch you?'

'No.' Vehemently. 'It's fine.'

'D'you think . . .' – Jules gazed up at the trees – 'you're like you're sort of *ashamed* of him?'

'No.'

'So why does he never come down here?'

'Because it's difficult.'

'Why's it difficult?'

'It just is. He has to look after my sisters.'

'Does your dad have a funny accent?'

'No.'

'What sort of accent?'

'Just normal. Just English. He speaks English like normal.'

'Don't you want him to meet us? Me, and Caz, and Mel and people?'

'It doesn't . . . It isn't . . .'

'At the beginning,' said Jules, cheerily malevolent now, 'you used to talk about Scotland all the time. About your dad and your sisters. You never talk about them any more. Aren't you proud of them? Don't you want to tell us about Scotland any more?'

'Got bored.' Hen's voice seemed to be receding a little.

'Bored of what?'

'Bored. Just bored.'

'Bored of telling us? You said Scotland was cool.'

'Doesn't matter.'

'What doesn't matter?'

Hen turned. 'Don't want to say. I just don't want to, all right?'

Jules's eyes widened. 'OoooOOOooh. I was only *asking*.'

'Doesn't *matter*. Just *leave it*, right?'

'Don't you love your dad or something? Don't you want him to meet us?'

'Just *leave it*.' Hen lengthened her step, trying to outpace Jules.

'I'd really like to go to Edinburgh, see what it's like. D'you think I could ever come and stay?'

'*No.*'

'Why not?'

'Just . . . It's difficult.'

'Why's it difficult?'

'He's got stuff to do. He's busy.'

'All the time? He's doing stuff all the time?'

'Look, just stop fucking winding me up, OK? Leave it. My dad's got nothing to do with you. That stuff, it's not yours. It's nothing to do with you or Caz.'

Jules looked wounded. 'Fuck. God. I didn't know it was such a big deal.'

'I just don't want to talk about it. It isn't anything to do with you.'

'You're really ashamed of them, aren't you? Your family. What's wrong with them? They freaks or something?'

Hen didn't speak, just turned back to the path, put her head down and almost ran. Jules settled back to a more comfortable pace. The way she felt now was like she felt after she'd eaten a particularly complete meal.

Behind her, Izzy turned. 'Hang on,' she said, staring back up the road. 'Where's Ali?'

+

Ali was looking at Miss Naylor's wrinkles. There were two prominent ones which ran between her eyebrows from the top of her nose, four creases on her forehead as neat as foolscap lines and a few thin gatherings around her lips. There were the beginnings of crow's feet round her eyes – why, Ali couldn't think, since Miss Naylor wasn't exactly known for smiling – and the lines which ran from her nostrils to her mouth seemed to have become deeper in recent months. Every time Miss Naylor frowned, Ali had the sensation of watching time move. The frown made her older, the normal face made her younger. She watched the siltings of foundation round the corners of her nose, and wondered how Miss Naylor's life had brought her to this place.

The room was one of the better ones. It had a bunk bed in one corner where Miss Naylor had laid out a series of maps and papers, a larger bed in the centre of the room with a brown and pink duvet cover, a cheap wardrobe, a desk by the window and a basin. Apart from the papers and the duvet cover, there was nothing to indicate the personality of the room's occupant. No clothes, no jewellery, only some make-up by the basin and a bottle of anti-dandruff shampoo. There was no evidence of what Miss Naylor favoured as bedtime reading, no radio, no handbag, no sense of someone who had an existence beyond the school gates. She wondered again who Miss Naylor was. Had she once loved someone? Had they loved her back? What did she think about late at night when there was no one there? Were there still parts of her that remained human?

'And then?'

The late afternoon light was shining directly into Ali's eyes, and she was beginning to feel claustrophobic. They'd gone over it twice already. Everything, all the details from the moment she'd crept out of the swimming pool changing rooms to the moment she got back to the Manor. Which route she'd walked, where she'd stopped, what time she'd arrived at the station, which ticket she'd bought, which train she'd intended to catch, what she thought she was going to do at the other end. Whether she'd spoken to anyone, what they'd said, whether they'd given her anything, how long she'd waited, what she'd seen, what her mother had said on the phone when Miss Naylor rang, what her father would probably say when he was contacted. How long it had taken Jaws to search for her, what inconvenience it put them all to, how shamelessly inconsiderate . . . All the normal stuff. They'd confiscated her backpack and gone through it piece by piece. She'd said all she could say. And, so far, she'd said it quite well. She'd told them enough to pacify their suspicions, but not so much that they would find her openness surprising.

When she'd got to the station, there hadn't been too many people about: a few stragglers on the way back from shopping expeditions in Bristol, a greasy-looking man holding a cyclist's helmet, an old woman arguing with her middle-aged daughter. The car park was full to capacity with the cars of commuters, dusty in the silence and the early afternoon haze. Someone had been standing by the ticket booth, having a conversation with the guard. She could hear little snippets, stuff about timetables and delays. She had watched two little girls trying to give each other piggy backs and falling over. Their mother shaded her eyes against the sun and tried to joke with the man selling tickets. There had been something surreptitious in her gestures: the way she bent so close into the booth, the way she smiled with only one side of her mouth when she couldn't find the right change, the way she snapped at the children when they weren't really doing anything bad. Perhaps she was also planning to escape. If so, she wasn't doing it very well. Ali watched her, and learned. Best not to be like that. Best to look like everyone else, waiting and staring at the timetable boards.

Miss Naylor held up a crumpled five-pound note. 'How long did you expect this to last?'

Ali shrugged.

'You were going to get to Oxford and survive with this?'

'Maybe.'

'How, exactly?'

'Don't know.'

'You *don't know?* So you and your five pounds were just going to get there and see what happened? See if you could survive on the streets? Wander into a hotel and just hope that someone was handing out free rooms for the night?'

'Don't know.'

'Do you know what happens to people on the streets?'

'Yes.' Ali felt her mind recede. She remembered the trick she'd had when she was young of disappearing somewhere into her own head. She would slip so deep inside herself that the words rained down softly without ever quite touching their target. Her mother could shout all she liked, and Ali would just stand there like a pony in a snowstorm, patiently waiting till it was over and she could move again.

'So you know how many of them don't survive, or end up

dead or mugged or sick or raped? You know that some of them go missing and don't return? You know what it's like out there, do you?'

A shrug.

She tried a different tack. 'You are aware of how much concern you've caused your mother?'

'Mmmm.'

'And you don't mind? You don't mind the idea of your mother going frantic with worry, blaming herself, blaming us, blaming the school? You know she was just about to get in the car and drive all the way down here to look for you? That's all OK with you, is it?'

'Sorry.'

Miss Naylor rested her forehead on her hand. Although the gesture was supposed to imply exasperation, Ali was surprised to notice that she seemed tired. There was something in her shoulders and the angle of her spine which suggested a deeper weariness than that which came from interrogating a recalcitrant teenager.

Miss Naylor leaned back in her chair. 'Go,' she said. 'Just go. I'll think of a punishment later. And you can work out what you're going to tell your mother.'

Ali got up. Perhaps she should offer Miss Naylor something: a foothold, a clue, some small consolation. She stood in the grubby sunlight, looking down at Miss Naylor's hand where it rested on the desk. She tried to think of something to say, but nothing came. She turned and walked towards the door, feeling somehow dirtier than she had expected to. She no longer felt glad to have been found.

TUESDAY

'Results.' Miss Naylor slapped a pile of faxes down on the breakfast table. Hen heard the dry rustle of the pages, watched them creep, curling, back to the edge. 'We've been looking forward to these, haven't we, missies?'

Conversation had been desultory. Only Mel and Mina seemed to have enough energy to talk, but when Mel saw the faxes she stopped mid-sentence and put her hands to her face. 'Oh Jesus. Oh no.'

'Shall I read them out?'

'Couldn't you . . . ?' said Izzy.

'Aaaah.' Miss Naylor cocked her head to one side. 'Nervous, are we?'

'No. Just . . .'

'I could pin them to the board. I could stick them on the ceiling if you really want. The results will still be the same.'

Jules made a grab for the faxes. 'Can't we just look . . . ?'

'*Excuse* me, Julia.' The women in the canteen had stopped talking and were watching them across the tables. 'Melanie Baxter. Ready? B maths, C Eng. lit., Spanish B, French D, geography E . . .' Mel covered her face with her hands and groaned. 'Eng. lang. B, biology C, art A.'

'Catherine Fleming.' This time, it was the rest of the table who averted their eyes. They knew what was coming. 'All As except Bs in Eng. lang. and physics.'

Hen thought briefly of nudging Caz, of laughing, of taking the piss a little. But what would have felt right three days ago now seemed inconceivable. 'Isobel Mackeson. Mainly Cs. A in music and art, B in maths.'

'Lola Rettie.' Hen sat bolt upright, quite white. 'All As. We are clever, aren't we?'

Mel made vomiting motions. Hen blushed, fast and uncomfortable. The results didn't mean anything. They weren't even nice. She'd got them because she'd worked hard, harder than she'd ever bothered before. She wasn't sure why. The subjects were no more or less engaging and the teaching no better or worse than it had been in previous terms. True, they counted towards GCSEs, but so did other exams at other times. She'd worked because time spent not working seemed worse than the time spent working. She'd got them because work was the one anaesthetic which smoothed away food or home or Caz or guilt. And now, here, the results of all that work seemed just a handful of ashes. Her father would be pleased, but that was cheap consolation, and her mother . . . She didn't bother telling her mother about school stuff any more.

'Julia Prentice. Bs, mainly. A in biology and geography, C in French . . .' Pause. 'E in maths. Must do better, mustn't we?'

Jules looked over at Hen. The look was of such eviscerating hatred that Hen half smiled in shock.

Miss Naylor read out the others and slapped the faxes back

down on the table. 'You can check the percentages. Perhaps it will teach some of you a bit of maths.'

'Fuck,' said Mel thoughtfully. 'Fuck fuck fuck fuck fuck.'

+

They were sitting at a picnic bench, eating lunch. The usual packed stuff: a flabby ham sandwich, crisps, a carrot and a bar of chocolate so stale it had a white tidemark round the edges. The cycle ride had been fine so far. Or rather, it had been better than walking. Jules was glad to be out in the open. There was an air coming off the group now like the air before it snowed – tight, artificial, waiting. They'd only been at the Manor a week and already it felt like a lifetime.

Jules pulled away the bread from one side of her sandwich. One thin slice of bacon covered in what looked like rust, draped with a bit of rat's tail lettuce. What a rip-off, she thought, dumping the bread down on the table, folding the remaining triangle in half and stuffing it into her mouth.

The picnic table was one of four set out in a clearing with a concrete toilet block in one corner and three overflowing litter bins along one side. Perhaps on bright sunlit days this place might have been beautiful, but as it was, the creeping weeds and old Tesco carrier bags breathing in the wind gave it an air of perpetual autumn. Jules watched an empty bottle of tonic wine roll gently from one side of the bench to the other. Beside her were a little clutter of fag butts and the cap off a supermarket brand of vodka.

Hen, as usual, was fiddling with her lunch. She'd managed to pass her crisps on to Ali and the can of Coke to Caz. The sandwich had disappeared – Jules could see a pale square poking out from a patch of dandelions – and Hen was evidently trying to find a way to dispose of her carrot. First she'd taken a small bite of it, which she chewed for an unnecessary length of time. Then she examined the rest of it, smoothed out the bag her lunch had come in and put the carrot down on it. After a minute or so, she picked it up again and took another nibble. This time, when it came away, Jules noticed a tiny spot of what looked like blood on the top. Then she put it down again and, with one finger, began idly rolling it round the bag.

Caz had closed her eyes and was resting her head on her hands. The carrot rolled this way and that.

'Why don't you eat it?'

Hen seemed not to hear her.

'Hen,' said Jules, louder, 'why don't you eat it?'

No reply.

'Go on. Eat it. I dare you.'

'Will. In a minute.' Her voice was almost a whisper.

'No, you won't,' said Jules, remorseless. 'You'll just go on fiddling with it and then you'll throw it away when you think we're not looking.' Caz sat up, listening.

'I will. In a minute.'

'Bullshit. Course you won't. You never do.' The carrot rolled a little way towards Jules and then stopped. 'You haven't eaten anything today. You got rid of breakfast and now you're getting rid of lunch.'

'I *will*.'

'What's wrong with you? Do you have to do all this attention-seeking crap all the time? It's so fucking *boring*.'

'I'm *not*! I *don't*!'

'Yes you do. You do this every day.'

'Just leave me alone! Fuck *off*!'

Jules felt her brakes exhale. There was something exhilarating about telling the truth, even if she knew she'd probably get punished for it. She leaned closer to Hen, light and fast. 'None of us give a toss if you eat or not. None of us give a *fucking flying fuck.* We're all just sick of watching you doing your sad retard anorexic shit.'

Hen's eyes flickered wildly.

'You can starve yourself to death if you like. We don't care. You're so boring these days. You didn't used to be so boring.'

'I'm not. I'm not!'

'Oh yeah? So how come you look like Miss Scary Twiglet Woman? How come you look like a fucking *monkey* half the time?'

'I don't! I *don't!*' She seemed almost at screaming pitch.

'So why d'you do it then? Playing with your breakfast, throwing everything up. Why do you bother?'

'I don't! I'm not!'

'Course you bloody do. That's all you do these days. And you look like shit.'

'I don't . . . I don't care! *Just fuck off!*' She untangled herself from the bench and ran towards the forest.

'Lola!' Miss Naylor, who had been writing notes at one of the empty benches, looked up. 'Where are you going?'

Hen kept running.

'LOLA RETTIE. Get back here now!'

Hen slowed.

'Where did you think you were going?'

Hen said nothing. They were all watching her now.

'Lola. I asked you where you thought you were going.'

'Nowhere.' Her voice was quiet again.

'What did you say?'

'I said, nowhere, Miss Naylor. I was going nowhere.'

'Thank you. Well, if you're not going anywhere, could you come back here?'

She walked over to where Mel and Mina were sitting, folded herself onto the bench and dipped her head. When Mina touched Hen on one shoulder, she flinched.

Jules turned back to the table. There on the plastic bag, rolling slightly in the breeze, was the uneaten carrot. Oh, *very* clever, she thought wearily.

+

The afternoon ride seemed to last forever. The day had turned flat, and the light had taken on a brassy orange tint. The clouds slid lower, became darker, but did not change or break. What warmth there was still in the ground seemed sour and unwashed, and there were more flies around than there had been before. The air stuck in Jules's throat, making her feel out of breath even on the flat.

Despite the weather, they made faster time. After a couple of miles, the track joined a tarmacked cycle path which ran through the forest. In places it joined the road, and Jules felt the cars' slipstream shove at her as they passed. Miss Naylor rode up at the front, allowing them a view of broad blue bottom. She rode, thought Jules, as if she was taking part in the bloody Tour de France, bent down low over the handlebars, bum in the air, helmet trembling with effort. The others wobbled out behind.

They turned off the main road and onto a lane which wound through the hills, bordered by high beech hedgerows and vivid green limes. The verges had been stitched up tight with dog roses and brambles many years ago, and were now so overgrown that the lane seemed uncomfortably crowded. Jules

had the confused sensation of riding her bike down the course
of a deep silvery river with the trees and the shrubs forming a
trench around them. The lane bent upwards, and she could see
Miss Naylor shaking with the effort of forcing her bike up the
hill. It felt peaceful here, off the main road, with nothing much
except the sound of effortful breathing and the fizz of distant
insects. They rounded a bend and the road climbed slowly on.

When they got to the top they stopped by the entrance to
a field and sat down, breathing hard.

'Where's Isobel?' said Miss Naylor, leaning her bike against
a fencepost. Mel shrugged.

'Hasn't she been following us?'

'She was there when we came off the main road,' said Jules
eventually. 'I saw her.'

'Did anyone see her after that?'

The others looked at the sky.

'Someone better go and look for her.'

'She always turns up eventually,' said Jules.

' "Eventually" isn't good enough. We don't have time for
"eventually". This is supposed to be a competition against the
clock.'

'She'll get here. She always takes a bit longer.'

'Perhaps you'd like to volunteer, then. Go on.'

Jules slumped back against the gate. 'Do I have to?'

'Yes, Julia. You do have to. And next time don't be so
cheeky.'

It wasn't Miss Naylor's unconcealed sneer which really got
her, Jules thought. What really got her was Caz's turned-away
smile and Hen's pretence at making daisy chains, like she
hadn't been watching Jules all along, just waiting for her to get
it wrong again. Jules rode fast back down the hill, powered as

much by rage as by gravity. Fuck them, she thought. Fuck Caz with her beautiful indifference, fuck Miss Naylor for being the world's most vicious old lesbian, and most of all fuck Hen for everything: for abandoning her, for getting those results, for being an attention-seeking scrawny-arsed bitch, for being thinner than her, for being more fucking precious than all of them put together, for being fucking *clever*, for God's sake. All of them, every single one of them, could go and get stuffed. Particularly fuck Izzy. Izzy was a tragedy, a tedious burden, a useless waste of space. Izzy ought to have been put down at birth. Jules held her head high and glared at the lane. Izzy was nowhere, not halfway down the long straight stretch, not on the corner, not in any of the grassy lay-bys. She cycled on, flinging the stirrups around so fast that they kept recoiling and whacking her ankles. By the time she came round the bend at the top of the hill, she was snarling with frustration.

It was only when she was nearly back down where the main road connected to the lane that she saw a figure pushing a bike very slowly towards her. At first it was difficult to tell if it was Izzy, since she was bent down over the handlebars with her hair low over her face. Jules stopped. She could see even at this distance that there was something funny about the way Izzy looked. Oh God, she thought dully, she'll be crying. Does she always have to be crying?

'Izzy?'

Izzy made an unspecific high-pitched noise. Jules couldn't tell if it was speech or a sob.

'What's wrong?' Jules saw something moving on her arm and noticed for the first time a trickle of muddy blood. 'Are you all right?'

Izzy looked up. Her face was scarlet, not with sweat or

effort, but with something else. She seemed weirdly blown up, as if something had crept inside her and exhaled. All her features had blurred into each other, and her forehead was speckled with nettle-sting blotches. Her arms had swelled and taken on the mottled purplish colours of salami. She looked almost like a stranger, like a Down's Syndrome child, her flesh melting down and forming something – someone – else. On her legs, the skin had flaked and boiled as if someone had flung acid at her. And there was blood smeared across the palm of her hand. Jules felt many things at once: a kind of revulsion, a kind of fascination, a deep thrilling urgency, and – just for a second – an odd desire to cry. The blood, Izzy's blood, looked so beautiful against the green grass. But Izzy, Izzy herself, with the eczema and the swelling and the grey saliva at the corners of her lips . . . Izzy was not beautiful. My God, she thought, almost impressed, Izzy is stupendously ugly.

'Fuck,' she said, unthinking. 'Fuck *me*. You look *horrible*.'

Izzy tried to speak but nothing came out except a high stringy wheeze. Her lips were white with effort, and Jules could see two little pale spots at the side of her nostrils. 'Where's your medicine?'

Izzy shook her head.

Jules dropped her bike down on the verge, grappled the backpack chained over the back of Izzy's bike and began scrabbling through it. Izzy usually carried a small pharmacy of necessary medicines: stuff for the eczema, stuff for the insects, stuff for the hayfever, stuff for every likely and unlikely emergency. Jules had spent the last two years taking the piss out of her hypochondria. But this time there were only a box of plasters, a pair of scissors and a half-eaten packet of crisps.

'Where's your medicine?'

Izzy didn't seem able to let go of the bike. Jules realized that it must be propping her up as much as she was propping it.

'Didn't you bring it?'

Izzy shook her head.

'Why not?'

It took a while for Izzy to speak. 'Gone,' she whispered.

'Gone? Finished?'

A shake of the head.

'Just gone?'

A nod.

'Where gone? Don't you have more?'

Izzy swayed and closed her eyes.

'Wait there. I'll get Naylor.'

Jules swung herself back onto her bike and began to cycle back up the hill. The pedals rotated but they didn't seem to carry her along fast enough. Then she remembered something: Izzy shouldn't be sitting there on the verge, in all that dust and pollen. She turned round. There was nowhere else for her to go; it was all green round here, all fields and grass and glowering English summer.

'Just stay in the lane. In the lane. Away from the side,' Jules yelled over her shoulder.

She couldn't get the bike to hurry up. The lane bent its leisurely way back up the hill, meandering round the forest like it had all the time in the world. Jules heaved a few more yards, dismounted and began to half run, half clamber uphill, pushing the bike in front of her. How had Izzy got in such a state? Why hadn't she said anything while they were coming along the road? Why hadn't Naylor been watching out for her? Where the fuck had her medicines gone? And where did the blood come from? Jules gasped round the corner, feeling her breath thunder in her throat and her hands grow sticky on the plastic handlebars. It occurred to her that this journey was heroic; that she was a heroine. The thought made her want to cry again.

When she finally hauled her way to the top of the hill she found the others exactly as they had been, not speaking, sitting on the verge or resting against the gate. Caz had lain back and put her jacket behind her head. She was gazing up at the sky, watching the clouds slip by.

Miss Naylor saw her first. 'Where is she?'

Jules shuddered to a halt. 'Something's happened. She's all blown up. She's gone funny.'

'How do you mean, gone funny?'

'She can't breathe. She just . . . isn't breathing right.'

The others sat up and were watching her. 'Where's her medicine?'

'Not there.'

'Why not?'

'Don't know. She said it was gone.'

'Come on. You'd better show me.'

Jules gasped once and swung herself back onto the bike.

'Shall I come?' said Mel suddenly.

Miss Naylor ignored her. 'Stay there. Wait.'

Jules felt a bud of something like joy swell in her chest. *That'll fucking show them,* she thought, glancing back at Caz and Hen. Caz had stood up and was watching her. But Hen was still lying on the grass, staring up towards the tracing-paper moon, not looking at any of them.

The bends of the lane felt almost familiar now. Jules's brakes shrieked as she hurtled round the corners. Miss Naylor followed, the zips of her tracksuit top flapping in the breeze, her eyes narrowed, intentful. Jules had just enough time to notice how absurd Miss Naylor looked before she overtook, spinning past her and down out of sight.

They found Izzy where Jules had left her, half in the lane, half out of it. The bike was flung down next to her and she was using her backpack as a pillow, propping herself up so she could breathe. Miss Naylor dropped her own bike and ran over to where Izzy was sitting.

'Where's your medicine?' she said sharply.

Izzy lifted her head a little.

'It's not there,' said Jules. 'It's not in her bag. I looked.'

'Well, where is it then?'

Jules bent down. 'Are you OK?'

It was clear that Izzy wasn't OK at all. The white spots at the side of her nostrils had spread, her eyes were dark with fear and her lips were turning grey. When she looked up, her eyes held Jules's remotely. The strange abstracted look in her eyes frightened Jules. It was the same look that Yves had given her as he lunged above her on Friday night.

Miss Naylor leaned past her and shook Izzy by the shoulder. '*Where's. Your. Medicine?*' She sounded as if she was talking to a slow-witted foreigner.

Jules could hear Izzy's lungs, a thin scream of air heaving in and out. The blood on Izzy's legs was beginning to congeal. She must have fallen off the bike at some point.

'*Isobel. Where. Is. Your. Medicine?*' Miss Naylor's face was so close Jules could see the glitter of new sweat on her lip.

'It's not there,' she said impatiently. 'I've looked.'

'Isobel. WE NEED. TO. FIND. YOUR. MEDICINE.' She touched Izzy's arm. 'You must know where it is.'

'*It isn't there.* She hasn't got it.'

'Well, where is it then?'

'I don't know. It doesn't matter. Just get her to the hospital.'

'She'll be fine. If we just find her drugs, she'll be fine.'

Jules spoke slowly. 'THEY. AREN'T. THERE. I *promise.* I've *looked.*'

Miss Naylor went over to her own backpack, groped around in it and produced a small chemist's first-aid pack from the bottom. Inside were bandages, gauze, some sticking plasters, a tube of Savlon and a leaflet. Miss Naylor tucked the sticking plasters back into the pack and began flicking through the leaflet, presumably searching for something which covered finding speechless thirteen-year-old girls covered in blood and unable to breathe lying by the side of country lanes in the middle of summer. The leaflet was evidently not forthcoming, and after a moment she flung it aside. Then she picked out the tube of Savlon and crouched down in front of Izzy. She ripped off the packaging from one of the antiseptic wipes and began stroking Savlon over the graze.

'There, now,' she was saying. 'There, now. Silly girl. Just being silly. Silly about nothing.' She was trying to speak softly but her voice sounded wrong, as if it might split if she spoke too loud.

It took a while for Jules to realize that Miss Naylor did not know what to do. As she watched the white first-aid leaflet fluttering over the grass, she felt a jab of loneliness so powerful it almost winded her. She understood that Miss Naylor knew nothing, that all the bullying of the past few years had been for nothing. Miss Naylor was as scared as she was.

'Ring for an ambulance.'

Izzy's foot jerked sideways, but she was too far gone to give any other acknowledgement.

Miss Naylor turned slowly, with the gauze still in one hand. 'No. You can't.'

'Why not?'

'It isn't necessary.'

Jules watched her. 'Do you . . . Do you know first aid?' she said conversationally.

Miss Naylor swivelled again. 'Find the medicine, for God's sake.' She turned back to Izzy's leg, wiping the gauze up and down as if soothing herself.

Jules went over to Miss Naylor's backpack, lifted her mobile phone from the top pocket and crept behind the nearby lime tree. She wasn't used to this kind of mobile, and it seemed to take forever before she found a dial tone. When she did, she stared once more at Izzy, grey-lipped and almost unconscious, and Miss Naylor bent over her knee, wiping and wiping. She knew that she wasn't doing this for Izzy; she was doing it against Miss Naylor. Izzy was ill, Miss Naylor was useless, and she felt only an uncrossable distance from them both. Then she dialled 999.

+

They were sitting in the TV room, watching but not really seeing. Jules was slumped in the depths of the sofa, arms crossed, her eyes half closed. She hadn't moved for the last half-hour, just sat there squinting at the screen. Caz had curled herself tight into one of the armchairs and was rolling her rings up and down each finger, listening to their faint metallic tinkle. Mel and Mina were together on the sofa again. The room seemed to be getting colder.

Nobody seemed much interested by the TV, but there was nothing else to do. They could have gone upstairs and sat around staring at the space where Izzy used to be, but somehow that idea didn't seem very welcoming. Or they could have gone outside, taken a walk, sat on the roof. But what would that have achieved? It would just have been another reminder of Izzy, and – though what had happened today did have a kind of sick thrill to it – nobody really seemed to want to recreate it. Ali got the impression that they were here staring at some stupid programme about plant life only because watching a screen meant that they didn't have to watch each other.

Jaws walked in and stood facing them. 'Izzy's all right. She's fine.' They watched her without interest, as if she was just another form of TV.

'She'll be back in another couple of days. Just shock from the fall and an adverse reaction. No long-term damage.' She sounded as if she had borrowed the words from someone else. 'But in the meantime, we need to contact her parents. The hospital needs to. We've got a number in Surrey, but there's nobody there. Has Izzy said where they might be?'

Jules shook her head.

Mina looked up. 'What happened to her medicine?'

'No one knows. Perhaps it fell out of her backpack. Her parents . . .'

'They're on holiday,' said Ali. 'I think.'

'Do you know where they were going?'

'She didn't say. Wasn't for long.'

'Did they leave a number?'

'Don't know. Don't think so.'

Ali glanced back at the television. There was a picture of a little insignificant plant, one small green shoot without any leaves. It was creeping out of the damp earth and, as the film speeded up, the little shoot started wriggling over towards another plant. Behind it, more of these pallid shoots appeared, grew tentacles, began spreading up from the ground. All the tentacles reached out greedily, swaying like little periscopes.

She heard Mel behind her. 'What happened?'

'She seems to have got separated from the rest of you and fallen off her bike. Maybe it was shock or maybe something stung her, but she had something called an anaphylactic reaction. If it happens again, it would have to be treated very quickly.'

The little shoots had started running along the ground, twitching, as if they were looking for something. Then they leapt skywards and latched onto this other plant – a perfectly innocuous thing, just sitting there being green and planty and minding its own business – and started squeezing it.

'Or what?' There was avarice in Mel's voice.

'Or things could get serious.'

'Like what serious?'

Jaws ran a finger along her neck, rubbing at the muscles. 'Or it might be fatal.'

Mel giggled. 'Wow.'

All the little snakey strands crept upwards, reaching out and binding themselves round and round the vivid stem. Ali could see the little plant growing pale and writhing slightly. It struggled upwards for a few seconds and then lurched sideways before letting itself be overwhelmed and falling under the swelling tendrils into the darkness. The tendrils moved on, staring across the livid air, crossing from plant to plant, looking for something to steal.

'So none of you know where her parents are?'

'Nuh.'

Ali heard rustling, and a faint, very faint, sucking sound. She watched the little shoots abandon the devoured plant and move across the earth.

+

Hen leaned over and prodded her fingers down her throat. A torn fingernail rasped at the back of her mouth and she moved slightly against the feeling. It was becoming increasingly difficult to get anything to come up. She'd stay lurching and retching for what seemed like hours. She loathed this. She loathed crouching over her own vomit, trying to rid herself of her insides. Nothing she told herself about it – that she'd feel better afterwards, that she had to because she was stupid, that if she didn't, she'd inflate quick as a car tyre – made it any better. It still felt as if she was trying to rip out her lungs, her heart, her guts. Only by thinking about the most unpleasant things her imagination could regurgitate was she able to do it at all.

The air was tight out here, as tight as it was inside. It wasn't particularly warm – the tiles on the roof were cool when she leaned against them – but the air was close and her skin was a little moist to the touch. The summer evenings felt flat and aged, as if all the freshness had gone out of the world. It felt odd being outside, but there was nowhere else to go. Someone was in the bathroom and she no longer dared use the toilet at this time of day. If someone came up, she'd just have time to hide the bag behind the loose bricks and light a fag. She looked down at the bag's contents. There were flakes of brown in there, glaucous strings of saliva, two or three green-tinged fragments of something that might once have been fruit. The rest was only bile. She had to close her nostrils and breathe through her mouth; the acid stench of vomit was so strong that it made her feel faint. She felt as if her insides had turned cannibal, as if something was devouring her from within. As if it didn't stop at her stomach but crept further and further, corrupting something more profound inside her.

When all of this had started, it had seemed a way of making things easier. If she just lost a bit of weight, she'd feel stronger about things, more able to deal with the daily slights of existence. She'd just be Hen with thirty per cent less fat, stripped of surplus, pure unfussed essence of Hen. She'd look better, be more pleasing to the eyes of her beholders. She'd feel lighter, airier, less encumbered by fear and old debts. Something like that, anyway. She couldn't actually remember how the thinking went any more. All she could recall was that she'd started off with a sense that life would somehow be simpler if there was less of her around, and now everything seemed infinitely more complicated. As she got lighter, the stuff in her head got heavier and heavier, until she could barely drag herself out of bed in the mornings.

Hen could no longer remember a time when she had felt anything other than panic. She couldn't remember curiosity or sadness or hope or exasperation. She couldn't remember the correct response to a lamb chop or a handsome man. She took her cue from others, or she got out of the way. What had seemed close before now seemed further away, as if she only observed the others, instead of being involved with them.

Somewhere far away was the sense of how things used to be. The past made her ashamed, but it also made her feel . . . well, nostalgic, almost. Nostalgic for a time when she hadn't felt so empty and so heavy both at once. Nostalgic for a time without worry or guilt or the inexorable need to expel the confusion inside.

She had, she supposed, been a greedy child. She'd loved food, kitchens, the blowsy scents of cafes and tearooms. She had, to her shame, clamoured to sit in cake shops and restaurants, licking pastry off her fingers, winning one or other parent into another slice of fondant. Her tastes weren't expensive, they were old-fashioned Scottish tastes: sweets and chain-store biscuits, cheap chocolate and Wall's ice lollies. She'd run miles for a mouthful of carbohydrate, climb obediently into bed for the promise of an electric-green tea-cake. She thought of herself now with disgust, a saucer-eyed dumpling shovelling offal into an insatiable gob. Now, she looked at food differently. Food wasn't a question of nice or nasty, it was a question of safe or unsafe. Raw tomato safe, cake unsafe. Boiled cabbage safe, pasta unsafe. She couldn't remember what foods she liked or disliked, all she could remember was the foods that made her fearful.

She tried thinking of the woman on the road again. Her face, her clothes, the blood on her legs. But she'd seen the image so many times, looped it round and round in her mind, that it was almost exhausted now. Overused, overplayed, emptied. It had become something else, something melded with the sight of Izzy raw and wheezing on the verge. The woman was not the woman any more. She'd crept away from the motorway into Hen's dreams, slithered through the cracks of her waking life, become not a nightmarish stranger on a road, but all the people she spent her life with. Hen couldn't think of the woman and find her repulsive any longer because she'd just end up thinking about Caz, or Izzy, or Miss Naylor. Not that the thought of Izzy wasn't revolting. Hen thought of her now, the last image of her sitting in the lane. She'd only seen her for a couple of seconds as she came speeding down the road. Izzy was sitting with her legs out in front of her and her back very straight. All she could see were Izzy's legs, a bright wrong red. Normally, Izzy's eczema just looked like a snowfall of skin. But this was different. This was as if Izzy had stripped herself down to a different self. There were fires, thought Hen, that lived for years behind the walls of houses, muttering along quite softly, warming the woodwork, smouldering in the skirting boards. And then something – some chance spark, some increase in temperature – would ignite them. She'd seen a film about it once, late at night, and been awestruck by the malicious beauty of the flames. Izzy looked like that, as if somewhere inside herself she was on fire. She had stared, fascinated, repulsed, at the stranger on the verge. Then the ambulance men had stepped in front of Izzy, obscuring her from view. When they bent over her with the syringe, Hen wondered how they could bear to touch her.

She closed her eyes, and the sight of Izzy by the verge wavered and became something else, someone else. It was her own disgustingness she saw in Izzy, it was the knowledge that Izzy was merely a reflected image of herself, her trembling thighs, her monkeyed face – her, bent over a bowl or a bag, being sick. She could see herself, up here forever, eternally vomiting up her hatreds. She was stupid, loathsome, thick; just a piece of oozing putrescent shit. She'd never be as good as Caz. She'd never come close. Sometimes when Caz looked at her these days, she thought she saw contempt in her eyes. Which was all she deserved, really.

She leaned against the tiles, feeling their roughness against her back, and stared into the bag again. She heaved once or twice, but nothing came up. Not even when she stopped thinking about Izzy and thought about maggots and Miss Naylor. Not even when she thought about the woman on the motorway. Nothing. There was nothing there any more.

+

'Ali?' said a small voice in the darkness. 'Will you read to us?'

Ali sat up. She couldn't see the speaker's face, but she knew it was Jules. Everyone had been unusually quiet this evening. The flat duvet over Izzy's bed seemed too neat and too empty for comfort.

'OK,' she said, groping for her torch. 'I haven't got that much, though.' She pulled open her top drawer and began ruffling around.

'Doesn't matter. Just something.'

Ali plucked out a handful of books. 'There's the library stuff.'

'No.'

'*Wuthering Heights?*'

'No way.'

'*Animal Farm?*'

'No.'

'There isn't anything else. You sure you don't want the library stuff?'

'No,' said Jules. 'No sexy bits.'

Ali got out of bed and shone her torch into the back of the drawer. There were two books left. Ali felt diffident about owning up to either of them. One of them had been given to her by her father years ago, and she'd bought the other one. She touched their covers and then withdrew her hand.

Jules sat upright, watching her. 'What have you got?'

'Children's books.'

'What sort?'

'Old fairy stories. Like *Rumplestiltskin* and *Cinderella* and *Puss In Boots*.'

Under her duvet, Mel snorted. But to Ali's astonishment, neither Jules nor Caz laughed. 'Perfect,' said Jules.

'Really? Are you sure?'

'Yes. Read them.' There was something in Jules's voice which didn't invite argument. Even weirder, none of the rest of the room seemed to want to contradict her.

Ali lay down, positioned the torch, and began to read.

WEDNESDAY

Jules was upstairs sitting on her bed. There was an odd smell in the room, strong and slightly acidic, which made her want to wrinkle her nose. It was probably the patch of damp on the wall. Jules was quite sure it had swollen since they'd got here, grown outwards so what had looked like a cloud when they arrived looked like a thunderstorm now. She was sure it used to have a distinct borderline, a wavering greenish grime separating the damp bit from the dry bit. Over the past few days the line had wandered almost to the corner of the window frame, and she could no longer tell which parts were diseased and which healthy.

The damp bit wasn't alone. The whole Manor seemed to exist to an alternative schedule, swelling and oozing like something half alive. At night the building made noises Jules had never heard any other building make: odd snappings, trickling in places with no taps, the rattle of glass on days with no wind. Sometimes when she crept to the bathroom in the night, the floorboards would be hot under her bare feet, and the walls wept condensation when she touched them. The light switch had given her a shock yesterday, the door handle stung her with static, and strange draughts crept up from the dark places below. Years of neglect must be taking their toll and now the building stank and drooled like something demented.

She would be glad to leave. When they'd first rolled up the drive she remembered looking up at this big sullen building and thinking that perhaps it contained possibilities. Now everything seemed off-kilter, damaged, wrong. When she had argued with Caz or Hen before, things had repaired themselves fairly quickly. But the events of the past few days, all of them, one after the other, did not seem mendable any more. She could feel something pressing dully at the back of her mind, like the beginnings of a headache.

She could hear Mel opposite bouncing on her bed. The bed didn't bounce properly because the mattress was too stiff, so every time she thudded down on it, her shoulders sagged slightly and the mattress made a faint crumping noise. 'Holi-*daaay*. Cele-*braaate*. Holi-*daaay*. Cele-*braaate*.' She began thudding up and down more rapidly, as if rising to the trot. 'Outta here, outta here, outta here, almos' outta here . . .'

Mina had a small pot of purple glittery nail varnish by her side and was gently stroking it onto the top of her pencil case.

'Shut up,' said Jules.

'Holi-*daaay*. Cele-*braaate*. Holi-*daaay* . . .'

'Mel.' Jules turned her head slightly. 'Can't you shut the fuck up?'

Mel stopped bouncing. 'WoooOOOoo. Holi-*daaay*, Cele-*braaate*—'

'MEL, will you fucking *shut up?* Don't want to listen to some fucking fat juvenile git.'

'HOLIDAAAY. CELEBRAAATE.' Mel took a strand of chewing gum out of her mouth and twiddled it insolently round one finger. 'Just because . . .'

'Just because what?'

'Just because you can't lighten up any more.'

'Give me a break . . .'

'Just because you found Izzy doesn't mean anything.'

'It's got nothing to fucking do with fucking *any* of that. Can't you just *be quiet* for a second?'

Mel considered Jules, her head on one side. 'You're dead chuffed with yourself.'

'Oh, please.' Jules picked up the magazine she'd been reading and hurled it away. 'You're sad, you know that?'

'True, though. And you've pissed off Caz.'

Jules got up. 'If you haven't got anything better to think about . . .' Her words were lost in the corridor.

+

Hen stood by the hatch in the canteen waiting for a meal she didn't want. She could hear the women moving around inside the kitchen, shifting metal tureens from one place to another. Hen didn't like the way the women looked at her as if there was something about her that belonged to them. She dreaded this daily trek up and down, fetching the food, finding somewhere to put it.

She picked up a plate. It was a dull turquoise green, the colour they painted the walls of public toilets. It was chipped, and a thin crack ran down the middle. Around the rim there was a smirr of grease, and when she moved it against the light she could see the grease shining at her. She tried to put the plate back and take another one but one of the women saw her and shook her head.

There wasn't much of a selection. Chicken or sausages – both wrinkled beyond recognition – some mashed potato, a few flaccid tomatoes, some baked beans and a bowl of salad. Hen watched the food and the women watched her.

'Go on, pet,' said one of them. She had sludgy brown eyes and a dribble of something down the front of her uniform. 'You look like you could do with a bit of feeding up. How about a sausage?'

She shook her head.

'Potato?'

'No thanks.'

'Got to eat something. Come on.'

The clatter of the kitchen began to press at Hen's head. The striplights shone down on the sausages, making them glisten, making everything look sick. The woman picked up a spoon and shovelled on a mound of potato. 'Here. This won't do you any harm. That and some salad. Are you on a diet?'

Hen couldn't speak. All that happened when she opened her mouth was a dull sort of creak.

'Go on.' The woman's voice was conspiratorial. 'If I had a figure like yours, I wouldn't worry about what I ate ever again.'

Hen pushed her plate towards the spoon. If she didn't take it, there would be a scene and she'd end up having to eat with Naylor again. The woman grabbed the plate and whacked two big spoonfuls of baked beans onto it before Hen could say anything. 'There.' She stood back. 'Nothing wrong with baked beans, is there?'

A bluebottle which had been fizzing for a while in the corner of Hen's vision swept round and down onto the plate. Hen could see its bluey shine, the way its little legs worked towards the food. The woman flicked at it with her free hand. Hen was beginning to wonder if she might faint again.

She took the plate and looked at it. Then, with the woman

and Miss Naylor still watching her, she walked over to the bin in the corner of the hall and scraped the contents in. She was aware of their gaze on her, but it no longer seemed to make much difference. She put the plate down on the side and walked out of the room. No one spoke; no one tried to call her back.

+

'Here,' said Rob, holding up a hand-rolled cigarette. 'Want one?'

Ali looked at the little white tube. It was skinny – not much wider than one of those hollow plastic toothpicks from the canteen – but neat. For a second, she wondered if she ought to take it. 'No, thanks.'

He smiled. 'I thought all teenagers smoked. I thought it was compulsory for teenagers to smoke.'

'No.' Ali sounded stiffer than she intended. 'They make me cough.'

'Quite right.' He put the little tube back into its tin and leaned back. They were sitting outside again, not far from the fence which marked the end of the Manor grounds. From time to time, Ali glanced upwards. The sky had turned an odd yellow colour, and the clouds had a sickly taint to them, as if the weather itself was ill. It would probably rain again before long.

She was fighting hard to suppress a feeling of unspecified urgency. Perhaps she shouldn't bother with this. Perhaps it would be easier just to go back to the Manor and submit to the inevitability of things. Perhaps she should not be sitting here with a strange man in a strange place plotting strange futures. What if she had misjudged and got Rob wrong? After all, wasn't this exactly what she'd been taught to fear? Men who offered things to children, men in cars, men who followed her through midnight streets, men concealing unknown weapons under overcoats, men who flashed, men who spat or thumped or raped or groped. Men who talked to girls when they didn't have anything to say. Men who looked at girls in *that* sort of way. Men who were interested in girls. Men who did anything other than act completely indifferent to girls. She was supposed to be suspicious of all of them, of what they might want and what they might take away. It was just a standard rule of life; women were safe and men were unsafe. So how was she supposed to judge them if she never got close enough to figure out how they worked? How would she understand which ones wanted to steal from her when she didn't even know what she had to offer?

When she thought about it, she wasn't scared of Rob in the normal way. She wasn't scared of being mugged or murdered or – God forbid – given the sort of confectionery that led to being shoved in the back of an unmarked van, driven to a nearby wasteland and becoming the subject of an unsolved police enquiry. She couldn't be mugged by a man who smoked roll-ups, anyway; it would be humiliating. And she'd long ago decided that she was too ugly to get raped. It wasn't any of that. It was just that she feared the infinite mysteries of other people's minds. Particularly now.

'So,' said Rob. 'How did your plan go?'

Ali put her hand up to fiddle with her hair, remembered that it would make her look nervous and put it down again. 'Fine. They were angry, but they're always angry.'

'And you still want to do this?'

'Yes. I think so.'

He looked over towards the river. 'I'm still not sure I understand your reasons.'

Now she came to think of it, Ali wasn't sure she understood her reasons either. It was just a feeling, a low-down lumpy feeling like dread or shame. 'I don't . . . I can't . . . I can't see why I'm here any more.' It sounded lame, but it was the truth.

'You're here to get educated. Same as anyone else your age. No one likes it, but everyone has to do it.'

'You sound like my mother.'

He smiled. 'Do I?'

'It isn't the education bit. I don't mind that. It's the other stuff.'

'How do you know the other stuff would be better anywhere else?'

'It wouldn't be so tight.' Ali's hands made a strangling gesture. 'It wouldn't be like you could never get free.'

'And you know if you get found there will be hell to pay?'

She nodded. 'I don't mind that. It's always the same.'

'If I get found, there will be bigger hell to pay. There's probably some law against aiding and abetting disgruntled thirteen-year-olds.'

'Fourteen,' said Ali.

'Thirteen or fourteen, you're still under age.'

'If you don't, then I'll just do it anyway.'

He looked up at her for the first time. There was amusement in the corners of his eyes, and something else as well.

Ali found she couldn't hold his gaze for very long.

'I believe you,' he said.

THURSDAY

Hen picked up the letter on the table. It was addressed in handwriting that she didn't recognize, weird handwriting that sloped backwards and forwards at the same time. The letter inside was written on paper so flimsy it was almost see-through.

Dear Hen, it said. *I hope you got back alright on Sunday. I am sorry about the argument. It must have been because I'm not a very good host – especially not in this dump!* ~~When I next see you.~~ *Life here is boring as usual. It would be nice to see you sometime. Maybe it would be fun to meet up and talk about music and stuff with you sometime. We could go to a gig. I've got some amazing new stuff – the best yet. Good funcky stuff. I think you might like them. I am sorry about the business with Caz. Nick is a mate but he can be unfair sometimes. He thinks about his reputation too much of the time.* ~~The darts.~~ *Don't tell him I said anything. Anyway. I hope you are going to have good holidays.*

Are you going to Scotland? My number at home is above.

Be cool, Adey.

There were two very small crosses at the bottom. If they're small, wondered Hen, does that mean they're like pecks on the cheek?

'What's that?' Caz extended her hand.

'Letter.'

'Who from?'

'Adey.'

'Eeeuwww!' Mel had overheard. 'He fancies you.'

'Don't think so. He just wants to talk about music.'

Fancying people, desiring them, seemed a faraway notion. What did fancying mean anyway? Was it a form of physical desire – in which case she felt only a vast and long-gone astonishment – or merely that you got embarrassed when they were mentioned? If embarrassment was the standard, then perhaps she did fancy Adey.

'Can I see?'

'N-no.'

'Why, babe?' Caz seemed soft all of a sudden.

'I . . . it isn't . . .'

Caz took the letter gently out of her hands, read it through and then passed it back. Hen looked down at the table where the ants still roamed. When she looked up again, Caz had gone.

+

Izzy was sitting on her bed staring at them. They were staring back. No one was speaking. They were just sitting there sidling glances at each other like people with secrets.

Izzy looked much as she had always looked. She wore the same shapeless colourless styleless clothes as she had been wearing two days ago, but the puffiness had gone and her breathing seemed even. Her manner had altered as well. She seemed older, loftier, as if she understood the world differently now.

And so they sat like that: Jules, Caz, Hen, Ali and Mel, silent. This was Izzy, for God's sake, thought Ali; this was the same girl they'd spent the last three years trying not to speak to. And now when she finally had something interesting to say, no one could find the words to ask her.

'What was it like?' said Jules.

Izzy began taking her belongings out of the small overnight bag and putting them back in the drawers. 'It was hospital.'

'And?'

'And.' She sounded sarcastic. 'It was like hospitals usually are.'

'Like what?'

'Like normal. Like crowded, people giving you injections, sitting around a lot.'

'Did they give you tests?'

'Yes.'

'What sort of tests?'

'Usual tests.'

'Like what?'

'Like the stuff they usually do.'

Jules's leg began to twitch rhythmically. 'D'you think you might have died?'

'Dunno. Could have done.'

'*Really?*'

'I don't know. Maybe.'

'What did they say?'

'They said it was lucky I got to the hospital when I did.'

'Wow.' Jules sounded impressed. 'God.'

Izzy stopped what she was doing and glared at Jules. 'Sorry. I'll try harder next time.'

'Didn't mean that. Just . . .'

'D'you know what went wrong?' said Caz.

'I didn't have my medicine.'

'Why not?'

'I don't know. It wasn't there.'

'How not there?'

Izzy looked at Caz as if she too was an idiot. Ali was surprised by the show of insolence; Izzy usually crept the floor when Caz spoke to her. 'It *wasn't there*. Someone must have taken it.'

'Like who?'

'Don't know. It wasn't there.'

'Thought your medicine was only for the eczema?' said Jules.

'Is. But there's hayfever stuff too.'

'But what you had, it wasn't hayfever. Jaws said you had sort of a reaction thing.'

'I did,' said Izzy stubbornly. 'But my medicine wasn't there.'

'So the medicine wouldn't have helped anyway?'

'Yes it would.'

'How?' said Jules.

'It just would.'

'*How* would it?'

'You wouldn't understand.'

Jules boiled.

Caz moved in. 'What was the ward like?'

'Just normal.'

'Were there lots of other people?'

'Few.'

'Were they nice?'

'Dunno. Didn't talk to them.'

'So what did you do all day?'

'Only been away about twenty-four hours.'

'Yeah, but you must have . . .'

'There was breakfast TV. Big deal.'

'What was the ambulance like?' said Jules.

'OK.'

'Did Miss Naylor try to be nice to you?'

Mel giggled. Izzy looked at her as if she'd been insulted.

'Did they give you nice drugs?'

'*Nice drugs?*'

'Yeah,' said Jules. 'You know, like morphine. Morphine's nice.'

'Morphine?'

'Yeah. Morphine's excellent. Morphine's like free coke. They give it to you free if you're ill.'

'I wasn't there to pick up a Class A drug habit.' Izzy's voice had taken on its old pompous tremor. 'Being in hospital isn't *nice*. The drugs aren't *nice*. They give you injections all the time and shove stuff over your face and talk to you like you're some kind of retard. None of it's *nice*.'

'Yeah, but did they give you morphine?'

Izzy put her hairbrush down on the bed and turned to face Jules. 'No, they didn't fucking give me *morphine*. I didn't go to hospital for some kind of *free drugs* thing.'

Jules lost her temper. She stood up, banging against Ali's shin. 'I'm only fucking trying to be *interested!*' she yelled. 'I couldn't give a fuck about your fucking hospital thing. I was just trying to *say* something!'

Izzy stared up at her, chin out.

'And it was me that fucking got you to the hospital in the first fucking place and if I hadn't rung 999 you'd still be sitting on the fucking *verge* with fucking Miss Useless Retard Naylor dabbing bloody *Savlon* on your knee and I wish I hadn't fucking *bothered* now.'

Jules turned and stumped across the room. 'Next time you can just fucking *stay there!* Next time you can just fucking DIE!' She walked out, slamming the door behind her so hard the wall shivered.

In the long silence which followed, Ali was not sure where to look. She got up slowly, trying to look as if she'd thought of a good reason not to sit there any more. Izzy went on fussing over her stuff, putting her pyjamas under her pillow. One by one, they all returned to their own beds. All except Hen, who just sat there, opposite Izzy, staring.

+

They were outside, sunbathing. There was real heat in the day now, proper roasting heat, the kind that changed the colour of skin after only an hour or so. Not that Caz needed much help. She was already tanned to the point of ambiguity, but, as she pointed out to Jules and Vicky, there was always room for a bit more.

Jules was swatting at invisible midges. 'Fucking bloodsuckers.'

'Put lotion on.'

'Doesn't work.' She rounded on Vicky, who was lying flat on her stomach beating a lazy tattoo on the cover of her book. 'Can't you stop making that stupid noise?'

Vicky smiled. 'You're just in a crap mood.'

'No.' Yes, actually. What should have been a moment of rare and startling beauty with Izzy had become something more familiar. She hadn't had any strict notions of how things were supposed to happen when Izzy returned, just that it included something along the lines of Izzy kneeling on the floor and sobbing extravagantly into the hems of her jeans. She hadn't intended to point out that she was a hero and she hadn't intended to make any kind of big issue about it, but she had hoped that her one dazzling moment of life-saving self-sacrifice would at least be greeted with some display of gratitude; large amounts of reward money, perhaps, or just a lifetime's worth of slavish devotion. But no. Instead, she was stuck once again with Izzy's ingratitude and the bitter knowledge that she had somehow managed to turn a good situation into a wrong one.

Caz sat upright. 'God, it's depressing. I can't stand how fat I am.'

'You're not,' said Vicky, watching Caz's ankles so she wouldn't have to look further up at her stomach or – God forbid – her tits. 'You're so thin and brown it's disgusting.'

'I'm not. Look like a bag of chips.'

'It's me that's fat. Must of put on about three stone this term.'

'You're fine.'

'I'm not. I'm repellent.'

Jules lay down flat on her bath towel and turned her face away. Couldn't they just shut up, she thought savagely. People who looked like supermodels should be banned from ever saying anything about their own bodies, and from ever sunbathing in the company of normal people, the ones with fat bits and blobby bits and short bits and insufficient bits. And they should be banned from whining about anything ever again.

She was on the verge of getting up and going to find

somewhere less corrosive to sunbathe when Caz said slowly, 'We're being watched.'

Vicky shrieked and slammed the book down over her chest. 'Where? Who?'

'Over there. Two of the men from downstairs.'

'Fucking *perverts!* What are they doing?'

'Staring at us.'

'Freaks!'

'Don't move.'

'Why?'

'They'll know you've seen them.'

'Yeah! Course!'

'No. Hang on. Just wait.' Caz put on her sunglasses, turned over on her back and slowly began to undo the strap of her bikini top.

'Caz!' Vicky giggled. 'What are you *doing?*'

'Take your top off.'

'What? Why?'

'Go on.'

'Why? Don't want some creepy—'

'Just do it.'

Vicky, grumbling, undid her own bikini top and lay down flat, her arms pinned crosswise over her chest.

'Jules. Come on.'

'Why?'

'Explain later. Come on.'

Jules didn't like Caz's sunglasses. She didn't like it when Caz turned towards her and all Jules would see was just a black space where her expression used to be. Jules undid one strap and then put it back. 'Why do I have to do this?'

Caz didn't answer.

Jules undid the other strap and whipped the bikini off. She found that she could not look down at herself without blushing.

'Right. Now. Look casual.'

Yeah, *right*. Jules lay back, one leg crooked and one arm draped languidly over her forehead. She did not feel languid.

Time passed. When she opened her eyes again Caz was leaning up on one elbow. Her other arm was resting on one hip, and she was stroking one foot slowly up and down the other. Her hair was swept round so the tips of it just brushed the top of one nipple and – Jules wasn't quite sure she could believe this – she was pouting. Quite distinctly pouting. Oh, please. This was ridiculous. There was no way anyone would fall for that.

Jules started to laugh. 'You look—'

'Fuck off.'

'What are you doing?'

'What's it look like?'

'Fuck knows. Trying to look like Miss Stokeley Hot Lips or something. No bloke is that fucking dumb.'

Caz nodded towards the Manor. 'Oh yeah?'

Jules turned. Caz was right; the men were acting weird. A few minutes previously they had been talking placidly and looking out across the valley. But now, their behaviour had changed. They were talking with more animation than seemed strictly plausible, gesturing a little more grandly, laughing more loudly. One of them – the youngest-looking, tall, clean-shaven – kept running his hand through his hair and half rising to his feet. He kept looking at Caz and then looking away, as if something about the sight of her was too hot or too bright. It occurred to Jules that she could tell what the two of them were saying without having to hear the words.

Vicky giggled. 'Hel-*lo* boys.' She gave them the car-show-room pout.

'Go on,' said Caz. 'Don't lie there. Give it some.'

Jules sighed and turned on her side.

They lay silently for a while. Jules picked at the grass and Vicky practised the best way to push out her chest.

'Here we go,' muttered Caz. 'Told you so.'

Jules looked up. The young one was walking towards them. Vicky started to giggle and found, once she had started, that she couldn't stop.

The man walked up close and stood above them. 'Hello,' he said.

Caz stretched back a little. 'You're blocking my light.'

'Sorry.' He reversed.

'What about your friend? Doesn't he want to talk?'

'Is that OK?'

She nodded. 'Step right up.'

Jules squinted at them through the grass. The other one had ankles like a girl and little black strands of hair flaring out of the end of his nostrils. Physically, both were write-offs. The girly-ankled one was the man who had been watching her through the window as she climbed back in on Friday night.

The young one crouched down and turned to Caz. 'We've seen you around. Is this some kind of school field trip?'

Caz began to explain the swimming, the walking, the end of exams and the dispersal of a whole school year across the southern counties of England. She paused again, moving her foot up and down. 'So you like the view?'

'This part of the country has always been beautiful,' said girly-ankles determinedly.

'That wasn't what I meant.'

'How old are you lot anyway?'

'Seventeen.' Caz rolled over, turned her back on them and began putting on her bikini top again. 'I'm getting hot. Any of you want a walk?'

The young one leapt up and the one with girly ankles stayed where he was. Fucking marvellous, thought Jules. Absolutely fucking marvellous. So we get the sad git and you swan off into the distance with the other one.

Caz stood up. 'Won't be long,' she said. 'Don't do anything naughty.' She strode off, the young guy towing behind her like a dog.

Vicky levered her top back on and stretched. 'I'll just . . .' She got up and walked off, back towards the Manor.

Jules sat up with her back to girly-ankles and put her shirt back on. When she turned back to face him, he looked so nervous she almost laughed.

'I'm Brian,' he said.

Jules did not reply.

'Am I disturbing you?'

'Not really,' said Jules gracelessly.

A difficult silence. 'What's your school like?'

'Like this but worse.'

Pause.

'What's your favourite subject?'

Oh, please. 'Double chemistry.'

'Really?'

'No. Hate them all.'

'Why?'

'Because we're not learning them for any kind of fun. We're just learning them so we can pass another exam.'

'I see.' Another long pause.

Finally, Brian rose and turned. 'I'd better be getting back in.'

'Right.'

'Nice meeting you.'

'Yeah.'

She watched him walk back to the Manor. Dickhead.

There seemed no point in going on sunbathing now. While Caz and Vicky had been lying next to her she'd just wanted to be left in peace, but now she was properly alone again, she felt conspicuous. She lay back and listened to the whirr of insects above her head.

She felt out of her depth again, pushing against something she couldn't properly comprehend. She had no sense of what Caz was trying to do, only that to her men were by definition more interesting than girls. She thought about Caz walking off, not even bothering to check if she was OK, forgetting everything she'd left behind.

She sat up. If she wasn't careful, she'd probably just end up sitting here and making herself cry again. Crying was a good example of how things had changed in the last few days. She used to believe that crying provoked consolation from others. Now she knew that crying provoked nothing except the sound of its own sadness.

Jules shuffled on her shoes and set off. She had no idea where she was going. She couldn't hear anything, and she'd been so pissed off with Caz for abandoning her with Brian that she hadn't noticed which direction she was taking. She started walking towards the little plantation where Ali had her favourite tree.

Once inside the plantation she felt no clearer. It was dark in here, cool and shady with speckles of sunlight and soft mossy earth underfoot. This part of the grounds had a comforting quality which – had Jules been in a better temper – she might have felt grateful for. Many of the trees had evidently been planted when the Manor was first built and had formed great calm circles of open ground beneath themselves. It was just light enough to remove any feeling of creepiness and just dark enough to feel that, once within the wood, it would be almost impossible to be seen from the Manor. She stopped and took out a cigarette. There was silence except for the scuffle of wind in the leaves and the indistinct blare of a car alarm somewhere far away.

Perhaps Caz and the man weren't in here at all. Perhaps they'd disappeared off somewhere else. Perhaps Caz was doing something terrible right up close to where she was standing. Perhaps she was there behind one of the trees with the man, whispering. Perhaps the sound of the wind was not wind at all, but muffled laughter. Perhaps the trip to the wood had been nothing more than an opportunity to laugh. Perhaps it was a set-up and she'd been meant to get lost in the wood, never come out, be condemned to wander forever. Was she being watched?

She walked round a bend and there, under a tree, was Caz and the young guy. It was only when Jules came a little closer that she noticed something about the way they were both standing. The guy was leaning forward slightly, all his weight on his front leg, scowling; the standard posture of the angry man. He had his arm raised and was talking loudly, almost shouting. Caz was standing in front of him, a little flushed.

When she saw Jules she smiled and ran towards her. She seemed a little out of breath. 'Hiya,' she said. 'Was waiting for you. I'm just—' Before Jules could say anything, she ran off, giggling.

Jules looked round.

The young man walked over to her, right up close. 'Where's she going?'

'Don't know.'

He grabbed her by the arm. 'She said . . .'

For the second time in a week Jules became aware that men were stronger than women. She twisted her arm around in his grasp but it didn't seem to move, even when she pulled quite hard. She could feel him breathing.

'What's she playing at?'

She wished he would let go. She didn't like it.

'Come on. You must know. You and her and the other one, you were plotting something.'

'No. No. I don't . . .' She could feel his eyes trying to lock on to hers, but she didn't want to look at him.

'I don't know what you think you're doing, trying to provoke us. You're playing games.'

'What games? Don't know—'

He shoved his face close up to hers, close enough that she didn't have any choice but to look up and see the little spray of open pores just above his eyebrows. 'Yes, you do. You say you want it and then you run away.'

'I don't . . .' She was beginning to feel frightened. She was not sure at what point the balance had shifted, or how. She could not work out how, in the space of half an hour or so, things could have gone from all that stupid pouting and gig-gling to this low black anger. In answer he swept his arm back towards the path Caz had taken. 'Where's she gone?'

'I don't *know.*' Jules's voice rose. 'She'll come back.'

'You can't do this. You can't keep doing this and then run-ning away.'

What was he talking about? Why wasn't Caz coming back? Why wouldn't someone rescue her? What was he talking about? Why was he so angry?

'D'you do this to everyone?'

'I don't—'

He tugged again. 'Yes, you do.'

She didn't understand. 'Maybe it was a joke.'

'A joke? How was it funny, exactly?'

'I don't know.' She twisted her arm again, but he still wasn't letting go. He kept holding on, staring at her with his yellowy eyes.

'You're a bunch of fucking slags, you lot. Fucking *slags.*'

She reeled sideways. As she did so, he jerked at her arm and she stumbled slightly, knocking against him. She felt a hard-ness that shouldn't have been there. An erection. The guy had an erection. 'Let go! Please!'

'Where is she?'

'Let. Fucking. *Go!*'

He pushed his face down to hers again. '*Where is she?*'

'I don't know.' Jules began to cry. 'Please let go.'

There was silence for a second. Jules could feel the tears scorching down her face, big ugly real ones. She couldn't bear to look at him, couldn't stand him there, holding on to her so easily, couldn't bear the knowledge that she was trapped here just waiting for another Friday night.

Something about her crying seemed to change him. His grip on her wrist loosened slightly and his voice had gone quiet. 'You're not seventeen, are you?'

'No.'

'So how old are you?'

'Th . . . thirteen.'

'Jesus Christ,' he said, stepping backwards, finally releasing her arm. 'Jesus *Christ.*'

As soon as she was free, she turned and ran. Back down the path, back the way she had come. She could hear sounds behind her and sounds in front. It must be Caz coming to get her, coming to make sure she was OK. Caz hadn't meant to leave her there, Caz hadn't made him angry. As she ran, the sounds confused her – something crashing behind, something nearby. She pelted out of the wood, wailing.

There was a figure on the path just at the edge of the plantation, a female figure. But it wasn't Caz. It was Jaws. And Jaws was angry.

+

Hen pressed the buttons on the mobile and put it cautiously to her ear. She didn't trust mobiles. They were complicated objects, full of demands and ambition. She'd thought about having one until she'd pressed the phone-book button on Jamie's and realized that it had space for a thousand names. A thousand people. She barely knew twenty. And if she was to get one, and if she was to type in those twenty names, what then? Every time she scrolled through that thin list of names the mobile would exude a barely audible electronic sneer, a fractional squeak of contempt. Imprinted on the mobile would be the evidence of an unhappened life – a family, a school, friends who seemed somehow to be slipping towards unfriends. This was a machine that touched the minds of thousands. She touched no one.

Someone at the other end picked up the phone. 'Hello?'

Hen gasped.

'He-*llo?*'

'Um. Is Adey there?'

'Who is it?'

'Um. Hen.'

'Right.' The voice now had an interested and slightly suggestive note to it. 'Hang on.'

Hen waited. The pain in her thigh where she'd cut herself ebbed and drummed. After that distant frenzy, the release of the necessary bloodletting, it was always like this. The pain shifted from being a clean pain to being an ordinary pain. A sore, annoying, go-away sort of pain.

The receiver was picked up. 'Adey?'

Behind the langour, there was warmth in his voice. 'Hen. Hi.'

'Thanks for your letter.'

'I just . . . I just felt bad. After you left on Sunday. Shouldn't have been like that.'

Hen heard herself beginning to twitter. 'No, no. Really. No, I'm sorry. I shouldn't have left so fast. Without explaining.'

'So what was it?'

She hesitated. If she confided in him, maybe he would confide in her. 'Caz. She was running away. I thought I better go and see why she was going.'

'She all right?'

'She's fine. But . . . but she won't say what happened.' Pause. 'Do you know what happened?'

Adey sighed. It echoed so heavily in her ear that she held the mobile away for a second. 'It was only supposed to be a joke. She wasn't supposed to take it seriously.'

'Take what seriously?'

The line ticked. 'If I tell you, you won't be angry?'

'Why would I be angry?'

'Higgs . . . Caz . . . Higgs thinks . . .' He sounded as if he was having trouble getting the words in the right order. '. . . I don't think this, this is only what he thinks, right?'

'Yes?'

'He thinks Caz is a bit of a slapper.'

Hen kept her voice expressionless. 'Right.'

'So they go to his room, and they smoke a bit of blow, and they're talking. And then Higgs made out like they were going to have sex. OK? So Caz gets undressed, and she's lying in his bed bollock naked, and Higgs says he wants to try something . . .' He stopped, measuring something in his mind. Go on, thought Hen. Go on. '. . . something different. And Caz says she's right up for it.'

'Right.'

'Anyway.' He sounded squeamish. 'So he . . . he ties her to the bed, and then he says he just has to go and get something. So he goes out, and there's Caz, on the bed, waiting for him.' He paused again. 'Is this OK?'

'Fine. Really. Honestly.'

'And he goes outside, and he gets everyone together. Everyone except me, because I was with you. And they all stand outside Higgs's room, and then they all just burst in. And there's Caz on the bed, all tied up, and she looks so . . .' He caught himself. 'So whatever.'

'Yes.' She could feel herself blushing so stridently that it made her hair itch. 'Yes.'

'They didn't do anything to her. They just laughed.' He waited. 'You angry?'

'No. Promise.'

'And Caz . . . she's all right, isn't she?'

'She's fine. Really.'

'Do you think . . . do you think that she's a bit . . .'

'Yes,' said Hen hurriedly. 'Oh yes. She's always been like that.'

'That's what Higgs thought. So he thought he'd take the piss out of her for once. Thought she'd see the funny side.'

'Mmmm.'

'So . . .' – an abrupt, relieved shift – '. . . so you want to meet up? In the holidays?'

'Sure. Be great.'

'You've got my number?'

'Yes.'

'OK.' He sounded as if he wasn't sure this was the end of the conversation, as if he hoped it might not be.

'Adey, thanks. I'll call you, really I will. Soon as I get home.'

'No problem.'

Any lingering indecision she might have felt about seeing him again faded as she switched off the phone. How could she see him again, knowing what he'd just told her? She imagined herself in a noisy cafe in London somewhere, bracing herself against the scrape of chair legs and the reek of sweet food. She saw herself sitting opposite this strange pale man, trying to talk about something she couldn't talk about, staring at his little pigletty eyelashes. Why did he want to see her? Or rather, what did he want to see in her?

+

Jules was not looking at Jaws. Instead, she was looking at a small pot of pens on the desk. It contained three ordinary biros, a couple of fluorescent markers, a ruler, and an elegant silver paper knife decorated with arabic writing. Jules was wondering if the knife would be sharp enough to stab someone with.

They were sitting in the room Jaws had been using as a office. It was on the Manor's ground floor and had a view over the lawn to the woods. Every time Jules looked out she could see the path she had run down. It was dusk, and the light had almost gone, but the shape of the path was still distinct. Over to the left, the bright edge of the orange towel Vicky had been using for sunbathing shifted in the wind. When she thought of going out and walking across the empty lawns to collect her belongings, Jules blushed, though she was not sure why.

Jaws was not angry any more. She had stopped being angry about an hour ago, and now seemed only a little disheartened. 'What,' she said for the third time, 'was the point?'

'Don't know. Just said we ought to do it.'

'Ought to do what?'

'Take off our tops.'

'In front of the men?'

'The men weren't there. They were sitting on the bench.'

'But they could see?'

Jules nodded.

'And she didn't say why?'

'She just said, do it.'

'You didn't object?'

'It was embarrassing.'

'But you did it anyway?'

Jules sniffed. She could tell she was going to start crying again.

'You didn't want to, you thought it was embarrassing, but you still took off your bikini. Why?'

No response.

'Just explain. Explain how Caz could make you do things you don't want to do.'

Jules picked up a strand of damp loo paper from the desk and buried her nose in it.

Jaws leaned back in her chair and began massaging her forehead. 'I'm not angry. I'm just interested. Really interested. I want to know how Caz could persuade you to do something you didn't want to do. I think it's strange.'

From behind the tissue, Jules made an inarticulate noise. 'She didn't say.'

'Didn't say what?'

'Say what it was for. She just said to take our tops off.'

'And you thought it would be all right?'

No response.

'What do you *think* Caz was trying to do?'

As she started speaking, Jules's face began to crumple again. 'Think she wanted to show she could do things to them.'

Jaws nodded, expressionless.

Another long, miserable pause. 'She wanted to get rid of the men, so she pretended like she fancied them.'

'How do you mean?'

'She said it would get rid of them.'

'How?'

Jules shook her head.

'She was leading them on in some way?'

'Mmmm.'

'And then what?'

'She went to the wood with one of them.'

'How long were they in the wood before you arrived?'

'Dunno. A bit.'

'And when you got there, he was angry about something?'

Jules nodded.

'You think she wanted him to get angry?'

Another nod.

'So he would want to hurt someone?'

Jules dissolved again. Jaws got up and went over to the sink, poured out a glass of water and set it down in front of her. They'd been sitting here for what felt like a long time now, and Jaws was tired. She could see that Jules was doing her best and that she had long ago given up any attempt at deliberate concealment, but she could also see that Jules's urge to defend Caz was stronger even than the desire to vindicate herself. 'Never mind,' she said softly. 'You don't have to explain it all now.'

Jules looked up. Her face was a mess. 'Am I going to get detention?'

'No. There's no point.'

'Is Naylor pissed off?'

'*Miss* Naylor,' said Jaws automatically. 'Yes, she's angry. You all did something very stupid.'

'Is Caz with her?'

'I think so.'

Jules plucked wildly at her hair. Caz would probably have told Naylor something totally different. Perhaps their stories contradicted each other. Perhaps she had landed Caz in terrible trouble. She picked up the loo paper again and plunged it over her eyes.

Jaws watched her. 'Just one more question,' she said. 'Then you can go. If I need to talk to you again, I'll come and get you. Just tell me if you think Caz *meant* for something bad to happen.'

But it was precisely that question which was making Jules cry.

FRIDAY

As Ali reached the passageway she heard something slam. Something in their bedroom. The sound of drawers being pulled out and shoved roughly back. She tried to look through the crack in the doorway below the hinges. Nothing. The angle wasn't right.

Jaws was standing by the window, and Miss Naylor was over by Mel's bed with a pile of clothes in her hand. Both of them looked up.

'Search,' said Miss Naylor.

'Why?'

'Not your business. A search.'

'Perhaps,' said Jaws, 'It would be better if . . .'

Ali walked slowly across the room and sat on the edge of her bed. 'I'll stay.'

The sight of the two of them smashing through her flimsy privacy made Ali angry enough to remain. It wasn't just the intrusion, it was the pleasure that Miss Naylor was so evidently taking in it: the officious gestures, the sanctimonious frown. They'd have to order her out. And they wouldn't order her out because they knew she'd go right downstairs and tell the others, and they would come steaming upstairs even more enraged than she was.

Her indignation also outweighed the alarm at what they might find in her own drawers. She didn't smoke, so there were no cigarettes, she didn't have any drugs, she didn't steal or have stuff that she shouldn't. The only things they might find were the library books, the mobile and the money her father had sent. The mobile and the money were safely hidden above the hatch in the cleaning cupboard, and it didn't seem likely that they would be bothered by a couple of library books.

Miss Naylor pulled up the side of Mel's mattress and swiped her hand underneath.

'What are you looking for?'

'It doesn't concern—'

Jaws interrupted. 'Nothing to get fussed about.'

She upended Mel's drawers quickly, spilling out tampons, pens, a flutter of underwear. Ali watched an eyeliner and a pale pink lipgloss roll noisily to the floor. Nothing. No library books, no drugs, no drink, no fags, no mobile, no nothing.

She moved round to Izzy's bed. Ali watched a dribble of socks and formless shirts land on the duvet.

Jaws bent down and looked under the bed. 'Here.' She pulled out the two boxes containing Izzy's CDs and her Discman.

Miss Naylor placed the box on the bed and began flicking through it. 'Over there,' she said to Jaws, closing the box. 'By the door.'

When it came to her turn, Ali sat immobile. Jaws mumbled something inaudible and then began going through her drawers. What did they expect to find? Empty bottles of meths? Used needles?

Miss Naylor stood above Ali. 'Off.'

Ali shifted position slowly, inching her legs over the side of the bed. This was hers. This was all she had. Why did they have to meddle with this as well? Miss Naylor yanked the mattress up and swept her hand underneath. When she let it fall again, the undersheet fell crumpled over the edge, as if someone had slept there without Ali's knowledge.

She watched the back of Miss Naylor's neck and the ladderwork of lines around her throat. It occurred to her that Miss Naylor was a teacher who did not like children; a teacher, in fact, who did not much like people.

Miss Naylor picked up one of the books from the pile on the bed.

'This is a library book.'

Ali didn't reply.

'Well?'

Ali nodded once, almost imperceptibly.

'You'll pay the fine.' She swung the book in front of Ali's nose. 'You know there are penalties for taking library books off the school grounds? You know you should get a special dispensation for this?' She hurled the book in Jaws's direction, and the pages flustered as they fell. 'On the pile.'

They moved round to Jules's bed. Her top drawer contained the same muddle of make-up as Mel's had: one leaking foundation, a photograph, a watch with a broken strap, a comb furred with hair. The drawers below contained only a couple of folded T-shirts, two pairs of jeans, three fleeces in different colours, a denim jacket. Miss Naylor spread them out on the bed and sifted through them. In the top pocket of the jacket was an empty packet of B&H. She shook it a couple of times, sending a cascade of tobacco over the bedclothes, and then threw the packet over to Jaws. Ali waited for them to leave. Surely once they'd found evidence of smoking, they'd go?

But the cigarettes didn't seem to interest her much. Instead, she opened each of Jules's drawers again and began feeling round the backs of them. Her movements had become more forceful, the search more violently confident. What were they looking for? And why now? Had someone grassed about something? This is a police state, thought Ali. This is what they do in places where people have no rights.

At the back of the third drawer was a small rectangular metal tin, like an old-fashioned money box. Miss Naylor lifted it out and shook it. It obviously contained something – not coins or jewellery, but something soft and papery.

Miss Naylor put the box down. 'Penknife?' she said, glancing around.

Jaws shook her head. 'Downstairs. Sorry.'

She walked over to Ali's bed and put out her hand. Ali gave back a dead-eyed stare. Did she really think she was going to help? 'Lost it,' she said flatly, and looked away.

Miss Naylor went back over to Mel's drawers, removed the nail file from her sponge bag and picked up the tin. The lock was sturdy, and though the box was old-fashioned, it had evidently been designed to discourage intruders.

It took about ten minutes before the lock yielded. Jaws and Ali both heard the screech of surrendered metal and turned as Miss Naylor emptied out the tin's contents onto the bed. Of all the things Ali had been expecting – love letters, a year's supply of dope, condoms, cigarettes – it had not been these dull official packets now scattered randomly over the duvet. An asthma inhaler, two packets of antihistamines, a tube of steroid cream, two syringes still in their packet. Izzy's medicines.

Jaws looked at them and turned away. No one spoke.

Miss Naylor packed the medicines slowly back into the box, and put them in the pile of confiscations near the door. As she turned back, she looked at Ali. Ali could not tell if her smile was of vindication or collusion.

She moved over to Hen's bedside and began picking through the objects on the top – bottles of moisturizer, the old photograph of Hen in a boat with her family, a notebook full of lists in Hen's thin anxious handwriting. The top two drawers contained only clothes. There were two or three piles of thick wintry jerseys, woollen socks and a tracksuit with sagging knees. Everyone else's possessions reflected the season, from the tubes of suntan oil to the teeny bikinis. Only Hen existed in perpetual November.

Miss Naylor sat back on her haunches and tugged at the bottom drawer. The furniture in the Manor was cheap, bulk-bought, and the drawer would not run smoothly. Miss Naylor jerked at it, the muscles in her shoulder tensing. The wood shrieked and Hen's alarm clock wobbled from side to side, making the dial trip backwards. The drawer gave with a crash, thumping out of its sockets onto the floor.

There was a little pause, and then the smell hit her. The room was suddenly full of the sweet rotten scent which had been teasing round it in the last few days. Ali had first smelt it on Thursday or Friday and had thought it must be something coming up from the kitchens below. Perhaps someone had forgotten to put out one of the bin bags. Perhaps the kitchen staff were just preparing an unusually disgusting meal. But the smell had got stronger recently, more distinct and persistent.

Jaws bent towards the drawer. Neither of them said

anything, just dipped their heads and stared rapt at the contents. Ali crept off her bed and sidled over to Hen's corner.

'Aaaahhh,' said Jaws.

For a second, Ali couldn't make sense of what she saw. Inside the drawer there were colours, a jumble of bright plastic things. Fruit, rotting. Supermarket bags tied by their handles and full of dark squishy things. A soft blue fur of mould creeping round the edge of the lettering. A puff of spores dusted the bags as the contents settled again. The high sweet smell got stronger, closer to alcohol than to fruit. Ali could see the oranges falling in on themselves, the blackened bananas, the apples shrivelling into the corners. Something unidentifiable had begun melding with the drawer itself, darkening the wood. It had left a long marbled streak along the side. A slice of cheddar poked out of one of the bags, veined with decay. Ali recognized the roast potatoes from two days ago, a slice of what looked like bacon seeping greasily into a half-plucked bunch of browning grapes. There were dozens of bags, some empty, some full, all oozing into each other, all slithering from one state to another. Ali caught the stink of vomit and, as she closed her eyes, a faint movement in one of the corners. Two flies settled on the fruit and began to feed. At the back, something lifted unnaturally, breathing with life. There were bags full of toast or cereal or something much much worse. All the meals Hen had eaten – or not eaten – in the past ten days.

Miss Naylor turned. 'Get back,' she hissed.

Ali gave no indication that she had heard her.

'This has nothing to do with you.'

Jaws stood up. 'What do we . . . ?'

'Here.' Miss Naylor lifted one end of the drawer towards Jaws. 'Downstairs. The bins.'

How are they going to carry that, thought Ali. How are they going to walk down all those stairs, past Mel and Mina and the kitchen staff and the men, carrying that?

'Wait.' Jaws put her end of the drawer back down on the floor. Miss Naylor's lips snarled up at the corners as her fingers caught in the thin joints of the wood. 'I'll get bags.'

'No. Don't. It isn't the best . . .'

Jaws fled. Looking, thought Ali, like she was going to be sick too.

Miss Naylor made a clicking noise in the back of her throat and began trying to get the drawer back into its sockets. It jammed again, screeching against the cheap wood. Her forehead was smirred with sweat, and her foundation had begun to run again. It made her look artificial, as if she was made out of plastic.

Neither of them said anything. For a while, Ali felt almost comforted by Miss Naylor's presence. Maybe if neither of them spoke, it might be possible to pretend that it really was none of her business, that she really hadn't seen the contents of that drawer, that none of this bad stuff had happened.

Miss Naylor shifted. 'Probably best if . . .' She started again. Her voice didn't seem to be working properly. 'It's probably best if you don't say anything. To the others.'

Oh yeah? And how was she going to manage that? The two of them had just turned the room upside down, and she was supposed to say nothing? How to explain the small matter of the missing drawer? The absent fag packet? Izzy's CD boxes? The tin and the medicine? The overpowering smell of sick food?

Miss Naylor read Ali's face. It seemed to make her angry.

'Lola . . .' she began, 'Lola has a . . . difficulty. A problem.

She needs help. Telling people isn't going . . .' She stopped. 'You running around yelling your head off isn't going to make matters any better.'

Ali kept up the silence. She's pleading, she thought, she's actually almost pleading. For the second time that week, it occurred to her that Miss Naylor might, after all, be human. Though most of Miss Naylor's character remained foreign as monsters, Ali wondered if perhaps she sometimes experienced some of the same things as other people did, if she too might sometimes feel hope or fear or doubt. The thought of Miss Naylor as an equal made Ali feel angry. You can't make me, she thought. You can't force me to shut up. There's nothing you can do. You don't have any control any more. She lifted her head and looked Miss Naylor in the eye.

Miss Naylor got up off the bed and walked over to Ali, pushing up against the limits of her discomfort. Ali dropped her gaze and looked out of the window. Outside on the lawn there were buttercups staining the grass, a whole golden acre of them.

'Don't. Don't you . . .'

Ali hopped off the window ledge. 'Don't what?' she said softly.

Miss Naylor's face tensed. Her eyes blared and grew dark, as if something had peeled away and she had suddenly become more alive than she had been a second ago. As if she had stopped seeing Ali and saw instead a distant reflection. *She's mad*, thought Ali. *She's going to* . . . She began to turn away, but Miss Naylor swung her hand up so swiftly Ali didn't have time to avoid it. The two hard gold rings Miss Naylor wore connected with Ali's left ear. She felt them crack against her skull and the sudden belt of pain. Something began to thunder in her ears. She put her own hand up to hold her ear. It felt like it might have been bleeding, but when she pressed her fingers along the mark where Miss Naylor's hand had connected, it came away clean. Ali opened her mouth to say something and Miss Naylor clamped her hand over it, muffling Ali completely. Ali took a gasping breath and smelt the rot of vomit on her skin.

Miss Naylor's voice was deeper than usual. 'Don't you dare . . .'

Jaws came back in. She was holding a couple of large garden refuse bags and had been crying. She looked first at Miss Naylor standing by the window with her arm still half raised. And then at Ali holding her cheek, one side of her face scorched by the impact of the slap. She stood there for a long moment holding the bags, her mouth slightly open. And Ali saw something in Jaws's expression that really shouldn't have been there at all.

✦

Jules was having a fag in the rhododendron bush. The light was murky now, flat and yellow as greasy sheets, and the inside of the bush was cooler than Jules would have liked.

She hadn't even bothered asking Caz if she would like to join her. Every time she had tried to talk to Caz, it had somehow been impossible. Either Caz just changed the subject, or there was someone else around, or Vicky would appear, staring at them both with her small greedy eyes, wanting to know, wanting to be part of things. Jules still had no idea if Caz's story tallied with hers, or what she had told Miss Naylor or – worse – what she had really intended when she had left Jules in the wood.

She heard rustling, but there was no time to hide. She sat on the branch, hoping absurdly that the shade would cover her.

Mel's eyes were very black. 'Guess!' she said dramatically.

'Fuck!' Jules swayed and put a foot out to steady herself. 'Don't *do* that!'

'Do what?'

'Scare me. Retard.' She glared at Mel. 'How did you find me?'

'Followed the smoke. Obviously. You're signalling like a bloody Red Indian.'

'Shit!' Jules hurled the cigarette to the ground. 'I'll get busted!'

Mel ignored her. 'Guess!'

'What?'

'Just guess.'

'*I don't know.*' She jumped off the branch.

'There's been a row. A really amazing one.'

'And?'

'*And . . .*' Mel paused, resplendent with gossip, 'and Ali says Miss Naylor hit her.'

'Hit her? Why?'

'Because they had a row.'

'About what?'

'Don't know. She said Miss Naylor was so angry she just hit her.'

'Why?'

'Told you. Don't know. Something to do with a search. Naylor and Jaws were in the room looking for something and Naylor just . . .'

'*Fuck!*'

'What?'

'There was an empty packet in my jacket. *Fuck fuck fuck.*'

'Yeah, but . . .' Mel followed her out of the shrub. 'Isn't it amazing? They could sack her for that.'

Jules started to run.

'It doesn't matter!' called Mel after her. 'It's empty!'

But Jules kept running over the summer lawn, back towards the Manor.

+

Upstairs in the bedroom a small crowd was gathered around Ali. She was sitting on the window ledge with her arms crossed and was evidently feeling hemmed in.

'. . . again?' Caz said as Jules came through the door.

Ali raised her hand to the side of her face. 'Here.'

'Can't see any mark.'

'No.' Ali's tone was dry. 'Sorry.'

'Ali!' Jules thumped to a halt. 'Did she find anything?'

Ali paused for what seemed an unnecessarily long time before answering. 'The library books, Izzy's music . . .'

'The fag packet?'

'Yes.'

'*Fuck!*' Jules kicked the leg of Izzy's bed. '*Fuck! Arse!*'

'It's not a problem.' Caz turned to face her.

'It *is* a fucking problem! That's the third time I've been busted. I'm out.'

'No you're not.'

'I am! She's got me twice before. She's been *gagging* to get me again.'

'Only an empty packet.'

'So? You think she *cares* if it's got fags in or not?'

Ali interrupted. 'She wasn't interested in the cigarettes.'

'D'you mean?'

'She was looking for something else.'

'Like what?'

Ali hopped off the ledge. 'Other stuff.'

'Yeah, other stuff and fags. She's been dying to bust me.'

Caz was watching Ali. 'You could get her for that,' she said. 'If you grassed on her, you could get her sacked.'

Ali turned.

'If you got in now, rang the school, told what happened, you could get her sacked. She'd be out. Teachers aren't allowed to hit girls.'

'But,' said Izzy, 'it's just her word against Naylor's, isn't it?' She inspected the side of Ali's face. 'Not like you can *see* anything.'

'Jaws saw her. If you got Jaws to help, you could get her out. Get her sacked.'

'No way,' said Izzy. 'Jaws isn't going to grass on another teacher.'

'She might. She hates Naylor, remember?'

Mel took a step towards the window ledge. 'Go on. It'd be amazing. Ring the school. Get her sacked.'

'Why don't you?' Caz's voice was light, careless. 'Get her out. Revenge.'

Ali's gaze flickered from one to the other.

'Revenge!' chanted Mel in a sing-song voice. 'Revenge! Ditch her! Get her out! Grass her up!'

The others began to join in. 'Get – her – out! Get – her – sacked! Ditch – the – bitch!'

Caz stood up and began to walk towards Ali. 'You could

make sure she never teaches again. It'd be amazing. She'd be stuffed.'

'Re-venge! Get – her – out! Get – her – sacked! Ditch – the – bitch!'

'Go on. I dare you. One phone call, that's all you'd have to do. Just call up and you'd get rid of her for ever. Fuck her over.'

'Get – her – out! Get – her – dumped! Re-venge! Re-venge! Re-venge!'

Caz raised her voice. 'Ring the school. Ring the governors. Ring the papers or something. Talk to the papers. If you talked to the papers, they'd do it for you. Get her . . .'

Ali half turned and saw Jules standing mute in the corner of the room. She could hear Caz beside her, getting closer, the whiteness at the corners of her eyes. As she hesitated, she felt the little shove of air against her cheek as each of Caz's words connected. Then she walked out.

+

Downstairs in the TV room, the curtains bloomed in the wind. Ali sat down in one of the chairs and folded her arms.

Jules was uncomfortable. There was something about the way life had been going recently that meant she kept having to ask Ali for things. She didn't like Ali and her slow glances. She didn't like the way Ali spent her life watching other people. And she particularly didn't like asking Ali for things. Not because it made her feel indebted, but because Ali always took so infuriatingly long to think about everything. Why did it have to be Ali who got hit by Miss Naylor? She does nothing but sit in trees for six months, Miss Naylor hits her and suddenly she's the centre of the universe. By rights, Jules considered, it should have been her fight, her slap and her glory. She was the one, after all, who had been hated by Miss Naylor for all that time. She would have known exactly how to make the best of the situation.

Jules could also see that the feeling was mutual. Ali's distrust was almost palpable. She was sitting down low in the chair, her arms clamped tight against her chest, watching Jules with her usual expression of considered stupidity.

Jules was suddenly furious. 'So what were they looking for, then?' It came out almost a shout.

'Other stuff.'

'Like what?'

'They took Izzy's CDs, the library books . . .'

'Why?'

'Dunno. They just did.'

'How come she hit you, then?'

Ali rested her head against the back of the chair and closed her eyes. 'We had an argument, she got pissed off, she hit me.'

Jules scowled at her. 'Can't see any mark.'

'It faded.'

'So how do I know it happened?'

Ali shrugged. 'Don't believe me. Not my problem.'

Silence. The curtains flapped against the corners of Jules's vision. 'What was she doing?'

'Told you. Searching stuff.'

'Why? What for?'

'Don't know. Why does she usually search stuff?'

'Because she's a nosy poking bitch.'

Ali smiled.

'Why was she searching now?'

To Jules's surprise, Ali opened her eyes and sat up. 'I don't know. She was doing it in a particular way.' She sounded thoughtful now, less defensive. 'Perhaps someone had tipped her off about something.'

'Tipped her off about what?'

'About searching. Told her to look for something.'

'What, like grassed?'

'Mmmm. Maybe.'

'The fags.'

Ali closed her eyes again. 'Told you. She wasn't interested in the fags.'

Jules was incensed. Didn't Ali care if she was expelled? Didn't she care that this was Jules's *life* they were talking about? Didn't Ali give a fuck about anything but trees and books? 'What else then?' She was shouting again.

Ali didn't say anything for a while. 'Izzy's CDs . . .'

'*And?*'

There was a silence so long that Jules wondered if Ali had fallen asleep.

But Ali was not asleep. She was thinking. From the way Jules was behaving, she had either forgotten about the medicines, or she didn't think they'd have found them, or – more likely – she genuinely didn't know they were there. It wasn't like she was playing innocent. It was more like she really *was* innocent. Should she tell Jules? Should she tell her all of it, or none of it, or just some of it? For a second, she felt only a kind of stunned and weary pity – for Jules, for Hen, for all of them.

'In your drawer,' she said, balancing each word with particular care, 'was Izzy's medicine.'

An electric silence. '*WHAT?*'

'Izzy's medicine was in your drawer. In a little black tin box.'

'Wha . . . how?'

'I don't know. It just was.'

'Are you saying,' – Jules's voice had risen a full two octaves – '*Are you saying I stole her medicines?*'

'I'm just saying—'

'I *didn't* steal her medicine! How *could* I steal her medicine? I *rescued* her!'

'I know, I know.' Ali flapped a placatory hand. 'I'm not saying you did.' She thought for a moment. 'Is that black box yours?'

'What black box?'

'A tin. Like an old money box. With a slit in the top. Sort of so big.' She measured out a rectangle.

'No.' Jules's eyes widened. 'No! That's not mine! I didn't steal her medicine! I totally absolutely did not—'

'Fine,' said Ali, 'All right, all right, I believe you.'

'I DIDN'T!' shouted Jules, 'I so utterly and completely didn't! Someone else did!'

'Whatever. There was something else. Not in your drawers.' She stopped again. Another endless pause. Jules wanted to turn her upside down and shake her till the words came out. 'There was something in Hen's drawer.'

'What?'

'I don't think it was the thing that they were looking for.'

'What was it?'

'Bags,' she said eventually. 'Food.'

'Food? What sort of food.'

'Rotting food. There was food in there. All the meals from last week.'

'How do you mean?'

'Just that. Food. All the meals Hen doesn't eat. It was in her drawer. You know there's been a funny smell for a while?'

Jules nodded.

'That's it. When Hen can't get rid of stuff, she hides it.'

The silence stretched out. But it no longer separated Jules and Ali. Now it made them complicit.

'But . . . but she's sick. In the loo. Every morning. Every meal.'

'There's only two loos on this floor, remember? And when someone else is in them, she's scared of being full, so she has to get rid of it somehow. She can't put it in the bin because she'd get busted. So . . .' Ali swallowed. She didn't like having to say this out loud. 'So she puts all the food in bags. Some of it's like sick stuff and some of it is just normal food she managed to hide.'

'Don't understand.'

'At meals, she takes the food, but she never eats it, right? She hides it, or she . . . she tries to get rid of it in the loo. There was other stuff, as well. Stuff she'd bought in Stokeley. Sweets and biscuits and stuff. Fruit. Rotting.'

Jules looked as if she too might be sick. 'That's . . .'

'Yeah,' Ali said drily, 'I know. Gross.'

'That's fucking *vile*.'

'Mmmm.'

'That's fucking *unbelievable*. Mutant.' Jules's eyes swirled. 'So we've been sharing a room . . .'

Ali nodded. 'Nice, isn't it?'

Jules sat blinking stupidly for a while.

'Miss Naylor was trying to get me not to tell anyone else and I wouldn't promise so she hit me.'

'Fuck,' said Jules softly. 'Fucking hell. Fucking . . .'

And Ali sat plucking at the polish on the chair's wooden arms, watching all Jules's certainties fall apart.

... FRIDAY

Ali paused outside the door, raised her hand and then lowered it again. She didn't feel particularly nervous. If anything, she felt unusually calm, almost serene. The pause was not because she was scared of knocking on Jaws's door, but because she would like to have found all the right words and assembled them in the correct order before she spoke. She needed to say something that didn't have Caz's snarl at the back of it, to say something made out of her own thoughts, not someone else's. Caz's vehemence had frightened her. Miss Naylor was a thwarted old bitch who deserved everything she got, but still. There was something a little too avid in Caz's instruction. And besides, this was her war, not theirs. If she could get Jaws to support her then perhaps she might be able to do something. Perhaps she wouldn't need to bother with her plan. Perhaps, at the final moment, it might be possible to rely on the solidity of adults after all.

Ali didn't particularly mind about the slap. The point of it, which she had understood almost at the same moment that she saw Miss Naylor's hand begin its trajectory towards her, was not what it was, but what it meant. Ali couldn't remember a single instance in all her time at the school when anyone had touched her. Not deliberately, anyway. Someone might brush past on their way to the library or whack her accidentally during PE. But otherwise nothing. At the beginning and end of term she would watch the others embracing each other in an ecstasy of devotion. But they'd somehow manage to do it without skin ever quite making contact with skin. *No one* touched. It wasn't done. It didn't happen. Touching was for grandparents and dogs.

When she had first arrived, it seemed sometimes as if she lived with a roomful of ghosts, and that only the faint vapour of someone else's smell proved their material existence. They – these girls with whom she spent so much of her life – shouted and banged and snored and cried, but they also glided between each other as surely as if they weren't there at all. In a packed corridor or a sweating gym, Ali would watch them shifting and feinting. When people did touch, they apologized with a sense of genuine horror. And now Miss Naylor had touched her. Not just touched her, but slapped her. That contact had broken something. Not merely the understanding that teachers did not hit pupils, but something else as well. Boys might hit each other to achieve their aims or prove a point, but girls didn't need to. Girls never got that close. There were other ways to ensure they got heard. And so when Miss Naylor raised her hand to strike Ali, she couldn't help thinking there was something a little bit crass in the gesture. Ali was not political – had never been in a position to become political – but she was learning. She was learning.

The floorboards squeaked underfoot. She raised her hand, paused once more and then knocked. Jaws opened the door. Her skin was very pale, almost blueish, and the little ploughed lines at the top of her nose seemed more prominent than usual.

She looked back at Ali and as she did so, Ali noticed the shape of a shadow moving against the wall behind her. She knew before she spoke that it was too late.

'I was . . .'

The shadow on the wall shifted slightly, came closer.

Ali tried again. 'I was just wondering . . . I was . . . to come and ask . . .'

Jaws shook her head. 'I can't.' She was almost whispering 'I can't.' She looked so hopeless, so empty, that Ali had the uncharacteristic urge to console her.

The shadow moved behind Jaws. 'Who's that?'

Ali didn't reply.

Miss Naylor's head appeared over Jaws's shoulder. Jaws didn't turn, she just ducked slightly. Miss Naylor didn't say anything for a while. Ali wondered wildly if Miss Naylor was waiting for Ali to censure her. If she started to speak now, would Miss Naylor accept what she had to say?

'We're going back,' Miss Naylor said eventually. 'Tonight. Tell the others. Go and pack.'

She took the door from Jaws's grasp and shut it. Ali started to run.

+

Hen and Caz were out on the roof, not speaking. It was a hazy afternoon, and the sun had blurred until the shadows weren't shadows any more, just blank spaces where the light used to be. Hen had been looking up at the clouds, watching the way they made the roof seem to slide away beneath her. There was something restful in this isolation and the sense of the huge spaces above her.

Then she'd heard the latch on the window and seen Caz's

face melting through the blank glass. Caz looked swiftly left and right and then slithered through.

'Hi,' said Hen.

'Hi, said Caz.

And that was it. They'd stood there, each with their separate cigarettes, their separate packets and separate lighters, leaning on separate bits of the roof, gazing up at separate bits of sky. They'd been like that for five minutes or so, each pulling the filter from their lips with a soft thump as they exhaled. Hen stubbed hers out under one of the tiles and lit another one immediately. The second cigarette was intended as a warning to Caz that she had no intention of leaving.

Just now, just recently, Hen didn't want to speak. Under normal circumstances, with Caz in a bad mood, she would have sat here, spooling through all the possible things she could say and coming out with the dumbest one. She would have found something – men, teachers, Jules, Izzy, the weather, whatever – to talk about. She would have burbled on for a while and sooner or later, Caz would have put down whatever sulk she'd picked up and they would have talked. Not meaningfully, not even generously, but just enough so that Hen knew she was still in there, still had access of a limited kind. But these were no longer normal circumstances. Hen had no idea how to speak to Caz any more. All those faces above her, laughing. When she looked at Caz now, she had the sensation of knowing too much, of holding information that she would rather not have had. Just at the moment, she wanted Caz to go away.

'Are you OK?' Caz spoke so softly that Hen almost didn't hear her.

'Fine.'

'Fine fine or fine fuck off?'

'Both,' said Hen boldly.

'It's just . . . I'm worried about you. We all are.'

'Why?'

'We worry. You don't always seem fine.'

'Like how?'

Caz sighed. 'You just seem . . . unhappy. Wrong. Like things aren't good.'

'I'm fine. *Really.*'

Caz was still smiling, but she went on, inexorable. 'It's just . . . the others talk about you. They say stuff. How you look ill. How you're not as much fun as you used to be. I've told them, Hen's OK, but they still talk about you.'

'They should stop bitching.'

'Know they should. But they're worried. They see you, the way you look . . .'

Hen looked up towards the clouds and the open sky.

'. . . and really it's not surprising.'

'What d'you mean?'

'They say you look terrible. So sad. Like a skeleton. I don't say these things, I think you look . . . different, but they do.'

'You think I look horrible?'

'I didn't say that. You don't look like you used to.'

'Horrible.' Hen's voice had flattened.

'Different. Not so . . .'

'Not so what?'

'Not so . . .' Caz looked away and took a long drag. 'I don't mean this unkindly, but not so good. Not so good-looking as you used to be. Your face is all bony now.'

Hen felt two things at once: a furtive delight, and the old fear again. Don't you realize, she wanted to shout, don't you realize, I did this for *you*? To be more like you, to get to that holy fucking golden place where you are. Each day, each meal, when I'm sick, I think of you, the shape of you, your impossible stomach, your perfect shoulders. *That's* what I want. *You* make me sick. But all she said was, 'Thanks.'

'I was surprised that Adey found you attractive. Blokes don't usually like girls too thin. But Adey's a funny guy. Higgs says he's odd. Got weird tastes. That he invents all these stories about himself, about other people. Higgs says he doesn't always trust him.'

'Oh? And you trust Higgs, do you?'

Caz looked at Hen and then looked away. 'I'm just saying this so you know. Higgs told me not to tell you. But you should know. Just in case something happens.'

'So,' said Hen, 'I'm ugly, I'm unsexy, everyone's bitching about me and Adey is a freak. Thank you.' She felt an urge – not unusual any more – to take the cigarette in her hand and jab its lighted end into her thigh. To leave it there for a while so it burned inside her.

Caz looked up at the sky and closed her eyes. 'OK then, I'll say it. Nothing to do with Higgs. Just look at yourself. *You're. Just. A. Sad. Fucked-up. Boring. Anorexic.* And you look like shit. Right? Will that do?'

'I'm not!' Hen was shouting.

'You look like one to me.'

'I'm *not!*'

'Well, how come you look like those people from concentration camps, then?'

'I *don't!*'

'Oh, come on. If you got any thinner, you'd be see-through. You look horrible. You know you do.'

'I don't,' said Hen desperately. 'I don't!'

'Oh yeah? So what do you see when you look in the mirror?'

'I'm not . . . I just . . .'

'You don't see anything funny? You don't think there's anything weird about locking yourself in the bathroom for hours and hours?'

'I just need . . . I just wanted . . .'

'So you admit you look like a freak?'

'No. *No.* I'm not. You're taking my—'

'And you steal stuff.'

'What do you mean?'

'Just that. You steal.'

Hen felt as if something tight had been slipped around her throat. 'What?'

'Izzy's medicine. In Jules's drawer.'

'I don't know—'

'Well, how did it get there, then?'

'Nothing. I didn't—'

'It's there. I know it is. I know you put it there.'

'You wanted me . . . You said it was revenge.'

'No, I didn't. *You* wanted to.'

Hen knew she should try to go and she knew that Caz would stop her. 'You said . . . to get back at them . . . because they grassed . . .'

'They didn't. No one grassed. Naylor saw us. She told me.' She leaned back against the roof again, her arms folded. 'Oh well. Like I said, anorexia makes people do such weird things.'

Hen was speechless for a while. Then she said quietly, 'Is this because I know about you and Higgs on Sunday?'

'Don't care what you know. Don't expect you to understand.'

'How do you know I don't understand?'

'Because you couldn't. You're too busy in your fucked-up little world to bother with anyone else.'

'You must . . .' The words came unfamiliarly to Hen. 'You must have felt pretty stupid yourself on that bed.' She wondered distantly if Caz intended to hit her. Caz hitting her, some sort of physical blow, would probably be a relief.

'It's none of your fucking business.'

'Oh? So I'm your business, but you're none of my business?'

And then, all at once, there was the sound of screaming. Hen wasn't sure where it came from, only that the sound wasn't from Caz. The sound was coming from the window. 'How *could* you? You fucking freak. You *freak!* How could you do that? How could you . . .'

The shape at the window resolved itself. It was Jules, yelling, her eyes wild, hair lifting and falling in the breeze. 'I don't fucking believe . . . It's *disgusting*. You're disgusting!' She scrambled out, banging her shins against the casement, not caring how she looked or how she got out there. She couldn't look at Hen properly any more. The only way she could bear to be in her presence was to create an unbreachable barrier of noise around herself. 'You're revolting, you're fucking twisted, you're—'

'Wha . . . what?' Hen looked utterly bewildered.

'The *bags*. Your drawer. How *could* you? What's *wrong* with you?'

Caz recovered herself faster than Hen. She was staring at Jules. 'What bags?'

'It's disgusting. It's revolting. It's . . . you're . . .'

'What is? What's revolting?'

'The bags. In the drawer. Hen's drawer. Food . . . sick . . . It's sick.'

'Oh, *that*.'

Jules stared at her. 'You know?'

'Course I know. We've been sharing a fucking room with this stuff for two weeks. I told them to look.'

'You *knew*?'

'Oh, please. Please stop being so stupid. Of *course* I knew. It was so *obvious*.'

'You *told* them?'

Caz folded her arms and looked out beyond them, over the rooftops. 'I didn't actually *tell* them, I just suggested.' The way she said it sounded entirely reasonable, as if she was the only sane person in an otherwise insane universe. 'It was so boring. I know you steal things, I know you're sick, I know you cut yourself. I always knew. You think it's a secret, but it's not. It never was. It's so *dull*, this stuff.'

'So you told them?'

'Suggested.'

'You said you told them.'

'I suggested. They decided. Who cares? It's over now.'

'So you grassed, basically.' Jules's voice had gone flat.

'Wouldn't you?' She gestured at Hen. 'Don't you find her disgusting?'

Jules opened her mouth to speak, but no sound came out.

Hen would have run at that moment if she could have done. But Jules was between her and the window, and Caz's gaze was pressing down on her.

'How *could* you?' said Jules eventually. 'How? *How?*'

Hen's eyes got rounder and rounder. 'I'm sorry,' she whispered, 'I'm sorry, I'm sorry, I'm sorry, I'm sorry . . .'

'You need help,' said Caz. 'You need help and you need a doctor and you need to stop it. You're gross at the moment, disgusting. You're thin and poky and ugly and you're no fucking fun to be with any more, and—'

Hen looked at her despairingly, from a long long way away. All she could think of to say was, 'I thought . . . I thought you liked me.'

Caz spat. 'We weren't friends. We were never friends. You just tagged along. You always tagged along. Both of you.'

Jules turned towards her, and her face began to work. 'Me? Me?'

There was something rough in Caz's face now. The lines at the side of her mouth were drawn inwards and she seemed alien. All that remained of her was the perfect body. 'Yeah, you. You as well. There was never anything. I only stuck with you because there was nothing better on offer. But every time, you fucked up. You couldn't deal with Yves, you couldn't deal with that dickhead in the wood, you couldn't deal with any of it. Every time I gave you a chance, you flunked it. You're just losers, losers all the way. Both of you. A waste of fucking space.'

Jules staggered slightly and put out a hand to steady herself. She didn't know how to counter this. She was used to hot fiery dramas, to screaming and slamming. When her mother lost her temper, she shouted, and the sides of her nose went scarlet. She was used to seeing people lose their cool, burn with righteousness. Not to this frozen ice-white rage. Not to the way Caz was speaking now, low and fast, so that the words slithered inside before she'd even noticed them. She didn't know how to counter this slick hard patter, as if Caz had practised for hours and all she had to do was open her lips and the words came slapping out like a mouthful of maggots.

'But *why?*' Jules was a child again, fraught with injustice, stifled by the immensity of the things for which there were no words. 'You *like* me. I'm your *friend*! I'm your confident.'

'Confidante. Not confident.'

'*Stop* it! *Stop it! Stop* telling me I'm wrong! I'm not wrong. I'm always wrong. You always say I'm wrong. I hate it, I hate it when you say it. I'm not . . .' The rest of the sentence was swallowed in a sob.

'Both of you,' said Caz, 'are as stupid as each other.' She sounded almost tired.

Hen was behind Jules, and her voice was splintering. 'Why?' she said. 'Why are you like this?' She reached out so she could see past Jules.

Jules whirled round. 'Don't touch me. Don't fucking *touch* me.'

Hen overbalanced, put a hand out to save herself, shoved against Jules. As she stumbled, Hen had an image of Caz, suddenly stilled. She was not moving, not doing anything.

But it wasn't Hen who fell. Behind her, Jules staggered, knocked off kilter as she grappled to get out of Hen's way. She rocked, her ankle slewing awkwardly to the right, trying to find a solid foothold against the side of the roof. And as she did so, the roof started to move. The tile beneath her foot came loose, screeched against itself and began slipping out beneath her. A trickle of cigarette butts spilled out from its sides. Jules's arms went back to save herself but there was nothing there, no one to catch her. Her lips opened but nothing came out except a faint whistling.

And Hen, with her hand on the roof trying to reach for her own balance, did nothing. Just watched. She watched because she couldn't take it in, didn't have the power to believe that it was possible that Jules wouldn't just naturally right herself, tip back onto the flat surface, stay on the right side of normality. But Jules didn't. Her arms flung out, and her leg smashed against the tiles. Her face grew wilder, less and less like herself. Her lips had turned out at the corners so they looked like someone else's lips, rubbery, ugly. And then life speeded up again and she fell. Off the roof, out of sight. And Hen just stood there, with one arm still extended into the useless air until she heard the flat dull sound from far below.

SATURDAY

The strap of the shoulder bag was beginning to hurt her neck. She hadn't packed much – only a change of clothes, the mobile and a book – but it was already weighing her down.

The traffic seemed so loud around here. Ali supposed she must have got used to the muted sounds of the countryside, but now everything shrieked and rasped and made her want to cover her face. The squeal of a taxi's brakes seemed unbearably sharp and when an ambulance shouldered its way through the cars she wanted to scream in sympathy with its siren. Signs and notices kept insisting on her attention: Special Offers, Free Gifts, 0% Annual Interest, One-Hour Photos, Roll-Over Cash Prize, Leeds v Liverpool, £5.99 Summer Sizzler.

It was hotter than it had been at the Manor, though this heat had no pleasure or freshness in it. She was sweating already and it was only nine-thirty in the morning. It must be something to do with the narrow streets, the way they tunnelled the heat into tight little spaces, pressing in, pushing down. All of it – the heat, the noise, the colours, the stink of drains and kebabs – seemed unfamiliar now. Which was stupid. She knew this place. She'd grown up in it. She'd been using the underground alone since she was nine and could feel her way around the city with the same unseeing ease as the natives who never lifted their gaze away from the pavement. If she thought of herself as belonging anywhere, then it was here in this city. She felt tenderly towards parts of it and anxious about others, she knew the best routes between one place and another. She could have told a stranger what to see, how to travel, how to live with authenticity. But this was different. Before, she'd always either been heading towards home or away from it. Now, there was no home. She wasn't heading towards something and she wasn't going away from it. She was just walking.

She'd spent the night in a cheap B. & B. near Paddington. It had been neither likeable nor comfortable, but the receptionists had picked their nails and asked no more than the necessary questions. She'd heard noises during the night – people coming and going, voices, the rasp of female argument. At one point someone had rattled the door and shouted something in a foreign accent, but Ali had just checked the lock and huddled deeper under the cheap sheets.

Leaving had been easy in the end. She'd simply taken her ready-packed bag from under the bed and gone. She'd run to the end of the drive and then, when she was sure she couldn't be seen, turned back to look. The Manor looked peaceful in the afternoon light. She could hear shrieking from somewhere at the back. Jules and Caz must be up on the roof having one of their perpetual cigarettes.

She had made it to the bus station in time, shown her ticket and climbed onto the London coach undisturbed. All the preparation she'd done on Monday had stood her in good stead. She knew the timetable off by heart, and exactly how long it would take to get to London before dark. All that time in the station had merely been a decoy to give her time to get away, a way of ensuring that when they came to look for her they'd waste hours, possibly even days, checking the stations, checking Oxford, checking the places where she wasn't.

She hefted the bag higher onto her shoulder and plunged down into the underground. She could feel the draught in her face, the warm cloying breath of the subterranean city. Someone had left a copy of that morning's paper lying on the back of one of the seats but she didn't pick it up. If they had alerted the police then she didn't want to know about it.

At the other end, the streets were quieter. South of the river, things were unfamiliar, as if she had stumbled across a city within a city. There was something subtly different about the height and spread of the buildings, the way the flyposters suggested decay rather than enticement. She'd forgotten the way you could travel for hours and hours, and still find yourself only halfway to your destination. In the country, you were at A and you travelled to B, and it was quite straightforward. It might take a bit of time, but you got there in a nice plain linear sort of way. Here in London, every journey was like a spy chase in a movie, full of dodges and blinds and long hours of aimless wandering. All of which suited her purposes wonderfully. Even if she had been noticed, it would take people a good long time before they tracked her route.

The street she wanted was one of a long line of similar streets. Victorian jerry-built red-brick houses, two storeys high, with streets so narrow that only one car could pass at a time. Dogs in windows, bright children's toys out in front yards, flourishes of feverfew and self-seeded hollyhocks. There must be a playground nearby. She could hear the sound of children shouting and the rumble of cars on the main road.

Number fifty-seven was a door like all the other doors – wooden, with a single glass panel at the top and a brass knocker. She stood outside the gate for a second, suddenly shy. She could see movement behind the net curtains and the sound of a car radio. She rubbed her lower lip with one dusty finger and then lifted the knocker.

When he opened the door, Rob smiled. It lifted his face, making him look temporarily younger than he actually was. 'Come in,' he said. 'Come in.'

+

They were sitting side by side. Her mother was scrabbling around in her handbag, looking for something down in the depths. Her elbow kept jabbing into Hen's side and though she had tried to move away, her mother's arms somehow filled up the gap. Her handbag was neat and girly, with flowery bead-work on the front and a trimming of pink feathers. She extracted a tissue and a pair of sunglasses, and thrust them at Hen. 'Take these.'

Hen took them, not looking.

Her mother yanked out a lipstick. 'Here, darling. Put this on. You look pale.'

Hen looked at the shiny pink surface of the lipstick, and shook her head.

'Why, pet? Just a little bit. A bit of colour.'

Hen could smell peppermint on her mother's breath. The duty sergeant behind the desk was making phone calls, tapping away at something with a pen. Somewhere music was playing, a radio station. Hen could hear the gabble of the DJ, the loud triumphal rhythm. Through one of the doors at the back was the smell of cooking, a fry-up in one of the houses round the back. The smell of the bacon was making her feel panicky.

Her mother sat back and then sat forward again, jolting Hen's shoulder. 'I got a postcard from your aunt Alice the other day. She's in France. She said, why didn't we come and see her? You and me by a swimming pool, living the high life. Wouldn't that be nice?'

Hen didn't reply.

'Darling.' Her mother leaned round and began stroking her hair. Hen jerked her head sideways. '*Darling.* Say you'll come. It would be good for you. Take your mind off—'

'No,' said Hen.

'Come on. It would be good for you. Bit of sun, nice food, wine . . .'

'No.'

Her mother sighed and sat back. 'You *are* difficult. Why not?'

'I don't want to.'

Her mother picked up her bag again and began scrabbling through it for something. Hen smelt bacon and perfume and the rusty stink of her mother's skin. *Flesh, the smell of flesh.*

Her mother pulled out a comb, leaned over and started trying to comb Hen's hair. Hen yanked her head away.

'Don't do that.' She picked up a strand and inspected the ends. 'It could do with a cut. When did you last go to the hairdressers?'

Hen tried breathing through her mouth so she wouldn't have to smell her mother any more.

'When we get back, we'll go to the salon, really splash out. You can have a massage and a pedicure and a manicure. Could have a whole day there, just us two. Lovely. We never get any time together, do we?'

Hen inspected her nails. She closed her eyes and then opened them again. It didn't seem to matter what she did: Jules's face was there. Jules's face at the moment she fell, rubbery, grotesque, paralysed.

Her mother nudged her again. 'Come on. It'd be lovely. Just the two of us, a real luxury day. No telling your father.'

Hen looked at the surface of her nails. They were ridged and pale with white spots all the way down their surface. Hen thought maybe if she looked hard enough she would see the bones shining underneath.

The duty sergeant looked up at them both, smiled briefly and then looked away again. 'Not long,' he said. 'Sorry about this.' Somewhere in all these official rooms, they were interviewing Caz. Hen did not want to think about Caz.

Her mother leaned over and nodded towards the policeman. 'Quite fetching, isn't he?'

Hen got up and went over to the stand near the door. There were different leaflets on display, one about Neighbourhood Watch, one about drug addiction, one about tagging your belongings. Hen picked out the leaflet about drugs and sat down again on the chairs opposite her mother. From here, she couldn't see the duty sergeant any more, and the smell of bacon seemed less pervasive.

'*Darling.*' Her mother looked wounded. 'Don't be like that.'

Hen opened the leaflet and started reading. It showed a slumped figure in a darkened room, holding something which could have been a syringe. The picture blurred, and she saw Jules's face again, the terror in her eyes. And then Caz, creeping to the edge of the roof, her mouth open, not speaking. She saw herself leaning over the parapet although she couldn't remember the movements which had brought her there. Someone screamed, but she didn't think it was her. She saw the figure on the pavement below, the bones, the way the dark blood splayed out on the tarmac. She remembered the woman on the motorway again, the ripped and twisted face, the black hair groping around her neck. The image of Jules and the woman blended, became the same, until Hen seemed to be looking down at the woman. Except that Jules wasn't Jules any more. Jules was a corpse.

She wanted to be sick, but she knew there was nothing there.

Across the room, on the opposite chair, her mother began to cry. The sound was quite soft, almost sing-song.

Hen watched her. She felt nothing at all.

© MARTIN SWAN

BELLA BATHURST is the author of the critically acclaimed history *The Lighthouse Stevensons*, which won the Somerset Maugham Award. Her journalism has appeared in the *Washington Post*, the London *Sunday Times*, and other major periodicals. Born in London in 1969, she now lives in Scotland, where she is at work on her next book, about shipwrecks and the men who live off their spoils.